The Black Garden

Joe Bright

The Black Garden

Copyright © 2020 by Joe Bright

Joe Bright Books
Studio City, CA

Cover photo by Benoit Dare

www.JoeBrightBooks.com

To my goddaughter, Rebecca

Thanks for always making me laugh and inspiring me not to take life so seriously.

CHAPTER 1

August 1941

Edward Calton was the only person who saw Carolyn O'Brien the day of her suicide. His white milk truck was parked at the curb with its engine still running. He wore a blue and white uniform with matching cap and had just finished putting two bottles of milk on Mrs. Steiner's doorstep when he saw Carolyn walking up Cedar Avenue, heading west toward Shady Bluff. It was a little after 5:00 a.m. The sun was coming up over the horizon and most of the town was still sleeping. According to Edward, Carolyn seemed perfectly at peace with the world, with her purse hanging from her shoulder and a red ribbon tied in her hair.

"She even gave me a smile and a wave," Edward told the police when they questioned him later that day. "All dressed up like she was heading off to church."

From Carolyn's home to Grant Baxter's was a forty-minute walk. The morning light muted the purple azaleas and red tulips that lined the home. Their fragrance awaited the heat of the day to draw it from the blossoms. Birds had already begun chirping in the trees as Carolyn crossed the front lawn and climbed the steps to the porch.

By now, Carolyn had tears in her eyes. From her purse, she removed a handgun that belonged to her father, George O'Brien. He'd bought it the year before, claiming his family needed protection from the Baxters. He also didn't trust most of the religious zealots in town who felt they were acting on God's behalf by persecuting George for doing unmentionable things to his own daughter. In public, George referred to them as the Klueless Klutz Klan. In private, he used less flattering terms.

Carolyn looked through the dark living room windows and saw nothing but her own reflection. She brushed the tears from her cheeks, straightened a stray strand of hair, and then pressed the barrel of her father's Enfield revolver against her temple. The quiet light of morning streaked through her light brown hair as she pulled the trigger, putting an end to her life and adding fuel to the controversy that surrounded her family.

CHAPTER 2

May 1958

I sat in my Chevy, parked in front of the O'Brien home, oblivious of Carolyn O'Brien and what she'd done. I knew nothing about Winter Haven, Vermont, or how its citizens felt about the O'Briens. My only contact with the family came through a telephone conversation I'd had with George two weeks earlier while replying to an ad in the Boston Globe.

Looking at the house now, I could see why Mr. O'Brien had hired me. With its peeling blue paint and lopsided rain gutters, the three-story Victorian screamed of neglect. An unkempt weeping willow stood inside the white picket fence. Tall grass and weeds ran wild through the yard.

I climbed the steps and knocked at the front door. To its right, a long porch swing hung from heavy chains that had been painted white at one time but now showed a lot of silver. The Platters' *The Great Pretender* drifted from up the street where a teenager peered under the hood of his car and had his radio turned up loud.

The door opened. A girl in her late teens or early twenties

stepped within the doorframe. She had long, dark blond hair and a quiet manner that could have passed as either shyness or self-confidence. Even without makeup and dressed in a baggy pink T-shirt, she was stunning. Perhaps it was the contrast with the home that caught me by surprise.

"Hello. I'm looking for George O'Brien," I said.

Her eyes were blue and aloof, yet within their innocence, I saw judgment as she studied my face. Widening the door, she gestured me in without a word.

The living room was decorated in classic claustrophobia. The pale blue curtains accented the dark blue sofa and lounge chair. The oak end tables and bureau matched the railing along the stairs that led to the second floor. The picture frames on the walls and piano all complemented one another. But once you put the whole picture together, you ended up with the home of a packrat who had collected more than he could accommodate.

The girl went down a hallway that led to the kitchen and came back with an elderly gentleman, hunched over and supporting himself with a cane. What little hair he had was light red and combed straight back.

"Mr. O'Brien? I'm Mitchell Sanders." I extended my hand. "We spoke on the phone."

Ignoring my hand, George shook his head and circled me, looking me up and down as if inspecting a cow at auction. The inspector here obviously disapproved of what he saw.

"You won't do." He shook his head and looked past me to the blonde girl, who went to the door and opened it for me to leave.

"But we had an agreement on the phone," I said, looking from the blonde back to George. "I came all the way from Boston."

"You're not what I'm looking for. Thank you for coming."

"But we had an agreement on the phone."

"You're nothing like what you described on the phone."

"In what way?"

"I asked if you were handsome. You said you were below average."

"What do my looks have to do with anything?"

"What do you think, Candice?" George ignored me and looked at his granddaughter.

I glanced at one and then the other, certain they were toying with me, but I could see no humor in their faces.

"He's very ordinary," Candice said.

The old man's eyes narrowed. He stroked his chin and regarded his granddaughter and then gave me another inspection.

"You brought luggage with you?" George asked.

"It's in my car."

"You brought enough for three months?"

I nodded. "Do you want me to get it?"

"Later." His cane tapped the floor as he moved from the carpeted living room to the linoleum in the hallway. He led me through the kitchen, past an unfinished game of chess, past their family cat, and out the back door.

The back yard was more horrifying than the front. It had a garden quality, yet was cluttered with odd items such as a bathtub, an old bicycle, a wagon, a table and a lawnmower that, judging by the length of the grass, hadn't been used in years. The tub, wagon, and other items were filled with dirt and had flowers planted in them, a sort of eclectic garden. Almost everything had rusted or turned black. Weeds and flowers twisted among the objects, giving it a Gothic look, which sounds more charming than it was.

A cement walkway cut through the right side of the bizarre garden before splitting into two paths, one leading to a gate in the back fence and the other leading to a one-room apartment.

"I love what you've done with the place," I said, looking around at the clutter.

George scowled, opened the studio door, and stepped aside. I stared at the assortment of boxes, paper bags, household furniture, clothes the family had outgrown, documents that no longer served a purpose, and God knows what else.

"This is where you'll stay. You may want to start by cleaning it up. There's a bed under there somewhere."

"What should I do with all the stuff?"

"There are garbage cans out the back gate."

"You want me to throw it all out?"

"You're attending Boston University, correct?" George asked.

"I'm studying literature," I answered, mistaking George's statement for interest. "I'm a writer. At least I'm—"

"Then you should be smart enough to figure out what's garbage and what's not." George fixed his eyes on me and waited for me to nod before returning to the house.

Looking at the mess, I realized I wouldn't be getting any sleep until I first found the bed, which I assumed was buried beneath the tallest mound of junk. Clearing a path, I opened the curtains and brought down a shower of dust. From the window, I could see George and Candice settling down at the table to finish their game of chess. They were strangers whose lives meant nothing to me other than a paycheck and an escape from Boston. It was my time of innocence, before I knew their histories, before I knew what the name O'Brien represented to this small Vermont town. I looked up at the second story of the house and then at the attic. I wondered about the rest of the family. Where were Candice's parents and George's wife? Why were this old man and young woman alone in such a big house? At the time, I had no idea how significant those questions were or how much I'd dislike the answers once I learned them.

CHAPTER 3

The morning sun glinted off the kitchen windows at the back of the O'Brien house. Behind the glare, I could see George O'Brien holding a pair of binoculars, looking out the side window where he apparently found something of interest through the open curtains of his neighbor's home.

I headed out the back gate to unload a box of junk I'd collected during my first night of servitude. I'd stayed up until one in the morning, first sorting through O'Briens' paraphernalia, and then desperately trying to find the bed so I could crawl into it. The mattress sagged in the middle, but I didn't care. It was soft and warm and had a fresh pair of sheets that George had brought out earlier. I'd slept soundly until the morning sun found its way to my face through a hole in the curtain.

Throughout the morning, I took five large boxes of garbage into the alley and had filled a dozen more with things that could be sold at a yard sale. During a couple of trips through the back gate, I saw George watching me from the kitchen windows. The other three times he spied on his neighbor with the binoculars.

By noon, I'd cleared a wide pathway from the door to the bed. Through the window, I saw George making a trip of his own out the back gate, most likely checking to see that my three years of college education had taught me the difference between trash and treasures. I expected him to come back in hauling a few items he couldn't bear to part with, but he went back to the house with nothing but his cane. Five minutes later he hollered for me to come in for lunch. I'd eaten no breakfast since this was my first real day at work and I wanted to make a good first impression. I found out later that nothing impressed George O'Brien.

I washed my hands in the studio's kitchen sink before going into the house where George sat at the table eating a bacon, lettuce, and tomato sandwich. Candice stood at the stove, watching a frying pan of sizzling bacon.

"How was your first night in paradise?" George wiped his mouth with the back of his hand.

"Wonderful. It's like Hiroshima at the end of the war."

"Have a seat." He motioned to a chair across the table from him.

"Perhaps I should help Candice with lunch."

"Candice can manage just fine on her own. Now sit. It's giving me a crook in the neck looking up at you." George had an Ebenezer Scrooge demeanor: bushy eyebrows and a constant scowl. "What have you done with all of my garbage?"

"I put it in the alley like you told me."

"I was out in the alley. You've got five boxes of paper out there. Where's everything else?"

"That's all I've come up with so far."

"You were at work half the night and all morning and all you've managed to find is five boxes worth of paper to toss out? Good Lord, what am I paying you all this good money for? I could hire the village idiot for half the price and get twice the productivity out of him."

"I've been separating things out. Most of the stuff is still in pretty good condition."

"You sound like my wife." George swallowed a bite of sandwich and wiped his hand over his mouth again. "That woman saved everything. All her school papers, all the way back to elementary school, are stuffed away up in our attic somewhere. God Almighty, what good are her old school papers ever going to do anyone? This house is filled from top to bottom with nothing but junk. If you can see an immediate use for it, keep it. Otherwise, throw it out. If I haven't missed it by now, I never will."

He pulled four blurry photographs from his shirt pocket and waved them at me like a lawyer presenting evidence of my guilt. I recognized them as some photos I'd thrown out earlier that morning. They were of a girl with light brown hair and were so far out of focus that you couldn't recognize her face. It could have been Candice, but I didn't think so. The hair was too dark.

"You kept all the garbage and threw out my memories. Don't touch the photographs without asking me first. This afternoon I'll send Candice out with you to supervise."

I looked up at Candice with a smile.

"Wipe that smile off your face," George said.

Candice glanced at me with curiosity, as though she found it odd that I liked the thought of her working with me.

"Have you considered having a yard sale?" I asked.

"Nobody wants my garbage, son."

"You'd be surprised what people—"

"Don't lecture me," he interrupted. "I'm three times your age and four times as smart." He grabbed his cane and got to his feet. "Now do as you're told and throw it outback." George trailed off down the hallway to the living room.

Candice brought me my BLT and set it in front of me, along with a glass of orange juice. "Still glad you came all the way from Massachusetts for this job?"

"Just happy to be putting my college education to good use," I said.

She put a second sandwich on another plate and took it to the living room. I listened to hear what kind of things they would say about me behind my back, but I only heard the hum of the refrigerator and a few birds chirping outside the window.

I didn't see Candice again until about three o'clock when she came to the studio to help with the dull process of sorting through boxes and paper bags. I suspected George had actually sent her to make sure I didn't throw away any more blurry photographs or anything equally insignificant. She picked up a small box and sat on a stool at the counter next to the sink.

She was dressed in sandals and baggy clothes, almost bohemian, though I doubt this was her intent. It appealed to me because I was into Jack Kerouac and Allen Ginsberg at the time and envied anyone who could live free of the expectations of society. I couldn't say if Candice fit into this category, but she did have the ability to occupy the same room as me yet forget I was even there—not that this delighted me.

She absorbed herself in the contents of her box, grinning to herself. She glanced up and caught me watching her. She had a foreign quality that I couldn't place. She held my gaze with no sign of embarrassment, regarding me with curiosity.

"You know, I never had a chance to thank you for standing up to your grandfather in declaring my ugliness."

She showed no sign that she appreciated my sense of humor.

"And you said it was such conviction," I prodded, wanting her to say that she hadn't actually meant what she said.

"We don't need your help, but Grandpa thinks we do," she said. "I didn't want him to waste any more time interviewing people."

"There were others?"

"Four."

"I don't suppose you were kind enough to call any of these men ordinary?"

"I was happy to see them go."

"Then I should be complimented that you stuck up for me."

"I would have been happy to see you go, as well."

I could see now that she hadn't lied to her grandfather about not finding me attractive. This bothered me a lot more than it should have. I wanted all women to love me. It didn't matter their age or if I found them attractive or not. I still wanted their approval. I told myself I didn't care what Candice thought, that she was nobody to me, just another pretty face who wasn't attracted to my average face. I certainly wasn't looking for a relationship. When September rolled around, I'd be back at college and the O'Briens would be nothing more than an entry in my diary. I would keep our relationship on a professional level: work for them in the day and have the evenings to myself to work on the novel I'd started during my freshman year of college.

The open curtains gave me a clear view of the odd garden and of George sitting in a rocking chair on the back porch. His cane lay across his lap as he moved back and forth in his chair. His eyes stared across the yard, through the studio window, and directly at me. His expression conveyed that he knew my thoughts and he disapproved, and should I try to make a move on his lovely granddaughter, he'd be there with his cane to put me in my place.

"Your grandfather doesn't trust me much, does he?"

Candice looked out the window. That thin smile I'd seen earlier crossed her lips again. "Why did you take this job?"

I could have told her the truth and explained the fallout from ending my engagement with Marie Manzini, but that story wouldn't paint me in the best light.

"I thought I'd get out and explore the world," I said, "get a change of scenery, meet some interesting people."

"In Winter Haven?" she asked, and I knew what she meant. With fewer than 8,000 residents, Winter Haven didn't seem like a hotbed of activity or culture. What little I'd seen of the town as I drove around looking for the O'Brien's house told me nothing happened here and that my summer would be as uneventful as I hoped it would be.

"I'm writing a novel," I said. "Boston's such an exciting city. There's so much going on. Then there are my friends and my family. I swear, I never have a minute to myself. How am I supposed to get any writing done? So, you know, now I'm here."

Candice gave me a bored look, reached into her box, and pulled out a Teddy Bear. It was missing one eye. She regarded it affectionately, brushed it off, and set it on the counter. At five o'clock, when Candice and I came out of the studio, she had the bear tucked under her arm.

On the back porch, George was asleep in his rocking chair with his mouth gaping open and the sun beating down on his face. The yellow cat was also taking in the sun as she lay on a marble table in what I'd now started thinking of as the black garden.

As I closed the door behind me, George blinked his eyes open, sat up, and wiped his hand across his mouth.

"Finished already?" His voice was dry and groggy.

"It's five o'clock," I said.

He held his wrist close to his face as he blinked and tried to focus on his watch. "Right on the nose," he said. "Never do more than is expected of you. That's a good motto. It'll get you far in life."

"I need time to work on my novel."

George nodded and straightened his back. "I'll keep that in mind when I consider whether or not to give you a bonus."

The man was unbelievable. I'd stayed up half the night and had even skipped breakfast, yet he still made me feel like a freeloader.

"Do you mind if I take a shower in the house? Mine is still filled with boxes."

"Now isn't that a shame?" George got to his feet and steadied himself with his cane. "Looks like you're going to have to do a little more work today after all." He turned and went into the house with Candice and her Teddy Bear behind him.

CHAPTER 4

That night I sat in my one-room apartment behind the O'Brien house, working on my novel. At least I tried. I pulled a small table over to the window and set up my gray Underwood Leader Portable typewriter—a 1947 model that had been gathering dust in my father's den until he passed it on to me during my first year at the university.

I had the curtains open and was looking up at Candice's bedroom. She was sitting near her window, looking off to the side, at a mirror I suppose, and brushing her hair. I sensed she knew I was watching her, that she wanted me to watch her. Otherwise, she wouldn't have sat so close to the window. Yet not once did she look out.

I drew the curtains closed and looked at a photograph that lay on the table next to the typewriter. It was a photo of me on my parents' sofa. Marie sat next to me, holding my hand, both of us smiling that same giddy smile that all people have when they first fall in love, the one that you later look back on with nausea. My mother had taken the picture. She was also the one who had insisted I bring it with me.

"Pull it out and look at it from time to time," she'd said. "So you can see what you're giving up. Maybe it will bring you to your senses."

Like all good parents, my mother would never allow me to escape my guilt. She'd give me little mementos of shame, such as the photograph, to remind me that I had sinned and was in need of repentance. Once, when I was twelve, my friend Randy and I were tossing a baseball around in the living room. I threw it too far to the right and hit a lamp—not just any lamp either, my mother's favorite, the one my father had given her for Christmas. Mom made me glue it back together and then had me put it in my bedroom so I could look at it every day and remember what a bad child I was. She couldn't help herself. It was her Catholic upbringing, and as we all know, nothing makes God happier than having His children walking around with a huge trunk of guilt strapped to their backs.

The lamp worked, too. That was the aggravating thing about it. Every time I had to switch it on or off, I'd look at the bad glue job and feel a knot of guilt tighten inside my stomach, the same feeling I had now as I stared at the photograph of Marie and me. She had brown hair and brown eyes that she'd inherited from her Italian ancestry and a strong spirit that she'd inherited from her father, who had immigrated to America and had worked hard to open his own restaurant. Papa Manzini, everyone called him. He had one of those smiles that won you over the moment he directed it at you. Five-foot four, two hundred pounds and a heart of gold—or so I thought until Marie revealed to me that he'd said I was too self-centered to ever amount to much. After that, I couldn't look at him without thinking of him as a very bad judge of character.

∞⊗

The next day, Candice and I went back to work cleaning out the studio while George went back to work watching us from his rocking chair on the back porch. It took five days to finish the job. Over that space of time, I told Candice stories of my childhood in Boston, about my family and friends, about college and the novel I was writing. She told me nothing. I'd noticed that her mouth was slightly out of proportion with the rest of her face. Yet, despite the grandness of her mouth, she did a remarkable job of keeping it closed. She never even laughed at any of my jokes.

At the end of my fifth day, I discovered the studio had a blue carpet, in dire need of shampooing. It accented the light blue walls and the oak counters. Candice told me that George had made them himself when he was younger. A true craftsman. It was a cozy little apartment after that. Had the place been in Boston, he'd have had no problem renting it at a decent price. The only two drawbacks were that George would be your landlord and your only view would be that awful-looking garden filled with junk. Then again, you did have a periodic view of Candice sitting in the window brushing her hair.

Moving into the studio had been a slow process since I had to first make room before I could haul in the things I'd brought with me from Boston. The last thing I brought in was a box filled with books I had stashed in the trunk of my '51 Chevy. As I carried it around the side of the house and through the studio door, I saw Candice watching me from the kitchen window. She then settled at the table to play her nightly game of chess.

I unloaded the books onto a shelf near the door. I had several favorites that I would pick up whenever I was in a writing slump. Often, just rereading a section or two would get me on track again. My own novel was a combination of several ideas. It had started out as a war story after reading Ernest Hemingway's *A Farewell to Arms* and *For Whom the Bell Tolls*. It then took on many fantasy elements once I discovered H. G. Wells and read *The Time Machine* and *The Invisible Man*. Now, with Jack Kerouac and Allen Ginsberg dominating my literary world, I was molding my story into something a little more offbeat.

Candice came out to deliver some towels and soap and to collect my dirty laundry. Her eyes wandered from my face to the bookshelf, paying little attention to the bag of clothes I handed her.

The girl had zero interest in me. I was merely a servant, there to appease her grandfather. Or maybe not. Later, as I was getting ready for bed, I kicked off my boots and was in the process of removing my shirt when I remembered I still had the curtains open. Looking through the window, I found Candice standing near the kitchen sink watching me. She suddenly took an interest in the stars. Closing the curtains, I sat down on the bed with a smile.

ৰ০৫৪

The next morning, I got my first glimpse at the neighbor George had been spying on. I came out of the studio and found her peering over the white fence that divided the O'Briens' yard from hers. A scowl graced her lips as she looked out over the black garden. Her name was Harriet Blanchard. George had mentioned her by name several times as he made derogatory remarks about her and her husband, referring to them as old geezers. Seeing Harriet now, I had to smile since she was probably George's age but with more life in her. George's bum leg and the fact that he walked stooped over made him seem older than he was.

"How are you doing?" I said.

Harriet looked up with a start. She smiled stiffly in an attempt to cover her embarrassment. She still had a lot of black streaking her gray hair, and judging by her pasty skin, she didn't get out in the sun much.

"I'm Mitchell Sanders," I said as I approached, "your new neighbor for the summer."

"So you're the one they hired to clean up this eyesore."

I hummed and looked behind me at the weed-ensnared debris that made up the black garden.

"Dora wouldn't have allowed this, but George just lets everything go until it looks like hell and he has to hire someone to come in and clean up the mess he made."

The back door opened. George stepped out and shook his cane in the air.

"Keep your nose out of my yard, Harriet. You got something to say, go say it to that deadbeat husband of yours, and leave my worker alone."

"You're a disgrace to the neighborhood," she said.

"You're a disgrace to the neighborhood," George mocked. "You sound like a damned parrot. Just once I'd like to hear you say something original. Now go back inside and finish knitting that afghan."

Harriet slapped a hand against her chest in shock. "Stop looking through my windows, you perverted old man!"

"You think I'd want to see your wrinkled old ass?"

Harriet's mouth twitched but didn't produce a sound. Her pale skin reddened as she marched across her lawn, climbed the steps, and disappeared through her back door, slamming it behind her.

"Next time that old buzzard shows her face over the fence, hit it with a shovel."

"She was merely admiring this lovely garden of yours, Mr. O'Brien." I gestured to the odd display of plants and junk. "My mother has a couple of pink flamingos in hers, but you've really outdone yourself."

"Nobody likes a smart-ass," he said. "I'm putting you to work in the attic today. Candice is already up there. Go give her a hand."

George remained on the back porch, gazing out over his unsightly domain as I took my three years of college education and climbed the stairs to the attic, a project destined to be as much fun as the studio.

The room was spacious with the ceiling following the contours of the roof. The front wall, where the roof peaked, held a regular-sized window, while both side walls contained four square windows near the floor, below the slope of the roof. Candice sat cross-legged on the floor, staring through one of the small windows. I knelt beside her and looked past the neighbor's house and down at Willow Lane, lined with trees and green grass. Down the street, in the front yard of a yellow house, stood two girls about Candice's age. Hula-hoops twirled around their hips.

"Friends of yours?"

Candice ignored me and crossed the room. I stayed at the window, gazing down at the neighborhood, wondering about Candice's friends—not the girls below me, but her friends in general. I'd been in Winter Haven for nearly a week. From what I could tell, no one had come to visit her, nor had she left the house. I figured a girl as pretty as Candice should have a dozen handsome men beating on her door, but where were they? Where were any of her friends for that matter—male or female? This was a lovely girl in the prime of her life. Yet she spent every minute of it with her grandfather, a man who had yet to say a kind word in my presence. I'd gathered that George was her only living relative. One evening at dinner, George had made a comment to Candice that started with: "When your mother was around." From that, I concluded she was dead. I suspected Candice's father and grandmother had also passed on. This I based strictly on the fact that they weren't around.

The attic was twice the size of my new studio apartment and had four times the amount of junk crammed into it. I opened a box near the window and looked in at an assortment of old clothes. Looking around at the multitude of boxes, I felt the pangs of depression move through me. One by one, I would have to pull each item from each box, inspect it, and try to figure out what wasn't garbage, and this I would have to do in the company of a girl who detested conversation.

"What do you say we haul all of this out to the alley and tell your grandfather we already inspected it?"

Candice sorted through a box without looking up.

"This is a waste of our time and you know it. Ninety-nine percent of this is going to turn out to be junk anyway."

"We're looking for the one percent that isn't," she said.

Besides the endless supply of old clothes, the boxes contained yarn, dishes, electrical paraphernalia, and of course the papers George had mentioned that his wife had held onto since her days in elementary school. From what I could tell, she'd been a fairly good student.

"Your family held on to everything, didn't they?" I held up a red high-heeled shoe and stuck my finger through the hole in the sole. Candice eyed me the way Marie used to whenever she disapproved of my behavior. *Women's Magic Curse*, my college roommate called it. He claimed that disapproving look had the ability to extract men's spines without us even realizing it. Like magic, we would start apologizing for things we hadn't done wrong and then do whatever the woman wanted. Once the woman had gotten her way, she'd lift the curse and we'd be left nursing our bruised egos and trying to convince ourselves that we were still the stronger of the two sexes.

Refusing to let Candice get the upper hand, I grabbed a pair of granny panties and held them up in a gesture of mockery. "Now this is one sexy pair of underwear."

And there was that look again. "That's all you men think about, isn't it? Sex."

"Oh yeah, these are a real turn-on." I tossed the panties in the garbage. "Besides, you're no saint yourself. I saw you watching me out the window, trying to sneak a peek."

"Don't flatter yourself. The last thing I want to see is your genitalia. I've seen Grandfather's before, and believe me, it's not that pretty."

"I'd like to think my genitalia is a little prettier than your grandfather's."

"You wish."

"I pray," I said.

"What are you two yapping about?" George said as he came up the stairs. I looked over my shoulder at him and wondered if he'd overheard our conversation. I gave Candice a little smile. She shot back with a narrow-eyed frown.

"I was just saying to Candice that since tomorrow is my day off that perhaps the three of us could go downtown and you can show me around."

"What about your writing?"

"You can't expect me to stay locked up in my room all the time."

George gave me a curious look, not sure if he should be offended by my remark. "You go show yourself around," he said. "Candice and I have better things to do with our time than play tour guide for you in this godforsaken town."

CHAPTER 5

Main Street had a quintessential New England charm: quaint shops, corner diners, and plenty of trees. People bustling along the sidewalks called each other by name and asked, "How are you doing?" as though they actually wanted to know. A narrow side street led to a park where children ran through the grass and squirrels escaped up the trunks of trees. Another street branched off toward a whitewashed church, glistening in the summer sun. This was the small-town charm I'd expected when I left Boston. The friendliness of the townspeople seemed so genuine that I almost felt at home, a delusion I doubt many small-town folks would have while vacationing in the city.

My sister Ann would have hated it. She was two years older than me and swore that manmade entertainment was vastly superior to anything God had created. Thus, the local shopping center would always surpass mountains and lakes. She also required variety, something Winter Haven didn't offer. The town had only one theater, eliminating all debates over which movie to see on a Friday night.

Ann now lived in Cambridge, along with her husband and daughter. We'd grown up on the opposite side of the Charles River, in Back Bay, not far from BU. The neighborhood was changing with houses being converted into apartments. In places like Winter Haven, change was more gradual and less unsettling.

I entered a sporting goods store and looked briefly at tents, sleeping bags, and mess kits. As a child, I used to beg my father to take us camping. He refused to go unless we went as a family. Since nothing could convince Ann to sleep on the ground, I led a childhood deprived of all camping experience.

I wandered over to the fishing poles, something I was more acquainted with—though my experience had led me to believe fishing wasn't my forte. I'd gone several times with friends and had never caught a thing. Once, we'd actually paid to fish inside of a fish hatchery. Not exactly sporting, but at least you were guaranteed a fish. Or so they told us. I'm probably the only person on earth who couldn't get a bite in a twenty-foot pond packed with hungry fish. It was so shallow I could watch the fish swim up to my bait, sniff it, and swim away. My friends claimed if I ever fell into the ocean, I wouldn't have to worry about getting eaten by a shark because there wasn't a fish alive that could stand the smell of me.

"I didn't ask how much they cost," a voice said. "I asked what the price would be for me."

I looked up, drawn by the tone of the conversation. In the golfing section, a distinguished gentleman and young man stood with a salesman wearing a blue shirt imprinted with the words *Can I help you with something, Sport?*

"That's the same question," the salesman said.

"That is not the same question," the gentleman corrected. "I'm asking what sort of discount I can expect."

"Of course, Mr. Baxter. Sorry. Let me grab the manager for you."

"Did I say I was ready to buy?"

"Well, no, but I'm not authorized to give discounts."

"Then you should have said that."

The salesman fidgeted and gazed toward the office at the back of the store.

"Would you like me to talk to the manager for you?"

The gentleman shooed him away with the wave of his hand. "If I want your help, I know where to find you."

The salesman's eyes moved from the two men to the golf clubs and then out across the store, where they landed on me. He passed the tents, the mess kits, and sleeping bags. He had hope in his eyes, encouraged by the sight of me holding a pole over my shoulder as if ready to cast the line out across the red and white tiles that checkered the floor.

"Sharp rod you've got there. One of our best sellers. Strong, durable, and guaranteed to catch fish."

"Is that a money-back guarantee?" I asked.

"You fish the right hole, it is."

"And would you happen to know where the right hole is?" I figured if I could come away empty-handed from a fish hatchery, there wasn't a fishing hole in the entire state of Vermont that could guarantee me a catch.

"I know several right holes," he assured me. "You planning on fishing around here?"

"Perhaps," I said, certain I wasn't planning on fishing anywhere. "I'm staying here in Winter Haven for the summer." I set the fishing pole back on the rack, not wanting him to waste his time selling me on something I had no intention of buying.

"Where are you from?"

"Boston."

He whistled lightly and regarded me with pity. "I don't know how anybody can live in a place like that. Too many people and too much noise. I was there once, four years ago. Went to see the Red Sox. I just couldn't get over all the traffic. It was like living in an anthill. I couldn't wait to get out of the place."

The man had a friendly smile and pleasant demeanor, but there was no recovering from badmouthing Boston. We had culture. We had sports. We had the Boston Common, Fenway Park, and Bunker Hill. We had the massacre, the tea party, and Paul Revere. What was Winter Haven's contribution to American history?

"What brings you to Winter Haven?" he asked.

"I'm helping some folks fix up their house."

"Who you working for?"

"George O'Brien."

The moment the name left my lips, the warmth evaporated from the man's eyes. His countenance dropped and his spine stiffened. Had I slapped him across the face, I doubt I could have gotten a colder response. He glanced to my right, to the distinguished gentleman, who was now focused on me.

"O'Brien, huh? Relatives of yours?"

"I found them in a newspaper ad."

The salesman's eyes scanned the store. "You have yourself a pleasant stay in Winter Haven. Let me know if I can help you with anything." He headed toward the door where a man and a woman were looking at tennis rackets. The attitude disturbed me slightly, but it didn't surprise me. Someone with George's lack of grace was bound to have ruffled his share of feathers. He'd offended me within the first minute of meeting him. No doubt his fellow-townsmen had received their share of ill will over the years.

"Want some advice?" a voice asked from over my shoulder. I turned and found Mr. Baxter dissecting me with his blue eyes. He was a robust man with graying hair and a cunning smile. I had a history teacher in high school who had that same smile, the kind that made me feel as though he'd caught me cheating. "Steer clear of the O'Briens," he said. "You play in the sewer, you're going to come out smelling like shit."

"That's mighty neighborly of you." I wasn't exactly a member of the George O'Brien fan club, but I didn't appreciate having someone tell me who to hate.

"Trust me. I've got your best interest at heart."

He walked back to the golf clubs and said a few words to the young man, who turned toward me with a smirk. He had a rock-star hairstyle, dark and slicked back like he was Elvis or Ricky Nelson. The Brylcreem glistened beneath the store's fluorescent lighting. He had the self-assurance of a man born into money. People had been saying yes to him since the day he could talk. No doubt he owed it all to the gentleman standing next to him.

The two of them watched me as I made my way toward the front door. Not wanting them to think they had scared me off, I stopped briefly at a selection of footballs and feigned interest in them. As I exited the store, I glanced back and found their eyes still on me. I walked to my car with a bad feeling in the pit of my stomach.

CHAPTER 6

From the studio, where I sat behind my Underwood typewriter, I could see George clearing off the table—probably putting away the chessboard. The light flowed out through the window and across the dark garden, giving it a romantically eerie mood.

The back yard was a point of curiosity for me. At first glance, it looked like nothing more than an assortment of junk. Yet on closer inspection, I could see that someone had taken care in the placement of the flowers scattered throughout the yard. It was almost artistic the way the flowerpot hung from the wire tied to the handlebars of the old bicycle, or the way the bathtub and wagon overflowed with flowers. The line of flowerpots sitting on the fence held a certain charm, as did the large tire near the back gate, with its center serving as a pot for a large plant. Even the porcelain figures seemed too well placed for it to be accidental. I couldn't imagine either George or Candice doing such a thing, which left the missing women of the family: George's wife or Candice's mother.

Looking up at the second floor, I found Candice standing at her bedroom window, looking down at me. I expected her to look away as she had the day she watched me taking off my shirt. But she didn't move, not even when I waved. The fact that she didn't wave back made me wonder if she even saw me at all, but she had to. The lights were on in the studio, and I was seated in plain sight.

Closing the curtains, I walked to the bookshelf, looking for something to read since I wasn't having much success with my writing. I grabbed *The Great Gatsby* and started to turn away when I noticed a gap in the lower row of books between *Robinson Crusoe* and *The Count of Monte Cristo*. No, I hadn't failed to slide the books together when putting them on the shelves. I was too anal-retentive for that. It was a family trait that started with my Grandfather Bryson, who was an ex-Marine and had been programmed to believe that everything had to be clean and orderly. My mother inherited the quality from him and I from her. That doesn't mean I could name the missing book. I did, however, have my list of suspected thieves narrowed down to two.

Confirmation came the next morning as I walked through the living room toward the stairs. It was destined to be another fun-filled day in the attic sorting through boxes of socks, underpants, and half-used toiletries. In the living room, on an end table next to the sofa, sat a copy of *The Invisible Man*. It had a torn cover, just like mine. I turned to the inside flap and found my name scrawled in blue ink. Another habit of mine, one I'd started at college when forced to room with people I didn't entirely trust.

In the attic, I found Candice seated on the floor with a box of papers in front of her. She looked up, over the sheet she was holding, and then put her eyes back on the page. She had her hair pulled back into a ponytail and wore a wrinkled yellow shirt. I came around behind her and peered over her shoulder, finding her looking at some schoolwork, with a C+ written at the top of the page.

"You mind?" she said, staring up at me.

"Are we working or studying?" I grabbed a box of my own and pulled it beside her. "Is that your grandmother's?"

"My mother's."

"Where is your mother?"

Candice set the paper on a pile on the floor, a pile she presumably had no intention of tossing out. Reaching into the box, she retrieved another paper.

"My parents were killed in a car accident."

"How about your grandmother?"

"She was in the car with them."

"When was this?"

Candice gave me a perturbed glance and placed the paper on her pile. Generally, I had no interest in other people's personal lives, but my encounter with Mr. Baxter had piqued my interest. Neither Candice nor her grandfather enjoyed talking about themselves. George often talked about politics or about the horrible people of Winter Haven. Other than that, he kept his conversation on the work he had hired me to do and on how inept I was at doing it.

Candice merely kept quiet and made me feel intrusive whenever I asked about things she felt were none of my business, which included almost everything. She'd gently roll her eyes, shake her head, and then look away, as she was doing now.

Later that morning, we cleared off an old-fashioned wooden table that was buried beneath a pile of colorful dresses. We pulled it away from the wall, making room for us on either side. Candice grabbed a wooden chair while I strolled through the clutter hoping to find one of my own. Spotting the corner of a wooden object, I shoved boxes aside and unveiled the top of a trunk, an antique with a curved lid and ribbed with metal bands.

"Grandpa said he wants to go through that on his own," Candice said abruptly. My father, the psychologist, could have turned to Freud to explain why Candice's reaction had elicited the opposite effect than she desired. I, however, needed nothing more than Shakespeare: *The lady doth protest too much, methinks.*

I grabbed the edge of the trunk and gave it a yank to see how heavy it was. It didn't budge, so I took a box, set it on the table, and stood facing Candice.

"Is there another set of keys to my room?" I asked.

The look in her eyes told me she knew where this was heading.

"I saw my copy of *The Invisible Man* downstairs."

Her jaw tightened.

"I don't want you in my room. That's my private stuff. You stay out of it."

"This is my house. I go wherever I want."

"Not in my room, you don't."

She rose to her feet and glared at me, seeking the proper thing to say to put me in my place. Instead, she crossed the room, gathered the school papers she had stacked on the floor, and disappeared down the stairs. Her irritation gave me a sadistic pleasure. Her quiet independence bothered me, and I felt the need to bring her down to my level. I wanted desperately not to find her so damned attractive. Or at the very least, I didn't want her to know how I felt. I'd always hated myself for finding conceited women beautiful, as though my admiration added to their narcissism. I once read in one of my father's psychology books that conceited people are actually insecure at heart. That appealed to me. It made them seem more human. It was hard for me to imagine someone who was completely self-assured.

With her gone, I wasted no time kneeling down at the wooden trunk, snapping open the latches, and lifting the heavy lid. I could see now why George wanted to go through this on his own. Inside was a jumble of photographs, all thrown together in a rainbow of colors, displaying smiling faces from a bygone era. To the side were several fat folders filled with documents.

I gathered a handful of photos and thumbed through them, happy for the chance to take a stroll through the lives of the O'Brien family. There were pictures of George and his wife Dora. I'd seen photos of her on the living room piano. I found pictures of Candice's mother. The name Carolyn was written on the backs of several, along with her age, which varied from picture to picture. She was even prettier than Candice. She appeared happy and outgoing while Candice always looked so contemptuous. Since most people smile when getting their picture taken, who could say if Carolyn was as happy as she appeared? As for being outgoing, I could only base that on facial expressions and by the way she danced around the living room in one picture and hung upside down on the porch swing in another. I couldn't imagine Candice ever doing either of those things.

Several photographs showed her holding her baby. She had to be happy there. The smile was too genuine, and I detected a sense of pride in the way she held baby Candice up to the camera. It made me feel good to know there was once such happiness in this house, yet sad to think it was no longer here. Carolyn was a young mother. Her age wasn't written on the backs of these photos, but she was definitely younger than twenty.

The pictures of Candice as a young girl and as an adolescent revealed what I expected: a serious, solemn child. A couple of photos showed her with her grandmother, Dora, but in most of the pictures she was alone—not with family, not with friends, just Candice sitting at the kitchen table or sitting on the back porch. I hoped the photos weren't a good representation of how her life had been, but I feared they were.

A good detective would have looked at those photographs and noticed the important detail I was overlooking. He would have seen the subtle nuances of emotion on the faces of the various members of the O'Brien family. He would have seen the background furniture, the color of the wallpaper, the fact that few things had changed inside the O'Brien household throughout the years. He would have seen all of those things, just as I did. But he would have also seen the most revealing thing of all, not what was in the pictures, but what was missing.

CHAPTER 7

George and I stood in the back yard, surveying his diverse collection of junk that he called a garden. He hadn't shaved, and his thin, red hair stood on end. I was quickly learning that to criticize anything around the O'Brien household was the same as volunteering to set it right. Thus, when I'd compared George's mounds of junk with my mother's pink flamingos, it was the same as professing how much I'd enjoy disassembling the black garden and transforming it into a respectable back yard.

"What did your wife think of the garden? If you don't mind my asking."

"You know why I hired you?" he asked.

"Why?"

"Because you're from the big city. And I always figured city folks don't give a rat's ass about anybody but themselves. I sure hope you don't disappoint me by proving me wrong."

And so began my adventure in the black garden, through the long grass, the weeds, the multitude of flowers, the porcelain gnomes, the bicycle, the bathtub, the tables, the tires, and yes, even a kitchen sink. Whatever could serve as a flowerpot was utilized. George wanted me to move it all out into the alley so the city could haul it away. I questioned his decision, claiming the city wouldn't appreciate us piling so much junk in their alley.

"It's my alley," George said. "And if the city has a problem with it, they'll figure out a way to get rid of it."

So out the back fence it went. It was a slow process, and with me doing all of the work alone, I calculated that it'd take a few weeks. Candice had stopped helping two days ago, ever since I'd accused her of taking my book. When I told George what she'd done, he didn't seem surprised. He said he'd speak to her about it, but so far, *The Invisible Man* had remained invisible.

I turned the wagon on its side, dumping the dirt, flowers, and weeds onto the ground. The wagon was badly rusted. I drenched the wheels in oil to get them spinning again. It saved my back since I could load the heavy items on it and roll it out the back gate. By late in the afternoon, I'd barely made a dent in the back corner.

While loading some tin buckets into the wagon, I looked up through the side yard and saw a car pull up in front of the house. It wasn't the type of event that would normally capture anyone's attention. But at the O'Brien house, it was monumental. Since my arrival two weeks ago, this was the first visitor I'd seen.

The driver couldn't have been older than sixteen. He checked his hair in the mirror before getting out and grabbing two large paper bags from the backseat. He took them to the front door, where I lost sight of him. He didn't stay long, five minutes tops. A short while later, I saw Candice in the kitchen putting food away. I knew an old lady in Boston who had hired a young woman to do her shopping for her. But she was nearly ninety years old and didn't have relatives living with her.

One by one, I took the flowerpots down from the fence. George had instructed me to throw them all out, but to keep the dirt. So I dumped each one out on the ground, flowers and all, and threw the pots in the wagon. I did the same with the pot that dangled from the handlebars of the bicycle. The bike tires were flat and rotted.

Vines interlaced the spokes, holding the bicycle firmly to the fence. I was on my knees using shears to free the bike from nature's grip when the back door swung open. Candice came down the steps, waved *The Invisible Man* at me, and set it by the studio door.

"Grandpa said you went crying to him about me going in your room."

"Did he tell you to stay out of there?" I stood and wiped the sweat from my brow with the back of my hand. Candice gave no answer other than a frown as she started back toward the door.

"The guy who came to the house," I said and waited for her to stop. "What was he delivering, groceries?"

"Grandpa doesn't like to shop."

"And neither do you, I take it."

That observation won me another two days of working alone under the blistering sun. I overturned flowerpots, pulled weeds, trimmed the grass along the fence, turned the alley into a trash heap, and took a verbal beating for all of it from George. He would sit in his rocking chair shouting orders at me, telling me how useless I was, while never lifting a finger to help. Whenever he had a particular point he wanted to drive home, he'd stand up, shake his cane at me, and tell me again how sorry he was for not hiring the village idiot, who would probably have had the job done by now.

After a day of dragging things out the back gate, I, too, wished he'd hired the village idiot. And sometimes I felt he had. Even when he wasn't complaining, I could feel his eyes scrutinizing my every move. At times I considered quitting, but the thought of going back to Boston and facing Marie, her friends, and my mother helped me see how good I had it in Winter Haven.

A large part of my problem with Marie revolved around a man named Jefferson Thomas, a black student at BU and one of Marie's pet projects. Jefferson Thomas had been named after the third president of the United States but in reverse order. Some of the faculty took offense to Jefferson, irritated by his irreverent attitude and outraged by his blasphemous name. Due to *Brown v Board of Education*, they couldn't expel a student just because of the color of his skin or because they found his name objectionable.

Last year, however, for no apparent reason, Jefferson's grades began to plummet, and suddenly the faculty had a case for expulsion. Marie and the other activists cried conspiracy, certain the professors were being overly harsh on Jefferson's work as an excuse to get rid of him. It was hard to build a case for racism against the university since many of the other black students at the school were doing well, but the activists felt certain that Jefferson was being singled out.

They held meetings with Jefferson, examined his work, and checked it against the work of students taking the same classes. Sure enough, answers that were correct on other students' papers were marked wrong on Jefferson's. The teachers had no choice but to raise Jefferson's grades while blaming the discrepancy on their assistants. Classes such as English were harder to dispute since most of the work consisted of essays and were more subjective. Suddenly, every class that could get away with it started assigning essays, and Jefferson's grades once again took a turn for the worse. Students held protest rallies, but the faculty wouldn't budge, claiming their grading had nothing to do with Jefferson's skin tone.

I'd first met Jefferson my sophomore year at a blues club. When the band that was playing that night took a break, Jefferson went up to the microphone without being invited. He pulled out a harmonica and started playing. The owner wasn't happy about it at first, but when everybody started clapping in unison with the tune, he let Jefferson play until the band finished their break. Afterward, Marie asked Jefferson to join us at our table. I liked the guy. He had a lot of charisma. On campus, he'd pull out his harmonica and dance around on the walkway, which was one of the things the faculty disliked about him. The Civil Rights Movement was already underway, but people still looked down on you if you hung around blacks. So I began distancing myself from Thomas even before the teachers conspired against him.

Marie tried many times to get me to participate in the rallies and to speak out against the injustice, but I always had homework to do or appointments to keep, anything that would prevent me from taking a stand.

"It's none of our business," I argued. "All you're going to do is turn the faculty against you."

And that was exactly what she did—not just the faculty either. Other students started calling her nigger lover and telling her to go back to Italy. The uglier it became, the less time I had available for dates or for study sessions. The next thing I knew, I was breaking off our engagement and moving to Winter Haven.

CHAPTER 8

George moved me around from job to job, depending on his mood. He'd have me in the back yard in the morning and in the attic in the afternoon, claiming he didn't want me to suffer from heatstroke. Apparently, the chance of heatstroke increased whenever the Blanchards were out in their back yard. Most of the time Harriet and her husband Carl would pretend they didn't see us as they went about their duty of watering the grass or filling the birdfeeder. George, on the other hand, had no acting skills. He'd scowl at them, huff as if the wind had blown a foul odor his way, and then he'd stand and tell me it was time for us to get out of the sun.

As disagreeable as George was, I started to feel sorry for him. His nastiness shielded him from the possibility of ever making any friends. I think he anticipated that everyone he met would treat him with malice, so he beat them to the punch by offending them first, which of course caused them to treat him as he'd predicted. A self-fulfilling prophecy, as my father's psychology books would have phrased it. However, to be fair to George, he wasn't always the one who started the confrontations. One morning while mending the fence that surrounded the front yard, I heard a car horn blare as it passed the house.

I recognized the driver as the young man I'd seen in the sporting goods store haggling over the price of golf clubs. The slick-haired rich boy. He drove a red, 1957 Thunderbird, its chrome sparkling in the noonday sun. The passenger was a blond-headed man with his face out the window as the car slowly rolled by.

"Rot in hell, O'Brien!" he yelled.

I looked back at George, who was standing behind me, inspecting my work. To my surprise, he lifted his right hand and extended his middle finger. It was a vulgar gesture, but coming from a sixty-six-year-old man, it was somehow charming.

His confrontations with the Blanchards, however, contained little charm and were often brutal. One evening at dinner, George asked if any of my university courses had ever discussed ways of provoking a heart attack. It was clear that Harriet Blanchard was the one he wished to send into cardiac arrest. Later, after I had retired to the studio and sat at my typewriter, I heard George and Harriet shouting at each other over the fence. I shut off my lights and parted the curtains. The sound was too muffled to make out much of what they said, something about leaves in the yard and a Halloween jack-o-lantern. Carl stood on the back porch of his home, not saying a word. He was a quiet, passive man, either too old or too tired to get involved. When Harriet went up the steps of her porch, Carl put his arm around her and escorted her inside, paying no attention to George, still shouting over the fence.

When George wasn't barking at his neighbors or keeping an eye on me, he usually tended to the flower garden that ran along the fence, just outside the back door. It was the only beautiful patch of earth on the property. George took pride in it. Ironically, directly in front of it stood the black garden, and on both sides of his patch of flowers stood long stretches of weeds. The man only had the ability to govern a ten-foot-square kingdom. When I commented on how all the long weeds growing around his garden detracted from its beauty, he put me to work on it.

To my surprise, George came out and helped. He put on his leather gloves and a Boston Red Sox cap and got down in the dirt. The two of us spent an entire morning on our knees pulling weeds. We started on separate ends of the garden, both of us working toward each other. We toiled in silence, which suited me fine. George was the kind of man you liked better when he said nothing. I looked over to see what kind of progress he was making and noticed he'd cleared a three-foot plot. Yet I failed to see what he'd done with the weeds he'd pulled. I had a couple of good-sized piles going, whereas George had nothing. I watched as he grabbed some weeds by the base, yanked their roots out of the ground, and shook off the soil. Without hesitation, he tossed them up over the fence into the Blanchards' yard.

"You ever read the book *How to Win Friends and Influence People?*" I asked.

He wrinkled his face. "Nope."

"It shows," I said.

"You ever read *The Holy Bible?*" he asked.

"Parts of it."

" 'Whatever you wish that men would do to you, do so to them.' That's Jesus's version of the Golden Rule." He squinted at the blazing sun and wiped the sweat from his forehead onto his sleeve. "One autumn I found a whole pile of leaves dumped over my fence. I figured they did unto me how they wanted me to do unto them, so I'm obliging." He stood and stretched his back as he massaged his fingers along the lower part of his spine.

"I'm no biblical scholar," I said. "But somehow I feel the true essence of that verse has been lost somewhere."

George peered over the fence and looked down at the weeds that now lay upon the neighbor's groomed grass. He looked proud of himself.

"Carl and Harriet Blanchard." He gestured toward the neighbor's house. "Couple old geezers, those two. I keep hoping they'll up and die so we can get some new blood in the neighborhood."

Pulling off his baseball cap and leather gloves, he scratched at his scalp. He was a thick-skinned old man, and I doubted many people could get the best of George O'Brien. You couldn't make him mad or spiteful because he was already there. The man woke up in a bad mood and remained in a constant state of bitterness all day. The challenge with George wasn't making him mad but making him happy. He seemed to be daring you to try and make him feel good. The thing people like George never seem to realize is that nobody cares enough about sour old buzzards like him to ever want to make them happy. It's easier just to leave them alone and let them wallow in their hate.

That night, after the lights in the house went out, I came out of the studio and stared up at the sky. The stars never looked so bright in the city. It was as though someone had fine-tuned the image on a television, making it sharp and beautiful. I had one of those feelings that you can never put into words and do it justice. I just felt good.

I looked over the fence to see if the Blanchards had picked up the weeds George had bestowed upon them. Even in the dark, I could see the clumps of blackness where the weeds lay. Climbing over, I gathered the weeds and took them to the back fence where I dropped them into the alley. I hadn't planned on doing it. I suppose it was the beauty of the sky that got to me. Also, I'd been thinking about George and how he was in this hate cycle that needed to be broken somehow. As long as he kept treating his neighbors with such malice, they would keep treating him likewise. It would go on forever if someone didn't interrupt it somehow. At that time, I had no idea how such a thing could be accomplished. Even if I had, I would have never thought I'd be the one to do it.

CHAPTER 9

The next morning, I opened the studio door and discovered a potted plant on my doorstep. No note, just a green plant in a rust-colored pot. I looked at the O'Brien house and felt the first bud of kindness I'd felt all summer. Who had put it there? Neither George nor Candice seemed a likely candidate, which was what made it so gratifying. I took it inside, set it on the table next to the typewriter, and opened the curtains so it could get some sun and so whoever had given it to me could see that I welcomed the gift.

It amazed me how good that small gesture made me feel. Not knowing which O'Brien was responsible, I treated them both with kindness, complimenting George on the woodwork he'd done in the studio and telling Candice how much I enjoyed the French toast she made for breakfast. They both responded congenially, so I still had no idea which one had put the plant at my door.

That day, George left me alone in the black garden, neither criticizing my work nor keeping watch from his rocking chair. It was a lesson in human nature I should have learned years ago. Perhaps I actually was egocentric, as Papa Manzini had claimed. Not that I thought I was better than others. I just tended to focus more on myself than I did on anyone else. But doesn't everyone?

After all, you are the center of your own universe, right? If you cease to exist, so does everything else—at least to you. Perhaps my problem wasn't that I focused more on myself than on others, but that I only focused on myself and rarely took an interest in anyone else.

"I see you're putting in overtime."

I looked up from the load of bricks I'd put in the wagon and found Candice standing on the back porch.

"It's ten after five," she said.

I looked at my watch, surprised that the time had gotten away from me. George had once told me he could set his watch by me since I always stopped work at precisely five o'clock.

"I'm still hoping to get that bonus," I said as I pulled off my leather gloves.

"Good luck with that." She had a playful glint in her eyes that I'd never seen before. "I was going to make a tuna fish sandwich. Do you want one?"

"Sure. Let me run and take a shower and I'll come in."

My hair was still damp when a knock came at the studio door. I quickly pulled on my blue jeans and was in the process of putting on a shirt as I pulled the door open and found Candice's lovely face staring back at me. Holding a plate with a sandwich on it in one hand and a glass of milk in the other, she fidgeted as her gaze moved from my chest to my eyes and back to my chest.

"Grandpa's in his office making his sales calls, so I thought I'd bring this out."

"You want to come in?" I finished buttoning my shirt and took the food from her.

"I'd better go back inside," she said, yet she remained, twisting a finger in her hair. "I wanted to ask you about last night … when you cleaned the weeds out of Blanchards' yard. Why'd you do that?"

I glanced past her, to the window on the second floor of the O'Brien home, Candice's bedroom.

"I couldn't sleep," I said. "Some people count sheep. I gather weeds."

"No, I'm serious. Why would you do something like that?"

"I don't know. I just don't like the way they treat each other."

She nodded as though she had spent many restless hours because of the squabbling that went on back and forth over the fence between her grandfather and Mrs. Blanchard.

"You sure you don't want to come in?" I stepped aside as an invitation for her to enter.

"Perhaps just a minute."

As she came in, I pushed the door closed with my foot and set the milk and sandwich on the table in front of my typewriter. A thin smile crossed her lips as she looked at the plant.

"What does your grandfather sell?"

"Photography equipment." She smoothed out the blanket on the bed and sat. "He used to be a photographer. He had a studio downtown. Then he fixed this place up and was going to move his studio in here." She gestured to the bedroom. "But he decided to be a salesman instead. He works for one of those catalog businesses."

That explained the trunk filled with photographs in the attic. It also explained why George was in so few of them or in the photos on the living room piano. The photographer is always the invisible presence, the artist granting the glory to everyone but himself. To me, George was anything but invisible. I had an easier time imagining him as a foreman on a construction site, walking around barking orders at men, than as a gentleman behind a camera, making people smile so he could capture it on film.

"Why do they hate each other so much?" I sipped my milk. "Your grandfather and the Blanchards, I mean."

She shrugged. "I don't think they even know anymore."

"You know, when I first moved in, I thought he liked Harriet. I'd see him at the window with his binoculars and wonder why he didn't just go over there and talk to her rather than waste his time spying on her. This was before I knew she had a husband."

"He doesn't watch her that much."

I raised my eyebrows to let her know I wasn't buying what she was selling.

"Not compared to how much he watches Margaret," Candice explained. "You wouldn't know because he watches her through the front window. She lives across the street."

"Does he like her?"

"Not according to him. But yeah, I think so."

"And what about her? Does she like him?"

"Margaret?" She shrugged and smiled like she had never considered Margaret's feelings. "She probably doesn't even know who he is."

"Did she just move in?"

"No. She's lived there forever—as long as I can remember."

"Do you like her?"

Candice went silent for a moment, watching me. "I don't know her," she confessed. "I've never spoken to her."

"Never?" I pressed.

Her eyes told me to drop the subject.

The elements of Candice's life were coming into focus, and it was a very disturbing picture. True, I'd suspected she didn't know Margaret very well, just as I surmised she didn't know any of her neighbors, but never to have talked to her neighbor in her entire life? I was no social butterfly, but I had at least spoken to all of my neighbors, even if just a casual hello. And that was in the city, where people were cold and suspicious of one another. Small towns were supposed to be friendly and close-knit. But then again, the O'Briens didn't exactly fit the small-town mold.

Candice flinched as knuckles rapped at the studio door. The quiet shame I'd seen a moment before disappeared, replaced by a stiff alertness. As I got up to answer the door, her breathing stopped. It seemed like an overreaction until I opened the door and saw the fire in George's eyes. I'd never seen him so rigid, so livid. His stare darted past me and bore into Candice, still seated on the bed, acting as though she'd been caught with her pants down.

"Get in the house, Candice."

"Is something wrong?" I asked.

"You know damn well what's wrong! I brought you into my house in good faith, and this is how you repay me? Pack your bags! You're no longer welcome here!"

"What are you talking about?"

"I want you out of here!" His usual orneriness had turned bitter. There was spittle on his chin. "Candice, I told you to get in the house."

George gave her a menacing stare as she slipped past us and out the door.

"As for you," he said, leaning closer to my face, "you've got one hour to pack your bags. I'll have your check ready." He headed down the walkway to the back steps with me directly behind him. My hands grew sweaty. Heat rose out of my collar.

"We were just talking for Christ's sake."

"Don't you use that language with me." He turned toward me, not happy to see me following on his heels. "And I don't want to hear any of your damned excuses. This is my house, and I want you out of it." He whacked my shin with his cane, not hard, but hard enough to let me know he meant business. "Now get to packing!"

Of all the pigheaded, closed-minded nonsense I'd ever heard, this won the grand prize. I stormed back into the studio and slammed the door. I didn't want the job anyway. I should have quit the moment I'd realized I'd been hired to be a maid and that my boss was Genghis Khan. Instead, I'd put up with his humiliation for nearly a month.

I pulled my suitcase out from under the bed, laid it open, and began pulling my clothes out of the dresser drawers. I threw them into the suitcase, getting more wound up, more incensed as I thought of that smug old man and his accusations. I no longer pitied his loneliness. I reveled in it. If anyone deserved to be miserable and alone, it was George O'Brien.

Fifteen minutes later, my suitcase was filled and closed. One box was crammed half full of books when a knock sounded at my door. I knew it was George even before I opened it. He'd come to apologize for being such an unreasonable bastard. I had no intention of accepting his apology.

Only it wasn't George. It was Candice. Her eyes were red. There was a sense of frustration on her face. The sight of her took some of the steam out of my fury. I looked past her at the kitchen windows and saw no sign of George.

"You have to stay."

"What's wrong, can't he come out and apologize for himself?" Returning to my bookshelf, I swept several books into my hands and tossed them in the box.

"He's not the one who wants you to stay. I do."

"I appreciate that, Candice, but no." I continued packing. "I've already put up with a lot more than I should have."

"He can be stubborn, but he's a good man. Go talk to him. Ask him for another chance. I'm sure he'll reconsider."

"You want me to apologize to him? I didn't do anything wrong."

"Who cares? Just do it. Please."

I shook my head adamantly. "I'm not going to apologize for something I didn't do. You should be in there begging him to apologize to me."

"He'd never do it."

"Then why should I?"

"Because I'm asking you to."

"Your grandfather is a pigheaded jackass. I see why people in this town hate him so much."

I felt the sting in my cheek even before I realized I'd been slapped. Candice was infuriated, her eyes filled with hurt and anger.

"Don't you ever talk about my grandfather like that!" Her finger bore into my chest. "I thought you were different. But you're just like everyone else in this godforsaken town." She went to the door and paused long enough to give me one more withering look before going out and slamming it behind her.

I rubbed a hand over my cheek, stunned at how quickly I'd lost her sympathy and had won her contempt. Perhaps calling the man she loved most in the world a pigheaded jackass wasn't the wisest thing I could have said. But what did I care? I was leaving. Soon, I'd be looking at their home in my rearview mirror and heading—where exactly? Back to Boston? Back to Marie and her horrible friends? Back to my father, who called me a coward for running away in the first place, who spoke to me with shame the day I left, asking me when I was going to grow up, when I was going to learn to face my problems? Either I groveled to George now or I groveled to Marie, her friends, and my parents when I showed up in Boston with my tail between my legs. I didn't like either scenario.

I went around to the front of the O'Brien house and knocked at the door, ashamed of myself for what I was about to do. I hated apologizing for my mistakes, but apologizing for something I hadn't done was far worse. George didn't make it easy on me either. When he opened the door, he was already waiting with check in hand.

"I gave you a fifty-cent bonus for all the extra effort."

I took the check with reluctance, doing my best to remain cordial.

"Could we talk about this, Mr. O'Brien?"

"I don't have anything to say to you."

I had my check now. If he truly wanted me gone, all he had to do was close the door in my face. But he didn't. He glared, enjoying my humiliation, wanting me to grovel some more. So I obliged.

"I'm sorry about what happened. I didn't realize you felt so strongly or I never would have invited her in."

"Candice knows better."

"Then go talk to her," I said in my defense. "Don't take it out on me. I didn't know she wasn't supposed to be in there."

That took the fire out of him. He studied me, put both hands on his cane, and leaned on it. The blaze slowly died in his eyes.

"My granddaughter's a virgin. Make sure she stays that way."

I had no response to that.

"Go finish your food. Then I need you to run to the store for me. That damn Conway boy never brought me my strawberry jam. The kid doesn't have a brain in his head. He forgets something every damn time. I'll get you some money when you come back in." He snatched the check from my hand and shut the door in my face.

CHAPTER 10

Candice stood at the sink with her sleeves rolled up to her elbows and her arms wrist-deep in the sudsy water. When I came through the back door with my plate and glass, she glanced at me and went back to scrubbing a bowl with a rag.

"It looks like I'm staying." I handed her my dishes, expecting a show of delight over the turn of events, but she said nothing as she plunged my plate and glass into the water. I glanced toward the hallway to make sure George wasn't within earshot.

"I'm sorry for what I said about your grandfather."

I patted her shoulder. She flinched and took a step away from me.

"I stood up for you." Her voice was low, but the tone was sharp. "I asked my grandfather to let you stay."

"And I appreciate it."

"Do you?" She held my gaze a moment before turning her attention back to the dishes.

"Now what? I apologized for what I said. I even apologized to your grandfather for something I didn't do."

"I heard your apology." She grabbed a dish towel and wiped her hands. "I was at the top of the stairs. I heard how you placed all of the blame on me. You're the one who invited me in, in case you forgot. I said no, but you insisted."

"I was being polite."

"At least the people of Winter Haven make it clear where they stand. I may not like it, but at least they're honest. But you …" She tossed the dish towel on the counter. "You act like you're our friend, but you're not. You clear the weeds from Blanchards' yard as if you're doing my grandfather a favor, trying to make peace between him and Harriet. Then I find out you hate my grandfather. So why did you gather up the weeds? It makes no sense to me. Then you apologize to my grandfather by throwing it all onto me. And now you come in here acting like we're old friends and like I should be happy that you're staying." She stared in defiance, daring me to defend myself.

She was just like Marie. Never happy. No matter what I said she would twist it to make me out to be the bad guy. I walked away without replying.

In the living room, I found George standing at the front window. The curtains were open four inches, just enough to make room for his binoculars. I cleared my throat to get his attention. He looked back at me without a trace of shame.

"You wanted me to run to the store for you?"

"Oh yeah, the strawberry jam." He pulled his wallet from his back pocket and fingered through the dollar bills, pulling out a ten. "Get the large jar if they have it. If not, get two of the small ones. Might as well get some bread while you're at it." He gave me directions to the market and then lifted the binoculars and returned to his post at the window, not even waiting for me to leave.

As I came down the walk and out the gate, I noticed a woman sitting on the porch of the home across the street. She was rocking back and forth in a wooden rocker. She raised her eyes from a book and stared across the street at me. She looked to be around sixty: graying hair, slightly overweight, with a lovely smile. I waved. She returned the gesture. When I walked around to the driver's door of my blue Chevy and slid the key into the lock, I glanced up and saw the binoculars peering through the curtains. I doubted Margaret could make them out from across the street.

The store on Pine Street was one of those small family-run markets, old with wooden floors and a set of stairs leading upward to what I figured was the owner's residence. The customers were mostly older people. I found the jam and bread and decided to grab a few things for myself that I could keep in the studio, saving me from running into the house whenever I wanted a snack. The O'Briens weren't fond of sugary or salty food and rarely had any on hand.

In one aisle, the teenaged boy who had delivered the groceries was stocking cans of soup on the shelf. "The Conway boy," George had called him. He barely looked old enough to drive, but he was taller than me and thin, with a disheveled ducktail.

The cashier at the front counter was a nice-looking woman in her late-thirties. She talked to the customers as she rang up their groceries. Periodically, her eyes left the conversation and followed me from aisle to aisle. When I set my basket of groceries in front of her, she gave me one of those looks that said she knew me. I knew the look well, having been blessed with a face that was always reminding people of somebody else. That wasn't the case this time, however.

"How are them O'Briens doing?" She pulled the strawberry jam out of the basket and punched in the numbers on the cash register.

"How did you know I was working for the O'Briens?"

"This is a small town. Word gets around quickly. And O'Brien company is big news around here. They're not exactly socialites."

"What's ole George got you doing?" asked a voice from behind me. I looked back and found two men and a woman eavesdropping on our conversation.

"A little of everything," I answered.

"You taking care of that daughter of his?" The man doing the talking was stout and had a mustache that drooped around the corners of his mouth.

"You mean his granddaughter?"

"People around here aren't sure what to call her," the cashier said as she rang up my bag of potato chips.

"What do you mean by that?"

"Devil's Spawn, that girl," the man said. "You be careful there, son. Don't want to be digging your bones up from under their front porch."

The Conway boy stood partway down one aisle. He scowled at the stout man while his finger squeezed the can of soup he was holding. I caught his eye, but he looked away and put the soup on the shelf.

"How much do I owe?"

"Six sixty-six. Now there's a figure for you. Good thing I'm not superstitious, I'd think we had a couple of warlocks and a witch living up there on Willow Lane."

"Mother." The stock boy's voice was restrained but sharp enough to convey his disapproval. I saw a trace of embarrassment shadow the cashier's face as she took my money and counted back the change. Was she ashamed of the words she'd spoken or from the knowledge that her son was the adult in the family and everyone in the store now knew it?

"Careful you don't wind up in a boiling pot hanging over a fire," said the man with the mustache. "I hear they eat their dead." He glanced back at the stock boy, challenging him to speak out against him, but the boy kept his attention on his work.

As I surveyed the room and the faces, the oddest feeling washed through me. It was sickening and profane. Where was that small-town charm I'd expected, the caring neighbors, the innocence? I could see now that the coldness of the big city had its advantages. Few people in Boston knew my personal business. Winter Haven was a large family, and the O'Briens were the relatives no one liked.

By association, their stigma was now rubbing off onto me. I didn't like that one bit. What I liked even less was confrontation. I rarely spoke my mind in the company of people I knew would disagree with me. That was my biggest problem with the Jefferson Thomas affair. Avoidance was my standard procedure. Few things agitated me enough to stir me to action.

I paid for my groceries, grabbed my bag, and went out the door. As I got in my car and started the engine, I looked back at the store and saw the Conway boy looking out the window at me. His face contained a mixture of emotions: some sadness, some irritation, but most of all jealousy. The boy hadn't spoken a word to me, but I knew what he dreamed about every night. I knew that when his mother sent him on an errand to deliver groceries to the O'Briens that his heart beat faster, that his palms got sweaty, and that he intentionally forgot items so he'd have a reason to come back later, to have one more look at Candice O'Brien.

CHAPTER 11

No matter how hard I tried, I couldn't shake the eerie feeling that pervaded my days following the incident in the store. My view of George and Candice became skewed. I watched them more carefully now, wondering why they'd chosen this life of solitude and what they'd done to alienate themselves from the town. Candice was slightly unusual, I suppose, but Devil's Spawn? That seemed melodramatic. And what had the cashier meant when she said she wasn't sure if Candice was George's granddaughter or daughter? I'd seen the pictures of Dora, George's wife. I'd seen the pictures of Candice's mother, Carolyn, whom I was quite certain was George's daughter.

Then my heart skipped a beat. I realized the detail I'd overlooked when going through the photographs in the attic trunk: Candice's father. I hadn't seen a single picture of him. And Candice went by the name of O'Brien. Perhaps the father was George's son and Carolyn was the daughter-in-law. But the snippets of conversation I'd collected over the past month told me otherwise. On top of that, I'd seen photographs of Carolyn as she grew from baby to young adult, and many of those pictures had been taken in and around the O'Brien house. So who was the father?

I could ask, but they wouldn't answer. Maybe I could talk to the Conway boy. I'd have to convince him not to say anything since George made it clear that talking about the O'Briens behind their backs was one sin he wouldn't tolerate, followed closely by the sin of talking about them to their faces.

George used a handkerchief to wipe the sweat from his brow as we worked in the back yard. The back half of the garden had been removed and was piled in the alley, up against the O'Briens' fence. If the city didn't start hauling things away soon, we'd either have to start piling things against neighbors' fences or start blocking off the alleyway. Neither choice was going to improve George's reputation.

Candice and I disassembled a platform constructed of cinder blocks and wooden planks and piled the material in the wagon.

"Was this your wagon or did it belong to Carolyn?" I knew this would grab her attention since she and George rarely spoke about Carolyn, and when they did they always referred to her as *your mother* or *mom*.

"How did you know my mother's name was Carolyn?"

"Some folks down at the store mentioned it."

"I'm paying you to do a job," George growled. "And that job doesn't entail poking your nose in our affairs."

"It's just that these people down at the store—"

"I don't give a damn about the people at the store." George's face deepened into a darker shade of red. "Don't talk to people about us. Not ever. You're only here for a few more months. Then you're going back to Boston, so stay out of our business." He glared as he wiped the handkerchief across his face, waiting for me to acknowledge that I understood and would obey. He trailed off down the walkway, climbed the steps, and went through the back door.

"What's going on here, Candice?"

She grabbed a cinder block and placed it in the wagon.

"I don't know what you two have done, but public opinion doesn't speak too highly of the O'Briens."

"I'm not interested in public opinion."

"You should be."

"We live in a world full of idiots, Mitchell. And the only people who care what they think are other idiots." Her look said she knew which category I fit into. She dusted her hands and followed her grandfather. As she climbed the steps, I noticed Harriet standing at her window looking out at me. I had the guilty-by-association feeling again, the same one I got when I was with Marie Manzini.

I pulled the wagon through the back gate and looked around for a spot to unload the cinder blocks and planks. I stared down the gravel alleyway, past the stench of the neighbors' garbage, past the end of the block, and into the next alley. This was the dirty side of the neighborhood, where people left their trash exposed for everyone to see. I wondered how many of these people had their own dirty little secrets hidden inside their cozy homes, how many of them hated the O'Briens, how many of them even gave them any thought.

When I dragged the wagon back inside the fence, I scanned the kitchen windows and found no sign of George or Candice. An idea ticked inside of me and my eyes rose to the second floor, to Candice's bedroom, and then to the small windows lining the attic. I pulled off my leather gloves and climbed the back steps.

George and Candice were in the living room listening to Radio Theater. I'd discovered they didn't own a television. Forty-five million households in American had televisions, and I had to end up in one that didn't. George despised them, said they were poisoning our culture and brainwashing people into buying a bunch of things they didn't need.

"Do you mind if I do some work in the attic? I need a break from the sun." I fanned myself with my hand. The look on George's face said he didn't buy my story, but he nodded and I headed upstairs to the attic.

I didn't know what I was looking for or even if there would be anything to find, but I had to give the wooden trunk another inspection. The first thing I did was verify the complete absence of Candice's father. There were hundreds of photos. Though some of them displayed faces I didn't recognize, none of them appeared to be Carolyn's husband.

I also inspected the documents stuffed inside folders. I found a deed to the house, a pink slip to a car, some warranties for various household appliances, and some certificates that validated George's claim of being a photographer. Buried among the documents I found Candice's birth certificate. Her full name was Candice Bonnie O'Brien. She was born January 5, 1939. Her mother's name was Carolyn Jean O'Brien. The space where the father's name was meant to go had been left blank. I couldn't say if that was what I was looking for or not, but it did seem significant.

I closed the trunk and gazed off into the dimly lit attic. Placing a box on the table, I started sorting through it, only half paying attention to the items as I pulled them out, glanced at them, and tossed them into another box I was using for the trash. I found broken watches, tarnished jewelry, and a book by Dr. Suess: *And to Think That I Saw It on Mulberry Street.* I smiled as I thumbed through the pictures. It made me think of the Christmas I went shopping with my sister Ann to buy a gift for her two-year-old daughter, Cynthia. She bought *Horton Hears a Who!* The following spring, their basement flooded and the book was destroyed, along with dozens of valuable documents. Among them was Ann's marriage certificate. I ended up driving her to the county recorder's office to get it replaced.

I closed the book and grinned. According to my watch, it was 4:10. I still had time.

George looked up as I descended the stairs.

"I'm going to run to the store and buy a few things. Do you need anything?"

"It's not five o'clock yet," he said.

"I'll make up the time when I get back." I didn't give him time to argue, just went out the door and hurried to my car. I knew he wouldn't approve of me messing with his time schedule. One morning, when I'd woken up late, he'd lectured me on the eight to five tradition he adhered to. I told him if I started an hour late, I'd merely tack an extra hour onto the end of the day. That wasn't good enough for George. Work started at eight and ended at five, though overtime with no pay was highly encouraged.

The county recorder's office was located on the second floor of the Winter Haven Courthouse, on Center Street, one block over from Main. The two-story gray-brick building had broad cement steps leading up to the entrance and narrow wooden stairs leading to the second floor. The county clerk was a thin-faced woman with horn-rimmed glasses and a wrinkled blouse that smelled of mothballs. When I came through the door, she was at her desk, chewing gum and gabbing on the phone. She looked at me but kept talking, telling whoever was on the other end of the line about a woman named Mildred who had been caught walking out of Redding's Department Store wearing not one but two brassieres, and apparently one of them wasn't paid for.

"Listen," she said into the phone, "I've got somebody here. I'll call you back in ten minutes." She gave me a smile as she approached the counter.

"What is it I can do for you?"

"I'm not really sure how this works." I rapped my knuckles on the counter. "Can just anybody look at a copy of someone else's marriage certificate or do you have to be family?"

"That's all public information," she said.

"The thing is, I'm not even sure when the marriage took place."

"Whose marriage certificate is it you want to see?"

"Carolyn O'Brien. I don't know the husband's name."

Beyond the lenses of the horn-rimmed glasses, the clerk's eyes darkened. Her gum chewing slowed and then came to a stop. I'd come thinking I might have to explain who Carolyn O'Brien was, but I could see now that no explanation would be necessary.

"You're not going to find a marriage certificate for Carolyn O'Brien." As she leaned on the counter, her voice softened like someone revealing dirty little secrets she didn't want anyone to overhear. "There was never a husband. Not even a boyfriend."

"But she had a daughter. Candice. Any idea who the father is?"

"Everybody knows who the father is." The clerk offered a thin smile and raised her eyebrows. "Let's just say that George O'Brien loved his daughter a little more than he should have."

I felt the color drain from my face.

The clerk faked an apologetic nod. A knot formed in my stomach. I could see my discomfort provided her with that sadistic pleasure we all get when we get to be the one to break the bad news to someone. This would give her something else to talk about on the phone when she finished telling about Mildred and her two brassieres.

"People say he's now doing the same with that granddaughter of his," the clerk said.

The knot tightened in my stomach. I'd come to the recorder's office with dozens of questions in mind, but suddenly none of them seemed important. I'd heard everything I needed to hear. I knew why people looked at the O'Briens as though they carried the plague. I knew why George and Candice chose to spend their lives inside their home rather than venturing out into the world. I knew why George had chosen to hire someone from out of town rather than someone from Winter Haven. And I knew what I had to do.

As I drove back to Willow Lane, I found myself welling up with hatred for George O'Brien—not just disliking him as I had before, but actually hating him. I parked in front of their Victorian home with its peeling blue paint and sat in my car staring at the front door. My mind conjured up images of George O'Brien in his younger days, wandering into his daughter's bedroom and slipping beneath the blankets with her, and images of him now, as he continued the tradition with Candice, a girl I had grown fonder of than I cared to admit. Devil's Spawn, I thought. I now understood its meaning, and it made me physically ill. I wanted to pound on the door and slap dear old grandpa across the face when he came to see who was there. But I knew I wouldn't—not me, not Mitchell Sanders. No, I'd do what I had done my entire life. I'd pack my bags and run away. It was what I did best.

As I came up the sidewalk, I checked my watch and saw that I'd missed an hour of work, but I no longer had any intention of making up the time. I knocked at the door but didn't wait for a reply before going inside, where I found George seated on the sofa reading a newspaper.

"You've been here long enough that you don't need to knock anymore," he said.

I nodded and glanced down the hall toward the kitchen, wondering where Candice was and hoping she was out of earshot. I didn't know how to begin. I didn't even know if I'd have the courage to say the things I'd thought of in the car. In fact, the longer I looked at George, the more certain I was that the best solution was to lie, tell him I had a family emergency and was needed at home.

He looked up at me again and checked his watch. "What are you standing around for?"

"You know, Mr. O'Brien, I'm not so sure this is working out," I said, deciding against the family emergency scenario.

"What isn't?"

"The job." I tried to keep myself from tapping my fingers against my legs, the way I do when I'm nervous. "It's not exactly what I expected, and I know Candice doesn't like my being here."

George folded his newspaper and laid it on his lap. "Who have you been talking to this time?"

"This has nothing to do with—"

"Don't bullshit me," he barked, annoyed at my spineless good manners. "If you have something to say, just come out with it."

I stared at his thinning hair and the wrinkles around his eyes. He was a hard man, but standing in front of him now, I couldn't imagine him doing the things the clerk had said he'd done. I could picture him losing his temper and slapping a child, but not molesting one, not impregnating his own daughter. I suppose we never truly know another person, not even those closest to us. There will forever be news stories of someone doing ghastly things, accompanied by interviews with family and friends saying what a great guy he was and how they couldn't believe he was capable of such an awful deed.

"Perhaps I've heard a few things."

"Such as?" George looked at me intently, daring me to say what I didn't want to say.

"That there's some question as to who Candice's father is. That it might be you."

George grabbed his cane and got to his feet. This wasn't a man who shied away from a confrontation. He might have been frail, but that didn't stop him from getting in my face, close enough that I could smell the grilled cheese sandwich on his breath.

"What do you think, Mitchell?" His voice was calmer than I expected.

"I don't know what to think."

"No, you wouldn't, would you? Like everyone else around here, you want someone to force-feed you the answers and tell you what your own opinion is." His eyes bore into me and I felt the shame of my accusation. With the shake of the head, he walked past me to the hall leading to the kitchen, where he paused and turned back toward me. "Do what you want. If you're not smart enough to make up your own mind about Candice and me, then I don't want you here anyway."

CHAPTER 12

I stayed awake half the night trying to decide if I should stay or go. I didn't drift off until well after three. Even then, my sleep was restless. I tossed and turned and had nightmares of George passionately kissing Candice and doing things no grandfather should do to a granddaughter. In my dream, she enjoyed it. She stopped in mid-kiss and glanced at me as I stood in George's bedroom doorway watching them. She gave me a mocking smile before kissing him again. In dreams, everything makes sense. Of course she was involved with her grandfather: that was why she didn't have a boyfriend; that was why he was so protective of her; that was why she'd seen his genitalia.

I woke up angry and still felt it twisting in me when I exited the studio and entered the back door of the home. On most mornings, I'd walk into the smell of bacon, eggs, pancakes, or oatmeal. Candice would be standing at the stove and George would be at the table hunched over his plate, filling his mouth. This morning, however, neither of them was in their usual positions, and the table was bare. I walked down the hall and found Candice crouched on the living room floor, picking up shards of glass from the carpet and putting them into a garbage can. The curtains were open, revealing a shattered window. George was unraveling the cord of the vacuum cleaner.

"What happened?"

"Some bastard threw a rock through our window." George pointed to a rock about the size of my fist that was sitting on the coffee table.

"Did you call the police?"

"Police aren't interested in our affairs." George went to the wall, plugged in the vacuum, and clicked it on.

The anger I felt toward George subsided. In its place grew a new anger, this one directed at the townspeople. George was no saint, but he didn't deserve this, nor did Candice. George's stubbornness didn't help the situation any. The frustration showed in his face as he ran the vacuum back and forth over the carpet, yet his unwillingness to call the police made it clear that he felt he could solve the problem simply by ignoring it.

I grabbed the local phone directory and turned to the section of county services, where I located the number for the sheriff's office. George was too busy cleaning to notice me pick up the phone and dial the number, and with the sound of the vacuum buzzing in his ears, he didn't even hear the conversation until I'd already reported the crime and had given the address.

"Hang that phone up!" George yelled when he turned and saw what I was doing. He turned off the vacuum. His face flushed red with anger. "Breaking windows is nothing new around here. Candice and I choose to take care of things ourselves. We don't need the police involved in our affairs."

"But you're not handling it yourself," I said. "What's going to stop them from coming back and breaking your window again or doing something worse?"

"They always come back." He gritted his teeth and held my gaze. "But the police don't give a damn about what goes on in this house. Inviting them here only gives them something to laugh about down at the station. If Sheriff Cornell and his dimwitted deputy show up here, I'm docking you a day's wages." He switched the vacuum back on and ran it roughly over the carpet, taking out his frustration on the slivers of glass scattered across the floor.

"What time did this happen?" I asked Candice as I crouched beside her and helped pick up the larger pieces of glass and stuff them in the garbage can.

She looked up at her grandfather. "One in the morning," she whispered.

Holing themselves up in their home hadn't successfully protected them from the ills of society. Those who abhorred the O'Briens always knew where to find them and went out of their way to assure them that they hadn't been forgotten.

"How you folks doing this morning?"

A man stared through the broken window. Sheriff Cornell, I assumed. He was wearing a gray Smokey the Bear hat and a dark brown shirt with a star-shaped badge above the left pocket.

"Get off my porch!" George yelled as he turned the vacuum off.

"You're the one that called and asked me to come out here."

"I never called anyone."

"Somebody did." Sheriff Cornell removed his hat and gave Candice a nod. He was around forty, with a receding hairline and round cheeks.

"I'm the one who called." I stood and opened the front door.

"Get your butt back in here!" George yelled.

I didn't even look back at him as I passed through the door and closed it behind me. A deputy, dressed in similar attire as the sheriff, narrowed his eyes at me as he climbed the steps to the porch. He was younger than the sheriff and moved as though he had a lot of excess energy that needed to be burned off. Fiddling with his wavy black hair, he stared through the broken window at Candice, with what I thought was a little too much interest.

"Apparently, this isn't the first time this happened," I said to the sheriff, who was tall, with tanned skin and dark eyes that studied me with suspicion.

"And who might you be?"

"Mitchell Sanders, a friend of the family."

"You're no friend of mine," George said through the broken window.

"You see who did this?"

"No. I'm staying in the studio outback. I didn't know anything about it until this morning."

"You know if George or Candice saw this happen?"

I stared through the window at the two O'Briens standing there watching and listening to the conversation. The sheriff could have asked his question to them, but he obviously knew them well enough to know he'd get nothing but belligerence from either one of them.

"No, I don't know," I answered.

The deputy leaned his head into the broken window. "You care to make a statement, Mr. O'Brien?"

"Yeah, I do. Get the hell off my porch. All three of you."

For an officer of the law, the deputy had no skill at maintaining a poker face. George's words irritated him. He looked to the sheriff for directions on how to handle the situation.

"Let's get off the man's porch." The sheriff led the way down the steps and out the front gate. His brown and white patrol car was parked at the curb behind my Chevy. Across the street, Margaret was watching from her doorway. Next door, Mr. and Mrs. Blanchard stood in their yard, keeping an eye on us. Having officers of the law scouting around the neighborhood was big news in a small town like this. I was certain they'd be talking about it at the dinner table tonight, and they'd get it blown out of proportion.

"That George is a very difficult man." The sheriff leaned against his patrol car and put his hands in his pockets. "Deputy Fritz and I would love to help him, but if he doesn't want my help, there's little I can do."

"Can't you watch the place?"

"We can drive by, but the chances of us catching somebody in the act are pretty slim."

"What they got you doing in that house anyway?" There was a calculating undertone in the deputy's voice. It had echoes of what I'd heard in the convenience store from the cashier and the man with the mustache.

"Right now I'm just throwing a lot of things out."

"What kind of stuff they got cluttering up that house of theirs?" The sheriff picked up the same tone as his deputy.

"You name it."

"Anything out of the ordinary?"

"Such as?"

"Oh, nothing in particular." He brushed the back of his fingers under his chin. "You know us lawmen, always on the lookout for clues. You do me a favor and keep an eye out, won't you? May just be the clue we need to find out who's been tossing rocks through these nice people's windows." The sheriff walked around the car and opened the driver's door. He glanced at the house and waved. Looking back, I saw George watching us through the broken pane of glass, looking less pleased than usual.

I remained at the curb as the sheriff started the car, made a U-turn, and drove down Willow Lane. I waited until the car disappeared from sight before making my way back through the gate. I was happy to see George no longer standing at the broken window, but I knew he'd be waiting. He'd be inside the front door ready to berate me for poking my nose in his business, even if my motives were well intended. I stopped at the foot of the steps, but rather than going up, I went around the house, cutting through the side lawn and heading to the studio. I still felt tired from the poor night's sleep and figured a half-hour's nap wouldn't hurt anything, while I gave George time to cool off.

But I never made it that far. As I rounded the corner into the back yard, I found George waiting for me. He stood on the porch, leaning forward on his cane, with his thin red hair tousled.

"I thought you were leaving," he said.

"I changed my mind."

"Well, if you ever pull a stunt like that again, I'll change it right back. Now help me get a new windowpane."

I followed him into the house, expecting him to give me some money and send me to town. Instead, he led me into his office. I'd heard him in there making his sales calls, but he always kept the door closed, so I'd never seen inside. It was next to his bedroom, just down the hall from the kitchen. Lots of framed photographs hung on the walls. There were a few shots of the family, but most of them were of buildings and objects: a broken-down barn, a horseshoe hanging above a door, the inside of an empty diner. There were even some shots of the black garden, which I must admit looked very artistic in black and white.

Across the room, on the other side of the desk, a door led into a smaller room. The door stood open and through it I could see a sink, print trays, bottles of chemicals on shelves, and several cameras on the counter.

"You have your own darkroom."

"I was a photographer in my past life." George walked around his desk where several windowpanes were leaning against the wall. He grabbed one, dragged it out a couple of inches, and waited for me to lend a hand.

"I don't think I've ever met anybody who keeps extra windowpanes on hand." I grabbed the other end of the glass and we slid it across the floor, out into the hall.

"I can get them at a discount in Albany," George said, "so I buy several at a time. Saves me a trip."

"How often does this happen?"

"They don't keep a regular schedule."

We carried the windowpane through the living room and out the front door where we set it on the ground and leaned it against the porch swing.

George pulled a screwdriver from his back pocket and handed it to me. "Start getting the broken glass out of the frame. I'll get the putty." He went to the kitchen and returned with a can of putty and two putty knives. He skillfully removed the wooden slates from around the window and brushed the broken glass from the frame onto the porch. Then, having me lift the glass and hold it in place, he refastened the slates, handed me a putty knife, and showed me how to seal the window into the frame.

He displayed an air of pride I hadn't seen in him before. I sensed he liked feeling useful and showing off his skills. What he didn't like was the attention from the neighbors. Carl and Harriet Blanchard were in their front yard, clipping the hedges that ran along the sidewalk. Harriet was wearing a light blue sunbonnet, but it didn't conceal her wandering eyes. Every time George caught her looking at us, he grunted with disapproval.

"Damn buzzards. Just waiting for me to die so they can pick at my bones."

I didn't bother pointing out that he was watching them every bit as much as they were watching him. Spending so much time around George, I began to realize that he was all bark. He liked to listen to himself complain, but I don't think the attention from the neighbors bothered him nearly as much as he wanted me to think.

I glanced at the Blanchards and found them both staring up at us, so I waved.

"Don't encourage them," George said.

"Too late," I said as Carl and Harriet returned the gesture, evoking another grunt from George. "I see your secret friend is out." I looked behind me, where Margaret was sitting on her porch across the street.

George looked at her and turned away bashfully. His cheeks flushed red.

"I don't like that old prune," he stated firmly and turned his attention back to the window, where he watched her in the reflection of the glass.

CHAPTER 13

George had a reel lawnmower. And by *reel*, I mean cylinder, a push mower with metal wheels and a wooden handle. Until I rescued it, the mower was part of the decor that made up the black garden. It was as rusty as every other metal object in that snarled jungle. I bathed the lawnmower in oil before managing to get the blade and the wheels to turn. Even then, it was sluggish and strenuous. I dragged it to the front yard and knew by the length of the grass that I was in for a workout. I'd already spent an hour picking rocks and garbage out of the grass before attempting the insufferable chore of cutting it.

"Perhaps you need to oil it some more." George was standing on the front porch, watching me struggle to push the mower through the tangled grass.

"What I need is a new lawnmower," I said. "Preferably, one that runs on gasoline." I'd cut no more than a five-foot stretch of grass, and already sweat was running down my face. I would have made faster progress with a scythe. At this rate, it would take most of the day to cut the front lawn and the grass on both sides of the house. The back would have to wait until I finished clearing away the black garden.

Many of the neighbors came out onto their porches and watched. It was my moment of fame: Mitchell, the lawn-mower man! Though, I suppose in reality I was only the sideshow. The real attraction was the unveiling of the O'Brien house. The place was an eyesore for the neighborhood. Seeing it transformed from hideous to semi-hideous was a sight to behold. George stood on his porch, supervising me and scowling at the neighbors. Maybe it wasn't his proudest moment, receiving so much attention for doing something as commonplace as cutting the grass. It emphasized the fact that in George's case, housekeeping wasn't commonplace.

When I finished, I expected a round of applause or some other congratulatory sign, but everyone merely went back inside their homes and let me rake up the clippings alone. Even George abandoned me.

The next day, I took to the willow tree with some pruning shears. The tree was beautiful, just unkempt. Candice brought me a glass of water after I'd pruned about three-quarters of the tree. The sun was blazing. I'd unbuttoned the front of my shirt to let my skin breathe.

Rather than going back inside, she sat on the front steps and waited for me to finish my water. I caught her looking at my chest and stomach. It made me feel good. There's no compliment in the world like being admired by a beautiful woman. Maybe my chest wasn't as defined as a bodybuilder's, but it was firm, and I hoped, in comparison, it was more attractive than her grandfather's.

The door opened and George stepped out and stared at my open shirt.

"Get in the house, Candice."

"Why?" She twisted around to look at him.

"Because I asked you to."

"I'd rather stay out here."

"*A Wonderful Time Up There* is on the radio."

"I'm bored with that song."

George gritted his teeth, frustrated that his granddaughter had inherited his stubborn streak. I bit at my lip and snipped another branch from the tree, hoping he wouldn't see how much enjoyment I was getting from his irritation.

"Button up your shirt," he said to me before going back inside the house. He came to the window behind the porch swing and watched until I'd obeyed his order. It wasn't sunburn he was worried about. It was the corruption of his granddaughter. This, at least, was my hope. This way I could justify my stay in Winter Haven. When I thought of the alternative, it made me ache inside.

"What is there to do in this town?" I asked Candice once George had moved away from the window. After my interaction with the people at the sporting goods store and the market, I'd shied away from town. I supposed that was what had happened to the O'Briens. It simply got easier to stay home than to put up with the judgmental looks and belittling comments.

"There's nothing to do here," Candice replied.

"Whew, what a relief!" I wiped the back of my hand across my forehead. "I've been debating what to do this weekend, but that should make it a lot easier. You want to come do nothing with me tomorrow?"

She looked behind her at the window. "No. I think I'd better stay home and do nothing here."

"Why don't you ever leave the house?"

"Does it look like I'm in the house to you?"

"You know what I mean. I've been here over a month and I've never seen you or your grandfather go anywhere."

"Where do you want us to go?"

"It's just not normal." I gathered the fallen branches and moved them out of my way. "Look at you, you're a beautiful girl. But you spend all of your time alone with your grandfather. You should be out with friends, but from what I can see, you don't have any. Someone with your looks should have men beating down your door, but where are they?"

I could tell my compliments affected her, even though they were accompanied by criticism. I doubted she even knew how pretty she was. She'd spent so much time isolated from the rest of society that she had no grounds for comparison. I was certain George loved her, but I was equally certain he wasn't good at expressing that love or showering her with praise.

"I'm happy with things the way they are," she said.

"Are you?" I waited for a reply but got none. "When's the last time you went to a movie?"

"I don't like movies."

"When's the last time you went downtown?"

"I don't like downtown either."

"What do you like?"

"To be left alone."

I smiled out of frustration. The walls she had built around herself were too high and too strong. I'd read in one of my father's psychology books that victims of sex crimes often blame themselves for the abuse, as though they deserved to be treated as objects, molested, raped, and even beaten. Such abuse wears on their self-esteem and the only defense they have is not to allow others to get close to them, either physically or emotionally. Being molested by someone who wasn't a member of the family would be bad enough but by your own grandfather? I couldn't even imagine how someone would handle that. Looking at Candice, I didn't know what to believe. George hadn't denied being Candice's father or molesting her, but he'd done a good job of making me question it.

"Do you really think I'm beautiful?"

I grinned. She looked so pure, seated on the step in her white dress. "Yes, of course. But don't tell your grandpa. I don't think he'd approve."

She smiled and looked over her shoulder at the window. George was nowhere in sight. Not that he would have been able to hear our conversation, but he was pretty good at reading faces, and I don't think he would have approved of the look on mine at the moment.

"It's been a long time since I went to a movie," Candice confessed.

"We should go some time."

She fidgeted and looked again at the window.

"What, I'm not good enough for you?"

"I think I could do better," she said with a hint of a smile.

I also felt she could do better, but I still laughed. She so rarely said anything funny. "I'm serious about the movie. We could go tonight."

"I'm not sure I'm ready for that yet."

"Going with me or going into town?"

"Town."

"You'll never be ready for that, Candice. You just have to jump in and do it."

"I really couldn't. I just couldn't." She looked again at the vacant living room window. "Grandpa would never let me go anyway."

"It couldn't hurt to ask."

She bit at her bottom lip and gave a little shrug.

"I'll ask him," I offered.

Candice gave me a faint smile, which I took as approval.

Late that afternoon, as we settled around the kitchen table for dinner, Candice watched me warily as she set a dish of spaghetti and meatballs in the center of the table. I smiled faintly at her, and then glanced at George and found him staring directly at me. His blue eyes weren't nearly as lovely as his granddaughter's. They had a glaring hate in them that matched the scowl on his lips.

I stared at the spaghetti.

"I'm going to have you start painting the house first thing Monday morning," he grumbled as he filled his plate. "People are starting to stare."

"Starting?" I said but could see George didn't appreciate my humor. "That's a big job. We're going to have to scrape the old paint off first. That alone will take several days."

"Let's not worry about the whole house. Just do the front for now. That's all anyone can see anyway."

"That's an interesting perspective."

George took a bite of his spaghetti. Underneath the table, Candice nudged me with the toe of her shoe. I didn't know if she wanted me to hurry up and ask about the movie or if she wanted me to forget about it altogether. When the phone rang, I waited until George got up before glancing at Candice for clarification. Her eyes went from George to her food, and I saw that George was watching us as he picked up the phone that hung on the wall beside the refrigerator.

"Hello," he said, cheerfully. Being a salesman and doing all of his business over the telephone, he made a habit of answering every call in a positive manner, in case it was a client on the other end. His face turned sour. "Sick bastard," he said and hung up the phone.

"Who was that?" Candice asked.

"Wrong number."

"Really?" I asked.

Candice kicked me and shook her head, telling me to let it go.

"You know, Mr. O'Brien, I was thinking about taking in a movie this evening."

"That's nice," he said in a tone that stated who cares?

"And I was wondering if it'd be okay with you if Candice came with me?"

Suddenly, he cared. He looked at Candice to see if she was in on the conspiracy. Her face remained expressionless, but the fact that my question didn't come as a surprise to her told George everything he needed to know.

"No. I'm afraid that's out of the question."

"I'm nineteen, Grandpa."

"But you still live under my roof."

"Would you like me to move out?"

"You're not going and that's final." He took a bite of his spaghetti and chewed angrily. Candice gave me one of those looks, the kind women often give men, telling them to be a man and do something. I'd seen my mother bully my father with that look many times.

"You can't expect her to spend the rest of her life locked up in this house," I objected weakly.

"You know nothing about any of this."

"I'd like to go, Grandpa."

George turned his dark eyes on her and set his fork on his plate. He was shaking his head, but his expression said that he was teetering, that he could be persuaded.

"If it's her safety you're worried about, I'll be with her all evening."

"Letting the wolf watch over the sheep doesn't exactly fill me with confidence." His eyes shifted from me to Candice and then back to me. "Let me talk to Candice a moment."

"I don't see why—" I began, but George cut me off with a scowl. I got up from the table, gave Candice a look of encouragement, and went out of the back door, where I settled down in George's rocking chair.

I stared at the large bite I'd taken out of the back yard. Three-quarters of the once eclectic garden was now gone and was cluttering up the alley. In its place were patches of bare soil interlaced with long grass and weeds. I remained in the rocking chair for a full five seconds before I heard knuckles rapping on the kitchen window. Turning, I found George glaring at me, motioning for me to get my butt up out of his chair and go into the studio.

From my desk, I stared at the back of the house, at the kitchen windows, where I saw the two O'Briens yelling at each other across the table.

It was like watching Marie debate Professor Gibson, the leader of the toss-Jefferson-Thomas-out-of-school committee. Gibson was a fiery, balding man of fifty. He taught political science and was fond of saying that the biggest mistake our forefathers made when they introduced slavery to America was that they didn't have the foresight to see that someday it would end and we'd be stuck with a bunch of worthless negroes running around expecting us to take care of them. He was the one teacher at BU that I absolutely detested, but I knew better than to ever disagree with him to his face. Marie, on the other hand, confronted him every time one of those racist statements left his lips. We all rooted for her, but Professor Gibson was too polished. He knew how to twist her words and twist history to his advantage, leaving her flustered and red-faced.

Watching the O'Briens from the studio window, I could see that George was the equivalent of Professor Gibson. He was browbeating Candice with his rhetoric, either telling her about men and their evil ways or telling her to be a good little granddaughter and keep the love in the family.

Candice, however, did something I'd never seen Marie do to Professor Gibson. She came around the table, kissed her grandfather on the forehead, and put her arms around him. Permission had been granted.

CHAPTER 14

Dressed in black and white, Candice said goodbye to George at the front door. By the way he held her and fussed over her leaving, you'd have thought he never expected to see her again. I stood in the living room, watching them and thinking how needlessly dramatic it all appeared. We were only going to a movie for goodness sake.

"You know our telephone number, right?" George asked. "If there's any trouble, call me. Don't put up with any nonsense."

"I'll be okay."

"The sheriff's department is on Front Street. They may be a bunch of idiots, but they're still paid to protect and serve. Go to them if you need to."

"Don't worry about me, Grandpa."

He furrowed his brow, gave her another hug, and opened the door for her to leave. "You be careful and enjoy yourself."

She kissed him on the cheek and stepped out onto the porch. I started out behind her, but George grabbed me by the arm, leaned close, and whispered: "Anything happens to her, it'll be the last regret you ever have. Now have fun."

The movie was starring Jimmy Stewart, an actor I admired greatly. He didn't steal women's hearts the way Elvis Presley and

James Dean did, but he was one of the most loved actors in show business and I knew I paled in comparison. I remember reading somewhere that with the advent of television people's self-esteem dropped dramatically. The theory was that before television the only people we had to compare ourselves with were the other people we met in our everyday lives. Television, however, broadened our scope of comparison. And most of us had a rough time competing with the models and movie stars that flashed across the screen. Even the stars could no longer live up to our social ideals. They relied on camera angles, makeup, and cosmetic surgery to remove their flaws. Since the O'Briens didn't own a television, I figured Candice hadn't been bombarded with images of handsome men, and I feared she'd take one look at Jimmy Stewart and realize she really could do better than me. So I happily announced that Jimmy was married with children.

Jimmy Stewart's marital status was of less interest to her than the people surrounding us as we stood in line waiting to buy our tickets. Most of them paid no attention to her and probably had no idea who she was, but her focus was on the gawkers and whisperers. She grabbed my hand and squeezed, keeping her eyes on the ground, as I handed our tickets to the usher and led Candice into the lobby.

"You want something to eat or drink?" I motioned to the concession booth where people were lined up to purchase popcorn and candy.

"I just want to sit down." She tugged at my arm, urging me inside, away from the staring eyes. We passed through the curtains that divided the lobby from the theater and took a seat toward the back. The darkness helped her relax. No one could see her here. Even if they could, she couldn't see their eyes.

"You ever been in here before?" I asked.

"When I was a child. Some guy spilled his soda all over Grandpa's head right in the middle of the movie. I think it was on purpose. Grandpa ended up hitting the man in the nose, and the owner or somebody asked us to leave."

"But was it a good movie?" I joked.

"I don't remember the movie," she answered evenly.

I feared she was destined to remember little about this movie as well. Shortly after the film started, two men came up the aisle looking for a seat. They forced a couple of kids to move over and took the seats directly behind us. Because of the dark and the fact that I wasn't paying attention, I didn't notice them until they started laughing and bumping the backs of our seats, pretending it was an accident.

"Sorry about that. I hope we didn't disturb you." The man put his hand on my shoulder as he spoke into my ear.

"Don't worry about it," I whispered, not thinking much of it. My attention was on Jimmy Stewart dangling from the edge of a building while a policeman strained to grab hold of him to pull him up. Candice grabbed my hand, watching anxiously as the tiles of the roof gave way and the policeman slid closer to the edge, tried to brace himself, and failed. As the officer plummeted to his death on the pavement below, I took the opportunity to put my arm around Candice as a pretense of comfort and protection. She leaned against me, still holding my hand.

It could have been a good moment.

One of the men behind us made a pining sound and said: "Ain't that sweet? I always get choked up whenever I'm in the presence of true love."

"Personally, I get more of a gagging sensation," the other said, and judging by the volume of their laughter, they found themselves very amusing. People in front of us turned to see who was laughing after the horrific scene we'd just witnessed on the screen.

"I sure wish my Uncle Grant was here to enjoy this show. I really think he'd like it."

"I'm sure he would. Your uncle was a swell guy."

"Shhh," said a short, curly-haired man from the side row.

"Shush yourself."

The gentleman got up and headed up the aisle into the lobby. The two men giggled. Candice's body tensed as she pulled away from me.

"I can't believe grandpa's sharing," said one of the men, leaning on the back of Candice's chair. "I thought this was only a family affair."

In the dim light of the theater, I could see a tear trickling down Candice's cheek. There was a tingling in my scalp and down my spine. The right thing to do was to turn around and confront them, but I couldn't make myself do it. Even my overwhelming shame couldn't spur me to action. My whole life I had shied away from confrontation. All I could do was grit my teeth and hope the moment would pass.

My rescuer came in the form of a beam of light passing through the curtains at the back of the theater. The curly-haired man returned, followed by a teenaged boy carrying a flashlight, which he shined in the faces of the men behind us.

"You guys want to keep it down?" He spoke with no conviction of authority.

"Hey, Billy, get that flashlight out of my face before I shove it up your ass."

The flashlight went out. The men snickered, proof that they could do anything they pleased without the worry of consequences.

"Now go back to selling your popcorn like a good boy."

Seeking direction on how to handle the situation, the usher looked at the curly-haired man. Rather than advice, he received a look of disappointment as the man grumbled and returned to his seat next to his wife. Spotting two empty seats behind the couple, I grabbed Candice's hand and urged her to come with me.

"Can't wait till after the movie, huh?" one of the men remarked. I looked back, wanting to see the faces of the men I hated. It was dark, but I recognize the silhouette and the glint of Brylcreem as the young man from the sporting goods store.

It wasn't Hitchcock's fault that I didn't enjoy the film. He had done a splendid job at directing. The movie was intense, haunting and, seductive—destined to become a classic. Still, I don't think Candice enjoyed it any more than I did. I couldn't keep my mind off the present situation. About halfway through the movie, the two men got up and left, which made me feel a little better.

Candice didn't want to get stuck in the crowd where she could be scrutinized and ridiculed, so before the final scene had faded from the screen, we were out of our seats and out the front door, into the warm night air. My goal had been to show Candice that life outside of the O'Brien home wasn't nearly as frightening as she thought. Instead, I'd confirmed her belief. Even though the harassment had only come from two faceless men, she now knew the world was against her and that everything her grandfather had taught her about the ills of society was true.

Behind the theater was a parking lot where I'd left my Chevy. Three streetlamps illuminated the area. In the pale light, on the far side of the lot, I could see two men watching us. Worse yet, they were seated on the back of my car. When Candice spotted them, she took my hand and looked up at me to see how she should respond. I kept walking but felt the butterflies flutter in my stomach. In the theater, I'd been ill at ease and cowardly. Now, I was petrified. I feared that the battle of words I'd anticipated in the theater would now turn bloody. I'd been in a few fights in my youth, but most of the time, I did everything I could to avoid them.

As we drew closer, the guy with the slick hair offered a smirk. His large blond friend sported a cheesy grin. Their plaid shirts and tan slacks told me they were rich kids. Their expressions told me they used that status to bully their way through life.

"This your car with the Massachusetts plates?" Slick patted the trunk of my car.

"Yeah, it's mine."

He rubbed his hand over the metal, treating the car with respect and admiration. "Me and my buddy were out here protecting it for you."

"I appreciate that. Darn thing's got a tendency to run off when I leave it unattended." I let go of Candice's hand and came toward them so they wouldn't know how scared I was. I knew I had a beating coming, and I wasn't overly anxious to receive it.

"'Course our services don't come for free." The blond slid off the car and stepped toward me.

"That's understandable," I said, hoping to diffuse the situation with humor. "Tomorrow you go to the movie and I'll watch your car for you."

Off to my left, an engine started. Headlights came on, shining in the opposite direction from us. Other moviegoers crossed through the lot, getting in their cars. Most of them didn't even give us a glance. Those who did apparently saw nothing curious about the situation. I could have shouted for help, but so far the only thing that warranted a call of distress was the feeling in the pit of my stomach.

"Why don't you run on home and give us a turn at the whore," Slick said.

My whole body went tense. The indignation I'd felt inside the theater pulsed through my veins. I was still trembling, but my cowardly self-control was beginning to slip.

"I sure hope that was your attempt at humor, buddy."

"I ain't your buddy." Slick's eyes never left mine as he hopped down from the trunk of my car. His smug look dissolved into a sneer. He stood a few inches taller than me. Still, I couldn't think of anything that would make me happier than releasing my anger on that pretty face of his.

"Wait for me in the theater," I said to Candice.

"You stay right here, Candice," Slick said. "My friend and I want a date. See if we're as good in bed as old grandpa."

"Go ahead," I said to her. "I'll catch up to you in a minute."

She started away, but the blond scurried in front of her, blocking her way. He grinned as he shifted from side to side, keeping her from going around him. I pretended to find his routine amusing as I calmly walked over, gave him a smile, and punched him in the face with everything I had. He didn't see it coming and hadn't braced himself. The hit took him off his feet and onto the seat of his pants. He had barely hit the pavement when a fist nailed me in the small of my back. It took the wind out of me. When I turned, Slick finished the job by slugging me twice in the gut.

"Stop it!" Candice yelled as Slick grabbed me by the shirt and threw me against the back of my car. A fist caught me on the chin, but my focus was on the blond as he got up from the ground and gripped Candice by the arm. She winced in pain, tried to pull away, then turned and slapped him. He gave Candice a little push, taunting her. His eyes briefly met mine before balling his fist and slugging Candice in the stomach. She buckled forward and strained for air as she dropped to her knees.

I shoved Slick away and headed toward the blond, but arms grabbed me from behind and held me in a bear hug. For a pampered rich kid, he was strong. I squirmed and kicked at his legs. His grip tightened, pressing his fists into my midsection. The blond let out a joyful yelp and bounced in front of me like a boxer. I expected a fist. Instead, he delivered two stinging slaps across my face, as jovial as a child tearing the wings off a fly.

"Go back to Massachusetts," he said and slapped me again.

I planted my foot solidly between his legs. He went to the pavement for a second time. Reaching behind me, I grabbed Slick by the groin and squeezed as hard as I could. This was dirty fighting, the way we did it in the city. In my Boston neighborhood, the boys used to ask: What do you call someone who fights fair? To which they answered: Loser. These men had me at a disadvantage, and I'd be damned if I was going to play by the rules.

When Slick lost his grip, I elbowed him in the face and went to help Candice to her feet. She wasn't crying, but she looked shaken.

"You're going to pay for that, asshole!" Slick said as he and the blond readied themselves for round two. They circled us, not giving us a chance to flee to the theater or to the safety of my car. I'd surprised them once and felt certain they wouldn't allow that to happen again. In the dim light of the parking lot, I could see a few people watching in the distance. No one appeared eager to get involved, with the exception of two young men weaving between parked cars as they headed our way. As they drew near, I could see they were in their mid twenties, slightly older than Slick and the blond. I didn't know if their presence should worry me or give me comfort.

"Hey, Vaughn. What we got here?" asked the smaller of the two men, as he entered the circle and slapped a hand on the blond's back. The gesture suggested friendship and sent a wave of fear up my spine. He had brown hair and a strong jawline. I looked past him, to several pockets of people standing off in the distance, watching us. Their passiveness infuriated me. It was what I would have done—what I had done back at the university when the opposition heated up against Jefferson Thomas. My greatest fear was that they'd watch apathetically while the four men beat me and raped Candice right there in the parking lot.

"Run, Candice!" I yelled.

Without hesitation, she ran for a space between two parked cars. She never even made it past their bumpers before Slick snatched her arm and pulled her close to him.

"You guys up for a little O'Brien pussy?" He smiled smugly at the newcomers, who perked up at the name O'Brien. I could see they hadn't recognized her at first and probably never would have, had Slick not mentioned her by name. I'd never felt so afraid and helpless. If I'd had a gun, I would have shot all four of them right then and there. It would have been a grievous error on my part, but I swear to God I would have done it.

The fourth man was the largest and the least handsome. His size and receding hairline made him look older than the others. It also made him the most threatening. He grinned at Slick's proposal and eyed Candice with interest. I knew right then that this was a man I would hate the rest of my life. That is until he put his hand on Slick's shoulder and squeezed so hard that it nearly brought him to his knees with pain.

"You're the only pussy I see around here, Todd." He increased the pressure until Todd/Slick relinquished his hold on Candice. She ran to me, and I held her close, staring over her shoulder at the two men whose names I didn't yet know. I saw then what Candice and George had failed to see in all of their years in Winter Haven. Not everyone was against them, and not all of the town's eight thousand residents had been born with tiny minds and tiny souls. I suppose it's human nature to focus on the negative, to amplify it in our minds until it overpowers the good that surrounds us every day. Sometimes we don't see the positive until it brings our enemies to their knees.

"Hold on there, Quinn," the blond-headed Vaughn said to the larger of the two newcomers. "You don't know the whole story. Mr. Massachusetts here said all men from Winter Haven were a bunch of wimps. We were just showing him that he was mistaken."

"Is that what happened?" Quinn asked me.

I shook my head. "When we came out of the theater, these two were sitting on my car and started harassing us."

"Sorry, Vaughn," Quinn said. "I don't even know this guy, but I already trust him more than I trust you. This is personal and we all know it. You two should know better than to mess with an O'Brien."

"I ain't afraid of no old man," Todd said.

"Who said anything about an old man?" Quinn asked. "You touch her and I'll personally break your neck. Now get out of here. If I even hear you looked at her the wrong way, Todd, I'll hunt you down and beat the living shit out of you. You understand me?"

Todd licked his lips and cocked his head, trying to look cool and un-intimidated. He started away, but Quinn grabbed his arm and spun him back around.

"Do you understand?"

"Yeah, man. Hell, I speak English."

Quinn popped him lightly in the mouth. "You watch that smart mouth of yours, too."

Todd started away and then stopped and looked at the man with the strong jawline. "Next year, Kirk, when I'm made supervisor, the first item on my agenda will be to fire your worthless ass." He pointed a threatening finger before joining Vaughn, the two of them walking between parked cars, making their way to the other side of the lot to Todd's red Thunderbird.

"We owe you one," I said. "I don't even know what the hell that was all about."

Quinn knew. I could tell by the way he looked at Candice.

"Don't mention it," he said. "I've been looking for a reason to pound on that Todd Miller. He bugs the hell out of me."

"Next time you come downtown looking for a fight, give us a call," Kirk said. "We hate it when someone else is down here having all the fun." He gestured to my license plates. "You're from Massachusetts?"

"Boston. I'm up here working for the O'Briens for the summer. We thought we'd take the night off and see a movie. We just didn't realize that it was a double feature."

"And a freak show at that," Quinn said. "Bozo and his pet monkey."

"Their families are lacking the gene that develops the brain," Kirk said with a laugh and then looked uncomfortably at Candice. "I mean the inbred part of the family."

"I don't claim them as family," Candice said. Her sharp tone surprised me but not nearly as much as what the comment implied. I was missing a larger piece of the puzzle than I had previously suspected.

"I'm Mitchell Sanders, by the way." I shook their hands. "The pretty one here is Candice O'Brien, as I suppose you already know."

Candice smiled at the compliment as the two men introduced themselves as Kirk McNight and Quinn Judson.

"We're heading over to Pete's Diner," Quinn said. "Why don't you join us?"

Kirk cringed and then covered it with a smile. He didn't mind saving Candice O'Brien's neck and even chatting with her in the solitude of the theater parking lot, but showing up with her in public was a different matter.

I related far too well. It was how I felt around Jefferson, and how I later felt around Marie once she'd offended many of the professors and half of the student body of Boston University. I knew people linked the two of us together. I saw their hateful glances and overheard their snide remarks. 'Guilty by association' was the way I explained it to my roommate the day he tried to convince me not to break up with Marie. I didn't need the hassle, and apparently, neither did Kirk.

"It's a nice place. A good crowd," Quinn persisted, ignoring Kirk's discomfort. "You can follow us over."

I looked at Candice for her reaction and found her staring at the ground. "Do you want to go, Candice?"

She shrugged, not looking at me.

"Yeah, sure," I said to Quinn. "We'd like that."

CHAPTER 15

Pete's Diner sat on the corner of Seventh and Sutter, three blocks over from Main. It was a bright place, red and yellow with chrome accents and a jukebox playing *At the Hop* by Danny & The Juniors. The diner was filled with the chatter of teenagers and young adults and the smells of hamburgers and French fries. The atmosphere was lively and friendly. Even the looks we received as Quinn and Kirk led us toward the back of the café didn't necessarily denote scorn, but rather the curiosity of seeing new faces in the room.

Kirk stiffly approached a table where a young lady sat sipping soda through a straw. She looked up at him and then checked her watch to emphasize that Kirk had kept her waiting. She started to say something, but when we stopped beside Kirk, she gave us a look and held her tongue.

"Candice, Mitchell. This is Nicole." Kirk sat and took Nicole's hand.

"Kirk's soon-to-be ex-wife," she said, pulling her hand away.

"You take it easy on Kirk." Quinn pulled a chair over from a neighboring table. "Todd Miller and his little crony were just begging us to whip on them. So we obliged."

"That's very thoughtful of you, Quinn," Nicole said as we settled around the table. She was tanned with short, curly hair. Looking around the diner, nearly every girl had a similar hairstyle. Candice, with her long straight hair, was the only one out of fashion.

"You're Candice O'Brien, aren't you?" Nicole asked. "I recognize you from Redding's Department Store." Her tone was accusatory, as though she'd caught Candice shoplifting and was now bringing it to her attention. "Last December, right before Christmas, your grandfather got into an argument with Mickey Bowry and hit him with his cane. Remember that, Kirk?"

Kirk shrugged. "Knowing Mickey, he had it coming."

"Maybe." Nicole looked at Candice, expecting her to enlighten us with her side of the story, but Candice's mind was on the diner, taking in the sounds blaring from the jukebox and the men and women her own age enjoying themselves. She was looking around at normal people doing normal things and it was all foreign to her. Her innocence was both endearing and frightening. I didn't know if my desire to hold her stemmed from love or a need to protect her. I took her hand. She turned her attention back to the table. We stared at one another, nodding politely and trying desperately to think of something clever to say. The only one who seemed comfortable with the situation was Quinn, who was staring up at the menu above the counter, trying to decide what he wanted to eat.

"So," I said, "I understand this town is quite the haven in the winter."

Quinn gave me a long stare as if trying to figure out if my comment was meant to be funny or if I was just dense. "You guys going to get something to eat? I'm starving."

We ordered hamburgers and sodas. Kirk told us about his job at Taft Paper, a mill just out of town that employed about thirty-five percent of Winter Haven. The president of the company was Howard Baxter, the man I'd met in the sporting goods shop along with Todd Miller—Howard's grandson. According to Kirk, Baxter was a shrewd businessman whose main talent was seeing to it that no one else in the community became more successful than he was. Apparently, two years earlier, in 1956, a group of local entrepreneurs had planned to erect Winter Haven's first shopping center. They had designs drawn up, purchased the property, and had even set a date for the groundbreaking ceremony. Then, with no good reason, the city council stepped in and shut the project down. Though Baxter adamantly denied all accusations, rumors circulated that he had played a major part in influencing the decision. Rumors flourished once again two months ago when Baxter began work on a shopping center of his own, which miraculously met with unanimous approval from the city council.

"But I can't hate him too much," Kirk said. "The man did give me a job."

"Hating your boss is the American way," Quinn said. "And hating Howard Baxter is just good old-fashioned common sense."

We ate hamburgers and talked about my favorite subject: Boston; and my worst subject: fishing. Kirk was one of those outdoor types who believed fishing was the closest a person could get to heaven without being dead. Not even the bitter New England winters could keep him away. According to Nicole, Kirk would hop out of bed at four o'clock in the morning, drive to a frozen lake, and bore a hole in the ice just to fish. The mere thought of it made me groan.

"We're planning on going this weekend," Quinn said. "You want to come?"

"We'd love to," Candice said, to my surprise. She hadn't said much all evening, and I thought she was having a horrible time.

"You have your own gear?" Kirk asked. "Or do you need to borrow some?"

"I'm afraid we're going to have to borrow some," I said.

"Have you ever fished, Candice?" Nicole asked. At first, I thought she was passing judgment, but when Candice shook her head, Nicole said: "You're going to hate it. Unless you're into meditation, 'cause it's real boring stuff."

"Hey! Don't go poisoning her against it before she even gives it a try." Kirk sounded genuinely offended. "Don't you listen to a word she says, Candice. You've never felt real excitement until you reeled in a five-pound trout. Ain't that right, Mitchell?"

"Oh yeah," I agreed wholeheartedly. "Though I have to warn you, you've never seen a true fisherman until you've seen me at work."

"Is that right?" Quinn said.

"Sometimes I scare myself. I'm that good." No one looked worried, least of all Kirk. They didn't know me, and I suppose they weren't sure how to take me. My college roommate once told me that whenever you meet someone new you should always start off by saying something stupid because it helps everyone relax. Of course, you always run the risk of looking like an idiot.

On the way home, Candice and I stopped at a bakery and I bought half a dozen donuts, thinking we could use them to sweeten George up a little. We'd promised to be home early, and he'd told Candice he'd have a game of chess set up for her when she got home. It was already a quarter after ten. He was sitting on the front porch swing when we pulled up. With a frown, he watched us come through the gate and climb the steps.

"You're late."

"We grabbed a bite to eat," I said.

"And we stopped off and bought some donuts." Candice held out the paper bag. "We brought you one."

George shook his head at it. "Any trouble?"

"No. Everyone was very nice," Candice lied.

My bottom lip was slightly swollen. Other than that we looked unmarred.

"We got invited to go fishing," Candice added.

"Of course, you turned them down," George said.

"Of course, I didn't," Candice replied.

George gritted his teeth and stared at me. I knew he was cursing me for being such a bad influence on his granddaughter.

Not only had I fed her junk food, I'd convinced her to abandon her dear sweet grandfather for an entire Saturday so she could spend the day at the lake—with strangers no less. She was slipping away from under his protective eye and it frustrated the hell out of him.

CHAPTER 16

On Saturday, the five of us drove out to Heritage Lake, seven miles outside of Winter Haven. The sky was a deep blue. The lake was its mirror. The encircling forest was a patchwork of green. At that moment I could understand Kirk's passion for the great outdoors. It was what I'd dreamed of as a child. Fishing wasn't necessarily part of that dream, but this was the setting. As we made our way down to the lake, carrying our fishing poles and tackle, I breathed in the scented air and was happy to be away from Boston, not just to escape the trouble with Marie, but away from the concrete and traffic. This was my peek into the world before man came along and transformed it to suit his needs. There was no stress in the mountains, just life the way God had intended it.

Quinn and Kirk had spent the previous night hunting for nightcrawlers and had caught at least four dozen. As we stopped at the edge of the lake, Quinn handed me a couple of worms and told me to show them how it was done.

"Please don't let me intimidate any of you," I said. "I'm just a mere mortal like the rest of you." I looked down at the fishing pole, hoping I could remember how to cast out the line.

"You're all talk," Quinn said.

"You think so, do you?"

"Yeah, I do."

"Well then, you're in for a pleasant surprise." I put one of the worms down on a rock and entwined the other onto the fishhook. Everyone stood around and watched me as I made a show of it. I was being a fool, and I'm sure they all knew it. "Stand back," I announced once I had the worm securely hooked. "I've got a very powerful swing, and I'd hate to drag any of you out into the water when I let this baby fly." I flung the rod back over my shoulder and gave it a flip, pressing the button down on the reel as I did so. The line hurled out above the water and made a small splash as the worm, hook, and sinkers hit the surface. It was a good toss but exceptionally anticlimactic.

As everyone else began baiting their hooks, I propped my rod between some rocks and helped Candice put the worm on her hook. Once everyone had tossed their lines into the water, we settled down on some large stones along the shore and waited.

"Meditation time," Nicole said, and she was right. We talked a bit about baseball and the last World Series, but most of the time we spent staring at the water. There was a nice breeze blowing in off the lake. It felt good in the heat of the day. I didn't have high hopes of catching any fish, but with luck, I'd catch a tan. Quinn stripped off his shirt. By the looks of him, he spent as much time in the sun as in the gym. His torso was well defined and he was the color of a bar of chocolate. Perhaps he was the least handsome, but he made up for it in body and personality. He told us a story about how he and his brother accidentally set their cat on fire. I laughed so hard that it made my side hurt, and I'm a cat lover. He said they managed to put the fire out before it did anything more than singe the fur, but from then on the cat went by the name of Blaze.

Candice's laugh sounded beautiful coming from her. The sun shimmered on her face and in her hair. I was touched by her happiness. For the first time since I met her, she seemed unguarded, as though she'd just realized the world wasn't such a bad place after all and that not all of Winter Haven was out to get her. Even after the conversation had died, she grinned as she stared across the water at the ducks swimming on the far side of the lake.

"Where are the drinks?" Kirk asked.

"Right where you left them," Nicole said. "In the car. I'd offer to go up and get them, but I'm having so much fun fishing that I can't bear to tear myself away."

Her remarks sounded rehearsed. By the look on Kirk's face, I had a feeling the drinks had been left in the car on purpose, a suspicion that was confirmed when he volunteered me to help retrieve them. I suspected he wanted to grill me on the O'Brien situation, which was fine with me. I had a few questions of my own.

We headed up the hill through the trees to our parked cars. Quinn and the McKnights had come in Kirk's '55 Buick, a red and white two-door sedan with a large dent on the passenger side. As Kirk opened the trunk and we lifted out the cooler, he started in with the questions, asking how I got the job, how I liked working with Mr. O'Brien, where I slept at night, and how Mr. O'Brien felt about my dating his granddaughter. I told him about reading George's ad in the Boston Globe, about my wanting to get out of Boston to escape my ex-girlfriend, and about my first day in Winter Haven when Candice saved the day by declaring my ugliness.

"She didn't," he said.

"She did," I assured him. "Actually, she called me ordinary, but ugly was what she meant. I think Mr. O'Brien now wishes he'd stuck to his guns and turned me away. He's sitting at home right now fuming that Candice is here with us and not there with him. If I'd known what I was getting myself into, I don't think I would have taken this job."

"It doesn't look like you have it too bad to me." Kirk stared down the hill to the lake.

"Candice is great. Her grandfather, though, can be a real pain in the ass. Is it true that he raped his own daughter?"

Kirk shrugged. "The O'Briens are hermits. Nobody knows them really. There are lots of rumors. The fact that he's letting you go out with Candice makes me doubt some of it at least."

"You mean that he's sleeping with her?"

"That's one of the rumors."

"There's nothing perverse about their relationship. That much I know."

If Kirk had pressed the issue, I suppose I would have had to admit that I really had no personal knowledge of George and Candice's sleeping habits, but he let the topic drop as we each took one side of the cooler and carried it down to the lake.

Candice was staring out at the glistening water as we came up behind her and set the cooler on the ground. Inside, they had a couple of six-packs of beer and a variety of sodas. I'd never seen alcohol in the O'Brien house, so I handed Candice a Coca-Cola and took another one for myself.

"So Candice," Kirk said, taking up his fishing pole again. "Mitch tells me you think he's ugly."

"Mitchell!" Candice scolded.

"It came up in conversation," I said. "Kirk was saying how handsome I was, and I said, 'That's funny, Candice thinks I'm ugly'."

"I never called you ugly."

"I think he's a hunk, personally," Quinn said and gave me a wink.

"Thank you, Quinn."

Nicole chuckled, but I could see Candice didn't quite know what to make of this show of affection between men.

"So, this is what men talk about when they're alone," she said.

"We need someone to build up our egos after the way you girls treat us," Kirk said.

"Oh, you poor abused men." Nicole put a hand on her chest.

"That's right," Quinn said. "After all we do for you, you treat us like dirt."

"And you love every minute of it."

"No, Nicole, we like being treated dirty, not like dirt," Kirk said. "She always gets those two confused."

"I got one!" Candice screamed.

By the bow in her fishing pole, it was a nice-sized one at that. I scrambled around stupidly, not knowing what to do, while Kirk grabbed a net and waded into the water. Taking hold of the fishing line, he helped Candice pull it close enough for him to get the net under it and swoop it out of the water. It was a bass, not huge, about two pounds, but that was two pounds bigger than anything I'd ever caught. Kirk handed the net to Candice, and she held it up with pride.

"Look at it! Wow, I caught a real fish!"

I'd never seen her smile so much. Being locked inside her house had protected her from failure, just as George had intended. It'd also protected her from success. I think she grew more in that one day than she had in the past several years.

By the time the sun lay upon the horizon, Kirk had caught three fish, Nicole two, Quinn and Candice one, and I had caught nothing. They harassed me about being the king fishermen until I finally broke down and confessed that in my whole life I'd never caught a single fish. When I told them about the fish hatchery, they all had a good laugh at my expense. We built a fire at a campsite inside the trees and fried the fish on a grill Kirk had brought. We were all sunburned except for Quinn, of course, and Nicole, who worked as a lifeguard at the local swimming pool.

We cut some thin branches from the trees, opened a bag of marshmallows, and roasted them over the fire. The forest grew dark and quiet, leaving nothing but the crackle of the fire. I was digging in the bag for another marshmallow when an animal shrieked in the nearby trees, followed immediately by the sound of something running through the underbrush. We fell silent for a moment and searched the darkness that surrounded us.

"Probably just some madman psycho killer," Kirk said. "We get those all the time out here."

"That's good to hear." I patted my heart with feigned relief. "I was afraid it was a deer or something."

"It's no joking matter," Quinn said. "These woods are treacherous. A woman was brutally beaten and left for dead out here one time." He paused and leaned toward the fire. He stared at Nicole, seated next to him, and said: "It was awful. Apparently, the animals got her and mangled her body. A friend of mine came up with the police to help search for her. As it got dark, my buddy got separated from the rest of the group and couldn't find his way out. It was a nightmare. He was out here hollering for help, and clear off in the distance he could hear someone hollering back, so he started off toward the voice. He was heading down this path and suddenly he heard the footsteps behind him. He turned around, but no one was there. He thought it was probably just a deer or something." Quinn looked at me with raised eyebrows.

"Anyway, after a moment, my friend heard this voice behind him, whispering, 'Give me back my necklace. Give me back my necklace.' Apparently, this guy who'd beaten the girl had stolen her necklace from her and she wanted it back. So, my friend, he sprinted as fast as he could through the trees, but it was night, so he couldn't see very well. He ended up tripping over a branch that had fallen across the path. It was pretty dark out now except for the moonlight shining down through the trees. He turned over onto his back, and standing over him was the dead girl, her flesh drooping from her bones, her eyes eaten out by worms. She started to laugh. 'Ha, ha, ha. Where's my necklace? You've got it!'"

Quinn yelled the last words as he lunged at Nicole, making her jump backward with such force she nearly fell off the log.

We all laughed as Nicole slapped at Quinn's arms and repeatedly called him an idiot. Quinn had a pleasant laugh, the kind that made every joke seem even funnier than it was. His teeth glowed in the light of the fire. Beyond him, Nicole caught my eye. She motioned past me to Candice, who wasn't finding this funny in the least. Rather, she was staring despondently off into the trees.

"That was a lovely story, Quinn. Thank you so much," Nicole said. "But perhaps we should find a better topic."

"Who was the girl?" Candice asked.

"It's just a story," Quinn said.

"If I weren't here, would she have had a name?"

Quinn looked at me apologetically. "Of course not."

Candice nodded and smiled darkly. She put another marshmallow on her stick and stuck it over the fire. She seemed satisfied with Quinn's answer, but it was too late. She'd killed the spirit of the evening.

CHAPTER 17

My headlights fanned out across the pavement and lit a path through the dark forest. In front of us, Kirk's Buick followed the curve of the road. In the passenger seat, Candice twisted her fingers. Her face was in shadows, only illuminated by the light of the moon as it flickered through the trees and revealed her sullen expression.

"I'm not attacking you," I said.

"Can we not talk about this?"

"Just tell me what that was about. It was rude. It was embarrassing. They went out of their way to be nice to us, and you treat them like they're the enemy. Why?"

She stared out the side window.

"Who did you think he was talking about? Your mother? Your grandmother? Is this related to the things your grandfather did?"

"What do you mean 'what he did'?" she asked. "What did he do?"

"You tell me."

"He did nothing. That's what he did."

"To you. How about to your mother?"

I took my foot of the gas and coasted around a bend. When the road straightened and I glanced at Candice, I found her glaring in disgust.

"Whatever happened, Candice, it's not your fault. You didn't do anything wrong."

"Neither did my grandfather," she snapped. "Do you honestly believe that about him? About us? You think you're so smart because you're from the city and have been to college. Well, I hate to break it to you, Mitchell, but they've taught you nothing because you're still an idiot." She looked away, out the side window at the dark trees blurring by. When she looked back at me, she had tears in her eyes, and the anger had disappeared from her voice. "I know what people say about us, and I'm sure you've heard it all by now. All kinds of ridiculous stories about things my grandfather did, but it's not true. None of it."

"Then tell me what happened."

Tears trickled down her cheeks.

"How am I supposed to take your side if you won't even tell me what your side is?"

Her hands shook as she wiped her eyes and stared forward at the taillights in front of us, winding through the trees. I could see her shutting down, going back inside herself. I expected her to remain silent for the rest of the trip. Instead, she began to cry and told me what had happened to her mother.

∞∞

In the spring of 1938, a sixteen-year-old Carolyn O'Brien was on her way home from high school when a car drove up beside her. It was Grant Baxter. He was nineteen, had graduated from high school the year before, and was one of the most popular boys in Winter Haven. He came from an affluent family. His father, Howard Baxter, had bought him and his sister everything their hearts desired, including the Plymouth Grant was driving that day.

He hadn't graduated at the top of his class or even close to it, but it didn't matter. His father had helped him get a job at Taft Paper and was grooming him to become a foreman.

It was late April, with a month left in the school year. Carolyn was a sophomore.

Grant had his arm hanging out of the open window and was tapping his fingers against the car door as he asked Carolyn if she wanted a lift home. He was a nice-looking young man, the kind any young girl would be flattered to be noticed by.

"My daddy told me never to take rides from strangers," Carolyn teased.

"Your daddy ever tell you how cute you are?" he replied.

She got in the car.

Grant talked about how he'd noticed Carolyn around town and how he thought she was one of the prettiest girls he'd ever seen.

Rather than driving her home, Grant headed into the woods, down a road not frequented very often. He told Carolyn he had something to show her. "A surprise," he said. She was innocent then, naïve, but soon that would end. To her, a drive through the woods was no more than a drive through the woods—until Grant stopped the car beside the road and indicated that the surprise was hidden behind the buttons of his trousers.

She tried to get out of the car, but he grabbed her by the hair and pulled her back in. She was wearing a yellow dress that buttoned down the back. He didn't bother unfastening it, merely yanked until the buttons popped off the fabric. He pulled the dress off her shoulders to undo her bra. When Carolyn screamed and lashed out at him, he punched her in the face, lifted the hem of her dress, and ripped off her panties. By the time he finished, the dress was nothing but a rag, and her face was bruised and bloody. Once he had satisfied his needs, he told her to get out of the car and left her standing beside the road, with his semen streaming down her inner thigh.

It was dark by the time she walked back to her neighborhood. George, who was forty-six at the time, had called all of her friends asking if they'd seen her. No one had. He drove all over town looking for her. His wife, Dora, was in Albany visiting her younger sister, who had just had a baby.

When George found Carolyn walking up the dark residential street, he slammed the car into park, jumped out, and ran to her, not even taking the time to close the door. By the condition of her dress and face, he knew something unspeakable had happened to his daughter.

Rather than explain, she simply put her head against his chest and sobbed.

He put her in the car and took her home where she finally managed to tell her story. George ran a hot bath for her and then phoned the police. Two officers came. They took Carolyn's statement and scolded George for having her bathe before they could examine her. The police couldn't have done much anyway. The only way to determine paternity was through blood tests, which couldn't be performed until the child was six months old.

George told them he wasn't going to let his daughter sit around with Grant Baxter's filth inside her, and that all they needed was Carolyn's word. Of course, when dealing with the son of one of the richest men in town, Carolyn's word didn't carry much weight.

CHAPTER 18

On July 2, I called the McKnights to see if they'd be interested in joining Candice and me at the city park for the Fourth of July. According to the newspaper, the community of Winter Haven gathered at the park every Independence Day for a fireworks display. People brought chairs, pillows, and blankets and staked their claim on a spot of green grass where they could get a good view of the hillside where the fireworks were launched.

When I got Nicole on the phone, she informed me that Kirk and Quinn had gone to Pete's Diner and that she didn't know what their plans were for the holiday. She was polite, but I got the impression she was avoiding making a commitment.

I drove to Pete's and found the men in the parking lot, talking about baseball with a few other guys. They watched me drive in. Kirk look past me at the passenger seat and seemed relieved to see that Candice wasn't with me.

"Taking her fishing is one thing, but this is different," he said once we were alone and I'd extended my invitation to the Fourth of July festivities. "We grew up in this town. People talk."

"I'll hold your hand, Kirk, if it makes you feel any better," Quinn said.

Kirk didn't even look at Quinn, just raised his middle finger at him as he went on talking to me. "Personally, I have nothing against her. I really don't even know her. None of us do. She didn't go to school, except maybe grade school."

"She didn't?"

"You understand where I'm coming from, don't you?"

"All too well," I said. I'd been there myself not so long ago and it was an ugly, cowardly place. I wanted to believe that I was past that now, that given the opportunity to rise above the stupidity of the masses that I'd be able to stand up for what I knew to be right. But the people of Winter Haven weren't my peers. Their opinions didn't bind me like those of my classmates back at BU or the folks from the old neighborhood. But that knowledge didn't stop me from detesting Kirk for his spinelessness.

On the evening of the Fourth of July, Candice and I arrived late, just as the sun made its descent over the horizon. The park was already full, and we had to squeeze in among those who had the foresight to come early. Candice couldn't recall ever coming to the park to see the display, not even as a child. She and her grandparents would sit by the windows in the attic and watch the show from there. George always told her it was foolish to fight the crowd in the park when they had a perfectly good view from their own home. He repeated those words to me that evening when I tried to convince him to come with us.

We spread out our blanket and looked out over the sea of faces, shadowed by the dying light. People talked and laughed as they waited for the first burst of color to fill the night sky. As we sat, I looked through the crowd and spotted Quinn looking at me. He sat on a blanket with Kirk and Nicole, a mere twenty feet from us. I nodded. He gave me an apologetic shrug.

I hadn't said anything to Candice about my invitation to Quinn and Kirk. As far as she knew, I hadn't even spoken to them since the fishing trip. It was better that way. They'd be the good people she'd hung out with once and who mysteriously disappeared from her life. As little as she knew about social norms, she might even consider that normal behavior. Or, then again, maybe she knew a lot more about human nature than I gave her credit for. I watched as she spotted Nicole through the crowd. Candice started to smile, but Nicole quickly looked away as though she hadn't seen us. Candice knew what that meant just as well as I did. Her mood darkened and she became self-conscious again, looking at the faces around us. If the people she considered her friends didn't approve of her, what hope of acceptance could she expect from strangers?

Her insecurity and self-contempt deepened a second later when a firecracker exploded at our backs, not five inches from us. Candice shrieked. I came up off the blanket as though stung by a bee. People laughed. A few applauded, one of them being Vaughn Deval as he stuffed his cigarette between his lips and gave me a smile. Beside him stood slick-boy Todd Miller, holding a handful of firecrackers. With the tip of his cigarette, he lit the fuse of another one and tossed it between Candice's legs, forcing her to scramble out of the way before it exploded.

People were seated on the grass between Todd and me. As I looked for a way around them, I saw Quinn rise to his feet. Anger lined his face, but Kirk grabbed his pant leg and shook his head at him. When Quinn retook his seat beside the McKnights, I felt a sense of abandonment—the way Jefferson Thomas must have felt when people who liked him refused to stand up for him.

As Todd and Vaughn walked away laughing, I settled back on the blanket and looked at the faces that surrounded me, seeing their amusement and hating them for it. I wondered how many of them recognized Candice, how many knew her story or merely a distorted version of it. Did they despise her? Did they pity her? Or was she just a girl who screamed when a firecracker exploded next to her, someone they would forget as soon as something new drew their attention? I imagine there was a mixture of all of those emotions among the crowd, yet my focus was on those watching us with judgment, those whose eyes said we hadn't been invited, that we had no right to be there.

My father used to tell me that the shortcomings we despise the most in others are the same one we ourselves possess, that on a conscious or subconscious level, we hate this particular aspect of our character and can't stand anyone else who bears the same weakness. I wouldn't have admitted it then, but what I hated most about the ignorance and judgment I saw seated around me in the park was that I knew it was the ugliest part of my own character. It was the way I treated Jefferson Thomas and all of those who openly supported him, even my own girlfriend.

A few days after I broke up with Marie, I ran into her two closest friends, Anita and Peggy, while walking across campus. They proceeded to tell me what a worthless human being I was and how lucky Marie was for discovering my true character before becoming saddled with me for life.

"I respect what Marie's doing," I told them. "I support her a hundred percent. I'd be right there with her if I had the time, but I don't. And what time I do have, I'd like to spend with Marie, but she's always too busy with a rally or a petition to ever have time for me. So don't try to make me out to be the bad guy here."

"That's the biggest load of poppycock I've ever heard in my life." Anita had one of those loud voices that made you wonder if she was hard of hearing. My college roommate used to refer to her as Megaphone, or Meg for short. At that moment, I felt her voice had risen a few decibels strictly to make a scene and draw attention to my humiliation. And it worked brilliantly. People slowed down as they passed and looked at me with raised eyebrows.

"Too bad Robert Ripley isn't still alive," Anita said. "He could have portrayed you in one of those believe-it-or-not cartoons of his. He could have titled it 'The Amazing Mitchell Sanders—the man born without a spine'."

Damn, I hated that girl.

I didn't like people passing judgment on me, even if they were right. I liked it even less when they were wrong, like the people in the park that Fourth of July. The excitement had seeped out of Candice. She no longer wanted to experience the festivities and the community spirit. I could see in her eyes that she wanted me to take her away from there, to drive her back to Willow Lane where we could watch the fireworks from the attic window with George. Part of me wanted to honor her silent request, but I couldn't do it. I couldn't let the people bully us into running away. It was what the O'Briens had been doing for years, and I was determined not to react as George had reacted by building a wall between Candice and anything that could possibly damage her, either physically or emotionally. We'd come to the park to have a good time, and by damn we were going to have a good time, even if we had to be miserable doing it.

"To hell with them." I put my arm around Candice and held her close.

She smiled sadly, but she had determination in her face. I was proud of her. Remaining there was a small act, but it showed that she wouldn't be intimidated and was willing to start fighting for her place in the world.

Someone stepped on our blanket behind us. We turned to find Quinn standing over us, with a cheesy grin on his face.

"You got room for one more?" he asked

We moved over to accommodate him. By the look on Candice's face, I was certain she'd fallen in love with him right there on the spot. I felt both gratitude and jealousy. He'd given her a sense of security I couldn't since I was even more of an outsider than she was.

As Quinn sat, we all stared back at Kirk and Nicole, who shook their heads at Quinn, not as a show of disapproval, but of surrender. They gathered their blanket and stepped through the crowd, looking apprehensive about their actions. People around us scooted over to make room as they laid out their blanket. We shared no words of apology or explanation, just a silent alliance as we stared up at the dark sky and waited for the display to begin.

For a small town, the show wasn't half bad. It didn't quite compare to Boston, but the city had a larger budget since it had more people to tax and squander from. The whole show lasted a total of twenty minutes and brought a glow to Candice's face that was nearly as bright as the sky. Every time she gasped with delight, I couldn't help but fall a little more in love with her. I saw Quinn watching her with the same sense of adoration I had.

When the last sparkle faded from the sky, some people let off fireworks of their own in the park. We watched for a while as we talked about music, mostly Elvis, whom Nicole freely admitted she was madly in love with. Kirk had obviously heard it all before and appeared unfazed by her declaration of love for the king.

"What's wrong with this country?" she said. "You don't send a man with that kind of talent into the army." Elvis had been in the army four months and according to Nicole, it proved that our government didn't know what the hell it was doing. "Personally, I think it's a tragedy. Don't you think so, Candice?"

Candice shrugged. "I don't really know that much about Elvis Presley."

"That's the most beautiful thing I've ever heard a woman say," Kirk said.

"Oh, you poor girl." Nicole put her hand on Candice's shoulder. "You have no idea what you're missing. Dwight D. Eisenhower may be the president, but Elvis Presley will always be the king. Boy, is he ever the king." She put a hand to her heart and sighed.

"She speaks the same way about me when I'm not around," Kirk said.

As Quinn and I folded the blankets, Candice stared across the lawn where children were running with sparklers, making designs in the dark. She smiled to herself, but there was sadness in her face, perhaps longing for a childhood she would never have. Growing up, she'd seen the fireworks from her attic, but she'd missed out on the laughter of the children and the smell of sulfur in the air. The things most people took for granted were extraordinary to her. I had no doubt that she'd read about this in one of her many books, but this was the first time she'd experienced it with all of her senses.

"I bet it's gorgeous here in the winter," I said, stepping up beside her.

"It's an absolute haven," she replied and took my hand. We followed the others across the grass to the street where our cars were parked. The area was nearly empty now, except for us and a few other stragglers, using up the last of their supply of fireworks.

I unlocked my car and put the blanket on the backseat.

"We're getting together at our place tomorrow to watch *The Jackie Gleason Show*," Nicole said. "Why don't you two come along?"

"That'd be great," I said. "I haven't seen Jackie Gleason in over a month and I really need a good laugh. You'll love him, Candice. The man is hilarious."

"I'd better talk to Grandpa. I hate leaving him alone so much."

"Bring him along," Quinn said.

Kirk gave him a sharp look, one that said he couldn't believe his ears—not that I blamed him. I couldn't think of anything that would take the humor out of Jackie Gleason faster than George O'Brien.

Candice looked at Nicole and Kirk to see if they shared Quinn's sentiment.

"Yes, bring him along," Nicole said

Kirk nodded in agreement.

"In fact, if you'd like to leave the hired hand home, you can come as my date," Quinn said to Candice.

It took me a second to realize he was talking about me. I shook my finger at him and told him to back off. Charmed by his comment, Candice laughed as I opened the car door for her.

CHAPTER 19

The Jackie Gleason Show was a Saturday night ritual in my family's home. My sister and I used to huddle in the living room with my parents and laugh until our sides ached. According to my father, Gleason's character, Ralph, was the embodiment of the frustrated American male, forever struggling to recover from the great depression. Ralph had a thousand get rich quick schemes, which always lost money and earned him the wrath of Alice, his wife. Their arguments would escalate into shouting matches with Ralph yelling: "One of these days, Alice! Pow! Right in the kisser!" And my father would slap his leg and howl with laughter.

The show had its critics, however, with George O'Brien topping the list. He claimed the show was made up of a bunch of degenerates who didn't have what it takes to make it in the real world, so they had to earn a living acting like buffoons. This criticism wasn't limited to Gleason and his gang but applied to every show on television. To George, it couldn't be an honest living if it seemed easy and paid a lot of money.

As we drove to the McKnights, he confessed that he'd never actually seen *The Jackie Gleason Show* and that his low opinion of the show stemmed from his common sense rather than from any factual knowledge. By the time we arrived at the front door, George had already made up his mind that he wasn't going to laugh no matter how funny it was. Nor was he going to like Quinn and the McKnights. He grunted rather than saying hello and then planted himself in the center of the sofa, daring us to entertain him. Your average person puts on his best behavior around strangers. George put on his worst. He wanted to hate Candice's new friends. He wanted to show her how right he was about the evils of the world and prove that these benevolent people were merely putting on a front while secretly planning their attack.

Their home was small but nice, with colorful drapes covering the windows, landscape paintings adorning the walls, and the smell of popcorn filling the air, but nothing could counteract the dark presence of the ogre seated on the sofa. He was like a black hole sucking the light out of the atmosphere. No one knew what to say around him. Any attempt at small talk ended with George frowning and grunting out a one-word response. When Kirk and Nicole brought out the popcorn and Kool-Aid, he took a glass and sat back with a moan of contempt, resolute in his decision to have a miserable evening. His frown remained as Kirk switched on the TV and Jackie Gleason appeared in a magnificent display of black and white. He was the great one, the master of hilarity—at least to most of us.

"One of these days, Alice! Bang! Zoom! To The Moon, Alice! To The Moon!" Gleason said, threatening to hit his wife so hard that he'd knock her all the way into outer space, which got Quinn laughing so hard that he choked on his popcorn. This reaction won Quinn a disdainful glance from George, who then pulled back his sleeve to check the time on his watch for the tenth time. A clock hung on the wall, right above the television, but looking at his watch was the only way George could draw attention to his annoyance.

It was the longest hour of *Jackie Gleason* I'd ever sat through. I hardly laughed at all. Quinn was the only one not affected by

George's mood. While he rolled with laughter, the rest of us merely grinned and were as happy as George to see the show come to an end.

"Would you care for some more Kool-Aid, Mr. O'Brien?" Nicole asked as Kirk switched off the television.

"No, thank you."

We sat in silence, staring around the room at each other and watching George check his watch again. Candice and I sat on the sofa with George—with her on one side and me on the other, the way George liked it. Kirk and Nicole occupied the loveseat, certain they had failed as hosts. Quinn, amused that George had wedged himself between Candice and me, sat in the lounge chair regarding me with a smirk.

"You a sports fan, Mr. O'Brien?" Kirk asked.

"Nope."

Kirk bit at his nails while Nicole tapped her toes on the carpet.

"Quite the weather we're having," Nicole said.

"It's been hot," I agreed and had to stop myself from smiling. The whole situation was ridiculous, us sitting around trying to entertain a man who had his mind set on not being entertained. We should have just talked about fishing or baseball or rock music without giving any thought to whether or not George was enjoying himself.

"Nicole bought one of those hula-hoops," Quinn said. "You want to give it a try, Mr. O'Brien?"

"We've got a comedian in our midst," George said without humor. "So this is what you youngsters do nowadays for fun. I heard you had some pretty wild parties."

"This one's quite a bash, isn't it, Gramps? I mean, Mr. O'Brien," Quinn said.

"Next time remind me to bring my Geritol. We can all share a bottle." George stood up and grabbed his cane. "Come along, Candice. Time to get home to bed. These people plumb wore me out."

"We aim to please," Quinn said, rising to escort us to the door. "It was a pleasure to have you here, Mr. O'Brien," Nicole said as she opened the door for us. "We'll have to do it again."

George moaned. "Give me time to recuperate, please. I'm an old man. I can't handle this much excitement." Stooped over his cane, he went out the door and down the front steps. I lagged behind, wanting to say something derisive about George so everyone would know we didn't blame them for the horrible evening. But Candice was standing right outside the door waiting for me, and I didn't want to belittle her grandfather in her presence. I opted for a smile and a raised eyebrow.

As I drove back to Willow Lane, I glanced at Candice, who sat beside me, clutching her fists and gritting her teeth. George was in the back seat humming softly to himself. He seemed happy about the way the evening had gone. It proved he was right about the people of Winter Haven and that he was better off staying at home, lounging on his sofa and reading the newspaper.

"No wonder no one invites you to parties, Grandpa." Candice didn't even turn around as she said this.

"What?" George put on an innocent routine. "I was a perfect gentleman."

"Like Attila the Hun," I said.

Candice turned in her seat. George's face brightened and then fell back into shadows as we passed beneath a streetlight. "You did nothing but insult them all evening. It was embarrassing. I can't believe you. You could have at least thanked them."

"For what, popcorn and second-rate entertainment? The whole program was nothing but yelling. I get enough of that living next to the Blanchards, and I certainly don't consider it entertainment. I wanted to leave five minutes into the thing. But like a true gentleman, I stayed and didn't make a scene."

"I'd hate to see you when you do make a scene." Candice sat forward again. She brushed the hair out of her eyes and chewed at her fingernails. In the back seat, George let out a low moan.

His humming came to a stop. He'd started the evening with great
hopes, a beautiful vision of life on Willow Lane returning to the
way it had been before Candice found interests outside of the
home. Things had started off well. He'd grumbled about leaving
the house. He'd complained about the television program. He'd
successfully demonstrated that her new friends were incapable of
showing him a good time. Yet somehow things had gone wrong
and he'd come off looking like the bad guy.

CHAPTER 20

"Look at that Harriet Blanchard. Nosy old weed. Always prying into everyone else's business." George stood at the kitchen window with his binoculars held to his eyes.

Candice and I sat behind him at the table playing a game of chess. She was massacring me and taking great pleasure in it.

"Don't you just hate people like that?" I said. "Bet she spies on her neighbors through a pair of binoculars."

Candice smiled.

"Got a wisecrack for everything, don't you?" George was one of those men who grew on you after a while. I started accepting that he was a miserable old cuss and that he never had anything positive to say. After getting to know him, I stopped taking his insults personally. He didn't hate me, not really, at least no more than he hated everybody else. It was just his nature. Sometimes I even found it amusing. My college roommate used to say: "People are the spice of life." I suppose that's a healthier attitude than going around hating everyone just because they're not like you. George just happened to be one of those rare spices you had to get used to and one you couldn't take in large doses.

After putting my king in checkmate for the sixth time, Candice threw up her hands and said: "That's it for me. I just can't take it anymore."

"What are you talking about? I'm the one who's losing."

"And you lose so badly. You're not even a challenge. What fun is that?"

"You're great on my ego." I swept the chess pieces off the table into the box. "I'll play you in a game of football and show you how much of a challenge I am."

"If the mind is weak, rely on the muscle," she chided as she folded the chessboard.

"Oh yes, you're a genius ... Blondie."

"Blondie? Is that the best you've got? You're a writer. You're supposed to be good with words."

"You're becoming a real pain in the butt, you know that? I liked you better when you were quiet."

"I'm sure you did. I was much less threatening to your intellect."

George watched us with bewilderment. I don't know if Candice joked with him this way or not, but I suspected she didn't. In fact, she'd only recently begun harassing me in such fashion. She was quicker than I was with the banter. She had a sadistic streak that enjoyed watching me struggle for something clever to say and constantly coming up short.

"I could really go for some ice cream," I said. "What do you say the three of us drive down to Pete's and get a sundae?"

"Candice and I will sit this one out." George set his binoculars on the shelf.

"Actually, I wouldn't mind going," Candice said.

I believe that was his moment of resignation, where George came to the conclusion that his granddaughter was too old to control anymore. He could tell her what to do, but he couldn't make her do it. He switched strategies at that point. Rather than telling her she couldn't do whatever she had set her mind on doing, he decided he would tag along wherever we went.

George owned a car. It sat in his garage and hadn't been driven in nearly a year. He said he hated dealing with the traffic, which in Winter Haven never consisted of more than a dozen cars sharing the same road, but I appeased George and offered to drive. He sat in the back seat, humming his little song and staring at me through the rearview mirror. Every time I checked the mirror, all I could see was his face, looking right back at me. I don't know if he was trying to make me nervous or just trying to figure out whether or not he liked me. I don't think the tune he was humming was even a song. It was just this nervous habit he had whenever he was put into an uncomfortable situation. To George, going to town was the worst.

We didn't end up going to Pete's, since George claimed he didn't like the crowd. Instead, we took a walk down Main Street, past the sporting goods store and theater. There was an ice cream parlor that George was eager to show us. He claimed he and Dora used to go there a lot. That was one of the few times I ever heard George mention his wife. I think he found talking about her painful.

We walked several blocks as George studied the facades of shops, looking as though he'd just returned to the town he'd grown up in and was finding it all unfamiliar. He rubbed his chin, gazed across the street, and then stopped and looked at the stores we'd just passed.

"Where was that place?" he asked. "It was called 'Haven's Ice Cream Parlor'."

"How long has it been since you've been downtown?" I asked.

"When you live in a place like Winter Haven, you come to town as seldom as possible. This town is run by idiots. They went and tore down the only nice place this town ever had and left us with the blight." He pointed past the end of the street, to a mill off in the distance. It had smokestacks that billowed white clouds into the air. "See that smoke? Taft Paper. Everything a Baxter touches turns to shit."

"I wish you wouldn't use language like that, Grandpa. It's not very gentlemanlike."

"It's hard to mention the name Baxter and not have the word 'shit' come out in the same sentence."

"Then don't mention the name Baxter."

It'd been twenty years since Grant Baxter raped Carolyn, but judging by George's emotions, he still bore the scars of that ill-fated day. He stared out at the mill with gritted teeth and clenched fists. These people had stolen his daughter's childhood and had brought misery into his home. Yet their world bloomed while the O'Briens' withered.

"George?" We turned and found a gentleman dressed in a suit and tie. He appeared to be in his mid-fifties and had a cheery demeanor. "George O'Brien, that you?"

George said nothing.

"Nice to see you out and about." Gray hair flowed from beneath his black hat. He smiled as if he'd just rediscovered an old friend. "I was beginning to wonder if you were still alive."

George grunted and walked past the gentleman, back in the direction we'd come.

"How are you getting along, Candice?" the gentleman asked, seeing that George was intent on not acknowledging his presence.

"Fine."

"Don't answer that man." George gave Candice a hard look. "He's not worth the breath."

"Sorry, you feel that way, George."

"How am I supposed to feel?" Blue veins protruded from George's neck. "You took what was a normal respectable life and turned it to shit. How can you live with yourself?"

"I was doing my job."

"Well, your job is shit." George headed down the sidewalk, back toward my car.

The gentleman stared uncomfortably at Candice and me for a moment before rolling up the end of the paper bag he was holding and walking away. Candice and I had to hurry to catch up with George. For a man with a cane, he could move pretty fast when he set his mind to it. His face beaded with sweat, and his breath was heavy and strained.

"I take it that was a Baxter," I said, "since you used the word 'shit' twice."

"Judge Ellington," George huffed. "He and the Baxters are the same breed."

I opened my mouth to ask how Ellington figured into this whole affair, but Candice shook her head at me. She was right of course. As far as George knew, I was ignorant of his daughter's rape. And even if I asked my question in a way that didn't give away my knowledge, bringing up old history wasn't something George could handle.

We drove home without a word and without our ice cream. George didn't hum on the way home, nor did he watch me through the rearview mirror. Rather, he kept his head down and put a hand over his eyes. I thought he might be crying, but when he got out of the car at his house, his eyes were dry.

He looked worn out by the excursion, limping up the steps and through the front door. "I think I'm going to go lie down," he said as we followed him into the living room. "Mitch, why don't you make yourself useful and go get to work on that back yard?"

"Today's my day off," I reminded him.

He looked at me, then at Candice, as though he didn't trust leaving us alone together. He was calculating, trying to think of some way of splitting us up while he took his nap. For a moment, I thought I would have the afternoon alone with Candice until she announced that she, too, was tired and was going to go up to her room to lie down. That left me with nothing to do but to work on the novel I'd been looking forward to neglecting.

CHAPTER 21

The rain pelted the window, accompanied by the tapping of typewriter keys as I labored at the table. The sound of the drops beating against the roof found its way into my story, where my hero stood on a corner trying to hail a cab in the pouring rain. It was dark out—not only in my story but also in Winter Haven. I leaned back in my chair with my lamp on, the curtains drawn, and my shoes off. I'd just finished page 203 and felt a sense of accomplishment. Another hundred pages and I'd have my novel. My hero was a lot like me, except he'd just returned home from the war, had women swooning over him, and was driven by strong principles that he wasn't afraid to stand up for.

Intermingled with the rain, a voice hollered outside. I turned off the lamp, parted the curtain, and gazed into the night. Candice stood on the back porch, wearing a nightgown that hung to her ankles. She whistled and clapped her hands together as she yelled for Star, her cat.

I leaned closer to the window to get a better view of the black garden. The yellow cat emerged from beneath the table that stood next to the bathtub. It hesitated a moment before forging forth through the rain, making a mad dash for the back porch, and into

Candice's arms. She held it to her chest and rubbed it behind the ears.

With a smile, I closed the curtains, switched back on the lamp, and looked at my alarm clock. It was already 10:40. After straightening out my manuscript, I went into the bathroom, grabbed my toothbrush, and squeezed out a gob of toothpaste. I'd barely started brushing when a knock came at the studio door.

It was Candice, her hair matted down and rain streaming over her face. She glanced down at her wet nightgown, which had become semi-transparent, revealing the fact that she wasn't wearing a bra. Crossing her arms over her breasts, she stepped inside.

"I locked myself out," she said.

I brought a towel from the bathroom and tossed it to her. As she dried herself, I tried not to stare too hard through the wet nightgown. Or rather, I tried not to let her see me staring too hard. My heart pounded. I was torn between my desires and what I knew George would do to me if I acted on those desires. As she dried her hair and wiped the rain from her face, I could see the outline of her body through the clinging nightgown. I'm not convinced that men are pigs. We just have a fine appreciation for beauty, so fine that we want to caress the beauty, to hold it and kiss it.

Like the pathetic gentleman my parents had raised me to be, I grabbed a long button-up shirt from my closet and handed it to Candice, telling her she should get out of her wet clothes before she caught pneumonia.

She changed in the bathroom and came out wearing my green shirt, which hung to her mid-thigh. She had nice legs.

"Where's your cat?" I asked.

"After I realized the back door was locked, I went around to the front. I set Star down, and she went through that little door of hers. I should have just left her out in the rain."

They had a little flap at the base of their front door so Star could come and go as she pleased. The cat was probably up in Candice's room, settling down on the bed and licking its fur dry.

After hanging her nightgown over the shower rod, Candice came in and sat down on the bed beside me. Seeing me glance at her legs, she scooted back onto the bed, curled her legs under her, and pulled the hem of the shirt down to cover herself.

"Why don't you just knock? Your grandfather will skin me alive if he finds you out here."

"You have something against being skinned alive?"

"Actually, I do."

"So do I. And trust me, he'll skin me for being stupid enough to lock myself out. He's unbearable when you disturb his sleep."

"You must disturb him a lot," I said.

"Very funny." She got up, went to the window, and parted the curtains. The weight of her situation lay heavy on her brow as she tapped a finger on her bottom lip and shook her head. It was dangerous for her to be in the studio, especially at this time of night and dressed in nothing but my shirt. Still, I was glad to have her here. I enjoyed the sight of her standing at the window, of her fiddling with her wet hair, and later, picking up my manuscript and thumbing the pages. Her eyes scanned through the paragraphs, her lips mouthed the words. I even glimpsed a smile or two.

"Can I read this?"

"You really want to?" I sounded reluctant, but inside I was beaming, happy to have an audience, and certain she'd be swept away with my eloquent prose and witty dialogue. "Okay, but it's my only copy. So be careful with it."

Leaving the manuscript on the table, she joined me on the bed again. I could smell the dampness of her hair as she combed her fingers through it to brush it from her face. Her blue eyes were clear, as though the rain had swept them clean. We stared at each other, not saying a word, and suddenly my heart was pounding. I wanted nothing more than to put my arms around her and press my lips to hers. I feared she was thinking the same thing.

"So, what are we going to do?" I asked, and then quickly clarified myself. "I mean, about getting you back in the house?"

She shrugged and didn't look away. I knew I was in trouble even before she leaned her face toward mine. I could feel her breath on my mouth, but I put a hand on her shoulder and stopped her before she made contact.

"Your grandfather would kill me."

A brief show of dejection crossed her face before she turned away and gazed at the shelf of books. She'd taken the risk and now wished she hadn't. I knew how she felt. The role of making the first move generally fell upon the male, and I hated nothing more than the sting of rejection, which was why I so rarely made any move at all.

I put my hand on her shoulder and rubbed her neck and upper back. She faced me again. I saw such innocence and pain in her eyes that I couldn't help but lean in and kiss her. It was short, a brief moment of my lips touching hers, but it was enough to tell me how deeply I had fallen for her. She put her hand on my cheek and smiled. I studied her face, the ovals of her eyes, the curve of her nose, the vastness of her mouth. The second kiss was longer, more intense, one of those out of body experiences that told me I was in way over my head. I could hear George's voice whispering in my ear, telling me his granddaughter was a virgin and he wanted her to stay that way. Other parts of my body disagreed with his counsel.

When I pulled away, she put an arm around me and rested her head on my shoulder. I kept my eyes on the bathroom door, afraid to look at her, afraid the next kiss would lead to my undoing.

"Tell me about Judge Ellington," I said.

"Is that really what you want to talk about right now?"

"Yeah."

Disappointed, she scooted to the head of the bed, propped a pillow behind her, and pulled the blankets over her legs. "What do you want to know?"

"Was he the judge at Grant Baxter's trial?"

"No. Back then he was just a lawyer. Baxter's lawyer."

SƆCR

In 1938, Randolph Ellington was thirty-six years old and had been practicing law for nine years. He was known for his polished rhetoric and well-placed outbursts of emotion. He'd called Dora O'Brien to the stand and asked her where she was on the night of the alleged rape. When Dora answered that she'd been in Albany visiting her sister, who had just had her baby, Ellington concluded that she could not vouch for what had taken place on April twenty-first, which left the whole testimony in the hands of George and Carolyn O'Brien.

Ellington then called on Howard Baxter. Howard told how he and Grant had gone for a ride that day in Grant's Plymouth. Howard was a low ranking executive responsible for implementing programs that would benefit Taft and its employees.

According to Howard, he and his son had disagreed on a new program that would give the workers incentive bonuses. They'd left together around three in the afternoon and hadn't returned home until eight that evening. Since the rape had taken place around four, this gave Grant an airtight alibi. On cross-examination, O'Brien's lawyer stated that he had witnesses from Taft Paper who would swear under oath that Howard had been at the mill during those hours, rather than riding around with his son. Howard didn't recant. Later, when the so-called witnesses took the stand, they could no longer recall exactly when Howard had left the mill that day.

George was given the opportunity to tell his side of the story, about how he'd found Carolyn walking home that night with her clothes torn and her face battered. He said he believed his daughter about the rape. Ellington asked him if he liked Grant Baxter.

"No."

"Why not?"

"How would you feel about a man who had raped your daughter?"

"Before April twenty-first," Ellington asked, "what was your opinion of Grant Baxter?"

"I thought he was an arrogant little snot-nosed brat." George was forty-six at the time. He had on a dark suit. He was still a photographer and still had all of his hair.

"So you didn't like Grant even before this alleged rape. Is that right?"

"That's right."

"You had a run-in with him at the movie theater several months ago. Isn't that true?" Ellington gave the jury a short look, so they'd know this was important.

"Yes."

"What happened?"

"He and his friends cut in the front of the line, and I told him to go to the back. So he started preaching about how a Baxter can do anything he damn well pleases." George was still naïve about the American judicial system and didn't yet see it as a game of rhetoric. He still thought that truth mattered.

"And so you assaulted him?" said Ellington.

"Is that what he told you? I merely pushed him aside and entered the theater in front of him. You can ask anyone." George was angry, which pleased Ellington. Angry men often said things that could be used against them.

"Was this the beginning of your plot against Grant Baxter?" Ellington paused and looked at George O'Brien with grave concern.

The prosecutor objected, claiming the defense was badgering the witness. The judge sustained the objection. But it didn't matter to Ellington. The seed had been planted in the minds of the jurors.

"Who really did this to your daughter, Mr. O'Brien?" Ellington asked.

"You know damn well who did this!" He stared at Grant Baxter, seated at the defense's table, looking smug in his three-piece suit.

"You heard Howard Baxter testify, under oath, that he was with his son all day, Tuesday, April twenty-first," Ellington continued.

"I heard him lie under oath. Yes."

"Grant Baxter had nothing to do with this, did he, George?" Ellington offered the jury a sorrowful gaze, torn by the truth he was about to reveal. "Isn't it true that you did this to your daughter?"

"Objection," the prosecutor said.

"That's a damn lie!" George yelled from the stand, his face turning a darker shade of red.

"Then to keep the truth from coming out, you fabricated this whole story about Grant—a young man whom you openly despise."

"How dare you!" George said before the judge had time to sustain the prosecutor's second objection.

As Ellington had declared, he was only doing his job. He'd been hired by the Baxters to see to it that Grant didn't spend one day behind bars, and he did just that. It was a sad day at the O'Briens' household when the jury returned a "Not Guilty" verdict. But the Baxters rejoiced.

The way Candice told it, Howard gave his son a heartfelt embrace and a pay raise that day. She saw it as rewarding bad behavior. And though she hadn't even been born yet and had never met Grant Baxter, I could see that she despised him and was shamed by the knowledge that he was her father.

"The same minute the jury declared Grant Baxter innocent, the entire town declared Grandpa guilty," Candice said as she sat at the head of my bed with her legs under the covers. "It's been twenty years. The Baxters have prospered. Ellington has become a judge. And my grandfather, the only innocent one out of the bunch, can't walk down the street without people whispering behind his back."

CHAPTER 22

I blinked my eyes open and saw a bar of muted sunlight falling across the carpet. The alarm clock on the nightstand said it was 6:30, an hour before I generally got up. George, on the other hand, had probably been up since five. That old man would pop right up with the sun. Then he'd call me and the rest of the world lazy for wasting our lives away beneath the sheets. I turned over and saw that Candice was still asleep. We were under the covers, Candice wearing my green shirt and me fully clothed, except my shoes and socks. I put my arm around her and held her close, just as I had last night before falling asleep.

When I kissed her on the forehead, her eyes opened briefly, and then fell shut again.

"Good morning, Sunshine," I said.

Her eyes opened again. They moved from my face to the room and then back to my face.

"I've been here all night," she said.

"I know. You wouldn't keep your hands off me."

She grinned, gave me a peck on the lips, and climbed over me and went into the bathroom, closing the door behind her. Crawling out of bed, I opened the nightstand drawer, grabbed a stick of Juicy

Fruit gum, and stuffed it in my mouth. I was in the process of putting on my shoes and socks when Candice came out, dressed in her nightgown and wearing my shirt over the top of it.

"Damn, that's sexy," I said.

"It's the latest fashion." She went to the window and parted the curtains. "How am I going to get back in the house before Grandpa notices I'm missing?"

"I'm going in right now," I said. "I'll distract him, and you sneak in the front door."

"What are you going to do?"

"I don't know yet." I ruffled Candice's hair as I passed her on my way out the door. My hope was that George would have gone back to bed after getting up and putting the cat out, something he did every morning, despite the fact that the cat could let itself out through the little flap at the front door.

As expected, the cat was roaming the black garden and the back door was now unlocked. I passed through the kitchen and came down the hallway into the living room where I found George sitting on the sofa, reading a newspaper. He subscribed to the town paper and read it religiously. I suspect he only did it so he'd have something new to bitch about. I doubt anyone in Winter Haven ever did anything to George's liking.

"You're up early," he said. His appearance startled me. His head looked smaller and older. It took me a moment to realize he didn't have any teeth. Until then, I hadn't realized he wore dentures. They sat on the coffee table, submerged in a glass of water.

I looked down at my watch as if I didn't know what time it was. "That bed's so comfortable that six hours feel like eight."

"Good. I'll start working you twice as long." He squinted up at me with his mouth wide open and his gums showing.

Past George, Candice appeared outside the front window, holding my manuscript against her chest. She smiled and bit at her bottom lip, emphasizing that she was being mischievous behind George's back. She pointed at George and then pointed at the hallway. I tried not to look directly at her, afraid I'd draw George's attention.

"Perhaps you can show me what you want done in the flowerbed and I'll get started," I said. George had mentioned the day before that he wanted me to weed his garden for him again, though I didn't think it needed it.

"Pull the weeds. Leave the flowers." George didn't even raise his eyes from his newspaper.

"What do you want me to do with all the stuff your neighbors dumped over the fence on top of your flowers?"

This got his attention.

"They what?" He popped off the sofa and marched into the kitchen. I gave Candice the okay sign and followed George from the room. He went right to the kitchen door and swung it open. There, of course, was nothing dumped upon the flower garden, other than the droplets of water from last night's rain. He studied it before looking back at me. "What are you talking about?"

I rubbed my eyes and stared at the garden as though I couldn't believe what I was seeing. "My eyes must be playing tricks on me."

"I hired Mr. Magoo." George went back inside.

I followed him back to the living room where he plopped down on the sofa and took up his newspaper again. The stairs leading to the second floor were dark, except for a dim glow of sunlight that streamed from one of the upstairs rooms.

"You're not going up there," George said.

"I was just thinking that since the ground's pretty wet outside ..." I never finished the thought, not because George was shaking his head, but because Candice reappeared at the window behind him. She wore the same expression my mother used to wear whenever I failed to take out the garbage or clean my room. Candice gestured to the door and then twisted her hand as if turning a key, indicating that the door was locked.

"Up for a game of chess?" I asked George, who appeared annoyed that I was still standing there bothering him.

"I thought you were going to get started on the flower garden."

"Now that I know how early it is, I feel a little tired."

"Then go back to bed."

"Perhaps I will," I replied, but rather than doing so, I went to the front door, unlocked it, and stepped outside into the morning air. "On the other hand, it is a lovely morning. Perhaps we should go for a walk."

Candice stood against the wall between the door and the window, giving me a hard look and motioning for me to go back inside. I winked at her and looked back at George, who was giving me a similar look, as he stared over the top of his newspaper.

"Is that a 'no' on the walk?" I asked.

George didn't answer, just put his eyes back on his paper as I shut the door. I went to the hallway and stared into the kitchen, chewing my gum and trying to think of a way to get him out of the room again.

"There's that Harriet Blanchard snooping over your back fence."

"That old crow." George popped up again. He preceded me into the kitchen. This time he didn't go outside but merely stopped at the window and looked out.

"Where?" he asked, studying the fence that separated the two homes.

"She ducked behind the fence."

George stared intently. Hearing the door open in the living room, I coughed a few times to cover the sound. Glancing back down the hall, I saw Candice creeping toward the stairs.

"She ain't out there," George said, turning toward me with an angry stare.

"There she is!" I shouted and pointed out the window, drawing his attention away from the hallway. Adding to the absurdity of everything I'd done that morning, their cat took that opportunity to leap upon the fence.

George simply looked at me as though I were the stupidest person he'd ever had the pleasure of knowing. "You know I don't tolerate drug users in my employment?"

"Perhaps I should go back to bed," I offered and did just that.

At breakfast, George poured me a bowl of Corn Flakes and milk and told me about a new addition they were building onto the high school and why that was a bad idea. He seemed annoyed that I didn't jump onto his bandwagon, but I knew nothing of Winter Haven's board of education and had no opinion one way or the other.

Candice came in with her hair pulled back in a ponytail and a sheepish grin on her face. She grabbed a bowl from the cupboard, sat at the table, and poured herself some Corn Flakes.

"Sleep well last night?" she asked me as she poured on the milk.

"I have no complaints."

"He was acting like a raving idiot this morning," George piped in. "The narcotics squad is coming out later with bloodhounds to sniff out his room."

Candice smirked as she spooned the cereal into her mouth. She glanced at me with the look of a partner in crime. She'd done something her grandfather didn't know about, something naughty, and she was pleased with herself. The two of us shared a secret that bonded us, and for the first time, George was on the outside.

CHAPTER 23

When I was in high school, a twelve-year-old girl who lived down the street from me was raped and murdered. My sister's boyfriend, Freddie Bailey, had come over one night and told us about it. He said a sanitation worker had found the body in an alley. The trail of evidence led the police to a guy named Paul Deacon, who also lived in my neighborhood. I'd gone to school with Paul. He was two grades ahead of me. I didn't know him well, but I hated him after hearing the news of the murder. My father was the psychologist who administered the psychological examination on Paul to see if he was fit to stand trial. That evening at the dinner table my father told us that he thought Paul was innocent. I didn't argue the point, but I felt my father was just a nice man who believed the best about people. I figured Paul had declared his innocence and my father trustingly believed him. The way I saw it, if the police thought Paul was guilty, then he was guilty.

A few weeks later, another girl, this one eleven years old, was raped but not killed. The rapist had told her that if she said anything to anyone that the devil would come and get her and her parents. Apparently, he'd said the same to several other girls he'd raped, and it'd worked in winning their silence. It didn't work this time, however. The girl told her mother, who went to the police and told them what had happened and who had done it. To my sister's horror, the rapist was Freddie Bailey. When the police picked him up and asked him if he'd killed the other girl, he confessed. I'd hated Paul Deacon when I thought he was the killer, but with Freddie I felt nothing but sorrow. I felt bad for his family, but mostly I felt bad for Ann, who cried for weeks afterward. As traumatic as it was, it did teach me not to be so quick to judge.

Now, as I thought about Judge Ellington and the Baxter family, I found myself wanting to hate them just as I had Paul Deacon, but I had to be honest with myself. I only knew Candice's side of the story, which might or might not be accurate. For all I knew, George had actually raped his own daughter. Stranger things have happened. How did Candice know any of this in the first place? I had a hard time picturing George telling her, and even if he had, could I trust his side of the story? If he had molested Candice's mother, Candice was the last person he would tell.

Thursday, after spending the day painting the front of the house, I drove downtown to the courthouse where I'd spoken to the county clerk about Carolyn O'Brien's marriage license. This time I stayed on the ground floor where the judge's chambers were located. Judge Ellington's assistant was a thin young woman with blond hair fashioned after Marilyn Monroe.

"He's in a meeting and won't be out until six," she said, speaking of Judge Ellington. "You're welcome to wait if you'd like."

I checked my watch. It was 5:20. I went outside and sat on the broad steps that led to the front door. To my right was a small park with a maple tree. A woman sat on the bench scolding her teenage daughter, telling her how she had disgraced the family and how no man would ever want her now. The source of contention was clearly the teenager's bulging stomach. Young girls were expected to maintain high morals while young men looked for girls with no morals at all.

The mother strained to keep her voice low, but I heard the words 'home for wayward girls' escape her lips several times, and every time she said it, the daughter cried harder. If the woman hoped to keep this pregnancy a secret, she had already missed her window of opportunity.

The girl looked about sixteen, the same age as Carolyn when she was raped. I wondered how George and Dora had handled the situation. The trial had announced the pregnancy to all of Winter Haven, so sending her away would have been futile. Did George keep her locked inside the house? Did she continue with school? Did her friends abandon her?

I heard voices over my shoulder and looked back to find Judge Ellington standing near the courthouse door, talking with two other men, all of them decked out in suits and business hats.

Getting to my feet, I approached and waited for their conversation to end. When Ellington glanced at me, I could see that he recognized my face but couldn't place me. Once the other two gentlemen left, he walked toward me and extended his hand.

"We've met, haven't we?"

"Mitchell Sanders. I'm working for the O'Briens."

"That's right, yes. How's Mr. O'Brien treating you?"

"Fine," I said. "He's a tough old man, that Mr. O'Brien. He can be a bit abrasive at times, but he's a good man."

I told the judge a little bit about myself before leading into my questions about Carolyn's rape and about the trial. We walked to Main Street, taking our time. It took us a half-hour to walk two blocks. Randolph Ellington was a tall, thin man with a narrow nose and bushy gray eyebrows. He had a presence that told me he was good at his job, a quality that hadn't worked in Carolyn O'Brien's favor.

"The thing I like the most about George O'Brien is that he's proud and unbendable," Ellington said as we stopped at the bakery window and looked in at the donuts and éclairs. "That also happens to be the thing I like the least about him. After the trial, George's own lawyer advised him to leave town. But to George, that would have been a sign of surrender, a confession of guilt. So he stayed and put himself and his family through hell."

"I never knew people could be so cruel," I said.

"You talk as if the whole town's against them. It isn't. Half of George's problems are in his head, and the other half he brought upon himself. Since the trial, George O'Brien hasn't exactly been the easiest man to love. He is spiteful to everyone, even to people who were once his friends. Jordan Patrick, who was a good friend of George's, told me that George once punched him in the nose for saying how cute Candice was. Jordan's only crime was his bad choice of words. First, he called Candice a cute little devil, not meaning a damn thing by it. Then he had the gall to tell George that she looked like him. George took it all wrong and hit him. All the while, there's Carolyn, just the prettiest thing you've ever seen, standing there with tears rolling down her face and her baby cuddled in her arms. It was a real shame."

"Couldn't they do a blood test to see if George was actually the father?"

"They did. It was inconclusive. I'm not saying George raped his own daughter, because I simply don't know what went on in their home, but I do know this much: Grant Baxter was innocent. But George couldn't accept that. He became irrational after the trial, started stalking the Baxters, following them around with that camera of his, taking pictures of everything they did. We finally had to put a restraining order on him."

"From what I hear, you're the one who blamed the rape on George in the first place."

Ellington stopped walking. He gave me a look that I felt certain he'd practiced and used throughout his career as a lawyer, a look designed to make witnesses feel small and unsure of themselves, just as it did me.

"George O'Brien was never convicted of anything," he said. "Was never even put on trial. But he put himself in prison nonetheless. I may be the judge in this town, but that's one door I can't open for him."

CHAPTER 24

Judge Ellington had planted a seed that germinated in my mind over the next few days. It started out as nothing more than a seedling of how to bust George O'Brien out of his self-made prison. Slowly, it grew roots, took on new possibilities, and sprouted into an escape plan that George was guaranteed to hate. He liked his cozy little cell and despised nothing more than people interfering with the dull routine of his life. I didn't have the details worked out, but I now had my eyes open to recognize opportunities when they arose.

The first opportunity presented itself in the form of George's spying. I wandered into the living room one afternoon and found him gazing through his binoculars out the front window. The voyeuristic theme that ran through George's life was one of devolution, regressing from the active role of photographer in his younger days to the secretive role of stalking the Baxters in his midlife and finally concluding with the passive pastime of ogling the neighbors. His hermitage had transformed him into a mere spectator of life rather than an active participant.

"Go talk to her, George."

He put down his binoculars and looked back at me. "Margaret? Hell no. That prunish old woman."

"How long have you been watching that prunish old woman?"

"I'm not watching anybody. Just keeping an eye on the neighborhood."

I went to the other window and stared across the street at Margaret's house. The sun streamed over her lawn while she sat in the shade of her porch, relaxing in her rocking chair. I understood George's pain. There were many times in my life when I had longed for a particular woman but was too afraid to do anything about it.

I opened the door and gave George a glance. "If you're not going to talk to her, I am." I was out the door before George could stop me.

"You say one word to her, I'll boot you out on your ear." He stopped in the doorway and glowered at me as I stood at the top of the steps.

"I'm just going to see if she has a cup of milk I could borrow for the cake I'm making."

"You're not making a cake."

"She doesn't know that," I whispered theatrically as if trying to keep Margaret from hearing me. I bounded down the steps, went down the walk, out the gate, and strolled across the street, while George's eyes burned the back of my neck. I was halfway across her front lawn before Margaret looked up from her book. Her graying hair was pulled away from her face, showing off her high cheekbones. She reminded me of my grandmother, slightly overweight and jovial. She closed her book, sticking her thumb in it to keep her place, and scooted forward to the edge of her wooden rocking chair.

"Afternoon," I said, stopping at the foot of her steps. "I'm making a cake," I started, and then realized this was not very believable, mainly because my clothes were filthy from working all morning in the back yard. "Or rather, Candice is making a cake. However, she got the eggs and flour and things in a bowl, then realized she didn't have any milk. I was afraid no store would let me come in, looking like I do, so I was wondering if I could borrow a cup of milk."

"Of course," she said. "No problem at all." She got up from her rocker, laid her book open on the seat, and went into the house. I looked back at the O'Briens' place. It looked pretty good, now that Candice and I had finished painting the entire front. I could see the dark spot at the front window where George was peering through the curtains. From across the street, you really couldn't see him or his binoculars. I gave him thumbs-up, knowing it would embarrass the hell out of him.

Margaret came out with a porcelain cup that had a flowery design on it. "You're doing a wonderful job with their home." She handed me the cup and stared across the street at the O'Briens'. "It's nice to see some activity over there."

"George decided it was time for a change. He's a good man. He wanted me to tell you hello and said his door's always open if you ever want to stop by."

"Tell him hello from me, too."

I felt I should invite her over for a piece of cake, but since we weren't really making one and I didn't know if we had all of the ingredients to do so, I simply thanked her and headed back across the street. When I came in the house, George was as eager as a junior high school boy waiting to find out if the new girl in town liked him. He left his post at the window and closed the door behind me.

"What'd she say?"

"She said I could borrow the milk."

"Besides that?" His eyes were wide and waiting.

"She asked if you personally would return her cup."

"No, she didn't," he said but didn't sound entirely convinced that I was lying.

I headed to the kitchen.

George stuck right on my heels. "Did she?" he persisted.

"Yeah." I sat at the table and took a drink of the milk. "And guess what? She's got a pair of binoculars sitting right by her front window. I think she's been watching you."

"Don't toy with an old man," he grumbled.

"It's true," I insisted. "And I asked her if I could borrow some sugar, too, but she said she thought you were already sweet enough. Of course, I had to agree."

George groaned. "Youngsters have no respect for their elders anymore." But I think he liked it. He went to the back window to see how much I'd accomplished that morning.

"Come with me," he said and opened the back door.

I swallowed the rest of the milk and left the cup on the table. Stepping outside, I followed George down the steps. He walked toward the studio, stopped, and turned back toward the house. Leaning forward on his cane, he squinted up at the roof.

"The backyard can wait for now, but those rain gutters have got to come down. They look like hell and don't do a damn bit of good when it rains." The gutters were nothing but strips of rust, hanging lopsided along the edge of the roof. By the looks of them, they hadn't served their purpose for several years. I couldn't understand why they had suddenly become a priority. However, the reason became clear when we walked around the house and entered the front yard. George went out of the gate as if he needed to put some distance between him and the house so he could get a better perceptive of the work that needed to be done. He paced the length of the sidewalk, shaking his head as he looked up at the old rain gutters. Casually, he stared up the street, and then glanced over at Margaret and gave her a wave as he came back through the gate.

The man was smooth, making everything look natural and spontaneous.

"Come to think of it," he said, "I've measured this out once before. I think I even know where I have it written down. Wait here for me." He went into the house and returned with a sheet of paper that contained the exact length of gutters needed, number of downspouts, wedges, elbows, screws, and whatnot to complete the job. This sheet of paper hadn't slipped his mind. He just needed an excuse to come outside and strut around where Margaret could see him.

"Do you know your way around Albany?" he asked.

"No."

"It doesn't matter. I'll get you the address of the store. If you get lost, you can always stop and ask for directions."

Candice came outside. Her hair was in a ponytail, and she was wearing a blue shirt several sizes too large for her. She had a nice figure, but you'd never know it because she always wore baggy clothes that George had picked out for her. Another one of his precautions to assure that history didn't repeat itself.

"It'll probably take you a few hours to get there and get back." George handed me the sheet of paper with the measurements. "You can start pulling down the old guttering first thing tomorrow morning."

"Where are you going?"

"He's going to Albany. We're going to finally do something about those rain gutters."

"He can go to the Home Center right here in Winter Haven."

"He's not going there. He's going to Albany," George said. "They have better quality and better prices. Home Center stocks nothing but junk, and they want you to pay twice as much for it."

"Don't be ridiculous," Candice said.

"I'll not give my business to Jordan Patrick. If I have to drive all the way to Albany for new rain gutters myself, then I'll do it."

It took me a second to recall where I'd heard the name Jordan Patrick before. But when I did, the whole trip to Albany made sense. If Judge Ellington's description of Jordan was accurate, then he was the nicest man in the world and was merely being punished for making a few bad word choices while admiring Candice when she was a baby.

"You can be so stubborn," Candice said.

"I have my pride."

"Which do you want, pride or rain gutters?"

"I'll take pride any day." George removed his checkbook from his back pocket, signed one, and gave it to me. "Take that and go on over to Albany like I told you."

"Perhaps we could pay for the rain gutters in cash," I said, "and this Jordan guy would never have to know who I'm buying them for."

"I won't give that man my business."

"Just use the check at Home Center." Candice spoke to me but never took her eyes off her grandfather. "No use driving all the way to Albany when you can buy everything right here."

I watched the grandfather and granddaughter stare each other down, George gritting his teeth, Candice remaining calm. George's breathing became heavy and he shook his head. Still, Candice gazed at him as if watching a sunset. I remained at their side, not knowing which one to obey.

"What are you waiting for?" Candice said, finally looking at me.

"Am I going downtown or to Albany?"

"You're going to Home Center," she said and motioned toward my car, encouraging me to leave.

"Who do you work for, my granddaughter or me?" George asked.

"Just go," Candice said.

"Tell him I was against it." George steadied himself and shook his cane at me. "Tell him if I ever see him turn his nose down at my granddaughter again, I'll tear his ugly mug off and feed it to that mongrel he calls a son. Tell him that for George O'Brien."

"I'll do that, Mr. O'Brien." I folded the check and stuffed it in my shirt pocket along with the sheet of paper. I still looked grubby, but I suppose it was a fitting look for a man heading off to buy rain gutters. Home improvement stores were always filled with people who looked like me.

Home Center was much smaller than I'd expected. They had a large warehouse outback where they kept their stock, but the actual store was no bigger than your average drug store. I'd imagined a huge building with dozens of employees where my chances of running into Jordan Patrick would have been slim. But when I came in, I only counted three customers and two employees.

Walking through the entrance was like stepping into the Everglades on a windless day. The air was stifling, only stirred by an oscillating fan that sat on the counter. One of the employees stood next to it, letting the air blow across his face as he used a calculator to tally up an invoice that lay before him. He was a stocky man in his late fifties with tanned skin and white dentures. As I approached, he raised his eyes and stared at me with a puzzled expression, like he was looking at an old friend he hadn't seen in years and barely recognized. He was wearing a red shirt with the name Jordan embroidered in yellow lettering over the pocket.

"The wonders of modern air conditioning," I said, gesturing to the fan.

"We had a new system put in last year, and it worked fine until we really needed it." He straightened up and put the invoice under the leg of the calculator so the fan wouldn't blow it away. "What can I help you with?"

"I need some rain gutters." I handed him the sheet George had written the measurements on. "All I've got is a car. Do you think that will all fit in my trunk?" I pointed out the large windows that graced the front of the store.

Jordan raised his eyebrows as he looked past me at the Chevy. "If not, you're going to have to go out and buy yourself a bigger car." He winked and gave me a smile. "We can deliver it for you if you'd like."

"You don't think it will fit in my car?"

He hummed and looked at the sheet of paper again. "It'll be tight if it fits at all, but we can give it a try." He pulled a blank invoice from a drawer and transferred George's information onto it while I looked around the room, deliberating on how to broach the subject of George O'Brien once it came time for me to hand over the check. Jordan seemed like a decent man, but I feared seeing George's name at the top of the check may bring out a darker side that didn't smile so much.

"You want me to call Jake Schuler and see what's taking him so long?" asked the other employee as he came over.

"No," Jordan said as a line of sweat trickled over his temple and past his ear. "I'll give him a call myself. Ring this up for me, will you? I'll be out in the warehouse putting the order together." Jordan wiped the sweat from his face and looked at me. "When Mike's done with you, drive your car around back and we'll see if we can get everything into your trunk."

"The warehouse is twenty degrees cooler than this and it doesn't even have air conditioning," Mike said as Jordan slipped out the back door. Mike was also dressed in a red shirt with his name embroidered over the pocket. But the resemblance didn't stop there. He had the same broad nose and hooded eyes. Yet he was thinner and had more hair than Jordan. I figured he was the mongrel son George had mentioned, a term spoken out of bias rather than fact.

"Jake Schuler was supposed to be here this morning to fix that damn thing." Mike gestured to the air conditioning vent. "If we sold ice cream, we'd be out of business by now."

When I drove around back, Jordan was standing in front of a large brick building that looked as though it had been around as long as Winter Haven itself. One of the three sliding doors stood open and Jordan waved for me to back my car into the dimly lit warehouse, next to a stack of rain gutters that stood along the wall. Jordan Patrick had a rugged look, with skin as brown and tough as leather, one of those men who would look more at home hunting deer in the mountains than confined in the brick walls of the warehouse.

As I shut off the engine and stepped out into the cool air, Jordan eyed my Massachusetts license plates. He handed me a box filled with fittings, which I set on my back seat.

"All this piping for the O'Brien house?" he asked as we stuffed the rain gutters into the trunk.

"This *is* a small town," I said. Since he hadn't seen George's check, the only way he could have known I worked for the O'Briens was through the Winter Haven grapevine. "Back in Boston, I don't even know who my neighbors are."

"If your neighbor was George O'Brien, you'd know." The gutters protruded a few feet beyond the end of the car, so Jordan grabbed a length of rope and tied the lid of the trunk to the back bumper. It was indeed a tight fit as Jordan had predicted, but we managed to get all of the gutters into the trunk. I was thankful for that since I didn't think George would appreciate Jordan showing up at his front door making the delivery.

"Mr. O'Brien can be a handful," I agreed. "Sure has a lot to say about you, though."

"I'll bet he does. What kind of lies has that man been telling you?"

"All lies, are they?" I could have told him the truth, as my mother taught me to do, but there were better things I could do with this opportunity than to help George along his path of self-destruction. So I did what any unethical, good-intentioned man would have done: I lied. "I figure anybody who can get George O'Brien to sing his praises can't be all bad," I said and saw the pleasant confusion in Jordan's eyes.

"I beg your pardon?"

"George couldn't say enough about you," I went on. "He said you're the one man who never turned his back on him, that you weren't swayed by all of the gossip going around."

"George said that?"

"Yeah," I said as if filled with admiration for the man standing before me. "It must take a lot of courage to go against popular opinion."

"Well ..." Jordan nodded. "A man's got to stand up for what he believes in, I always say."

I pulled my keys out of my pocket and opened the car door. "You're just like Mr. O'Brien described you. To be honest, I thought we'd get a better price on things in Albany. I even made plans to go, but Mr. O'Brien wouldn't hear of it. He said if Jordan Patrick doesn't get his business, nobody does. He can be pretty stubborn."

"You know I've always liked those O'Briens. Good people."

"They are, aren't they? And they're lucky to have a friend like you."

"You tell George hello for me."

"I'll do that," I promised.

CHAPTER 25

The next day, I climbed the ladder and tore down the old rain gutters. George followed me around as usual, barking orders and telling me I was doing it all wrong. Maybe I was. Who knows? When it comes to destroying things, I didn't realize there was a right and wrong way. All I figured was that the rain gutters had to come down without me coming down with them.

From my high perch above the front porch, I could see neighbors poking their heads out of doorways or gazing from windows, fascinated by the activity going on at the Victorian house with its new blue paint shimmering beneath the summer sun. Todd Miller's red Thunderbird cruised up Willow Lane and slowed as it passed in front of number 613. Vaughn's blond head peered from the passenger window and looked up at me, his head bobbing to the rhythm of the music playing over the car radio. Across the street, Margaret Hanson sat in her rocking chair, reading a book, only looking up when I let another rusty rain gutter fall to the ground. The girls in the yellow house down the street stood on their front lawn, swinging their hips as their hula-hoops twirled around their waists.

At noon, George yelled for me to come down and eat. As I descended the ladder, I glanced over at the Blanchards' home and saw Harriet standing at a window, watching us. I waved. She gave me a sweet smile. I doubted she was a bad person. She just had the misfortune of having George O'Brien for a neighbor.

"You'd think they'd never seen people work before," George said as I followed him through the front door.

My mouth watered at the aroma of a freshly baked ham. Candice had spent the morning cooking. Being the only woman in the house, she'd had no choice but to perfect her culinary skills at an early age. She had mastered an array of casseroles, roasts, and desserts. George's only compliments came in the form of moans of pleasure as he ate and by helping himself to seconds. He licked his lips as we came in the kitchen where Candice stood at the counter slicing the ham with a knife and making it into sandwiches. The table was decked out with dishes, milk, and potato salad.

"Kirk called," she said as we settled down at the table. "They're having a barbecue at the park on Saturday and would like us all to come."

"We're not going," George said.

"I told them we would."

"The reason I bought a home is so I wouldn't have to eat my food outside on the ground." George grabbed a spoon and dished himself a large heap of potato salad.

"I'm sure they have picnic tables," I said.

"Same thing. We're going to be out in the hot sun, waving flies away from our food and pretending we're enjoying it, while we're all secretly having a miserable time and wishing we could go home."

"I told them we'd go," Candice repeated.

George groaned and glared at me as if all of this were my fault. He knew he couldn't keep Candice away, and since he didn't want her going alone, he had no choice but to accompany her. To George, 'alone' was anytime he wasn't with her. I didn't count since I was the main person he didn't want her to be alone with.

ഇൗ

The red picnic table Kirk and Nicole had chosen sat beneath a cluster of maple trees, so George wouldn't have to eat his lunch under the heat of the sun. By the time we arrived, Kirk was already standing at a grill, lighting the charcoal as Nicole and Quinn laid the food and plates on a table. Other families and teenagers occupied nearby tables and those on the far side of the park.

"We've got steaks, punch, apple pie, and three different kinds of salad," Kirk said. "A little something for everyone."

Rather than delivering his standard protest, George reached into the front pocket of his baggy dress pants and pulled out a bottle of Geritol. Handing it to Quinn, he said: "There you go, son. Pour that in the punch and liven things up around here."

Candice cringed. I prepared myself for a rerun of our last get together. But Quinn changed that. He let out a howl of laughter that startled birds from the trees. His face turned red, and he held on to the picnic table as though he was afraid he might fall down laughing. The Geritol was funny, but Quinn's reaction made it hilarious. He had a way of viewing life that made you wish you could see the world through his eyes.

George's mood brightened, pleased his wit had elicited such a reaction. He might have brought the Geritol to drive home the point about how bad the last party had been, but Quinn's laugher turned it into a practical joke.

"Where did you find this guy?" Quinn asked Candice as George stuffed the bottle of Geritol back in his pocket.

"Well, I'll be damned. That's my grandma." Kirk walked out onto the grass and hugged a short lady with white hair. Linking arms with her, he escorted her to the picnic table.

"I was just driving by," she said, "and I said to myself, 'Now, that looks like my grandson.' And what do you know?" Her lines sounded as forced as Kirk's expressions of surprise.

"Why George O'Brien," she said if taken aback to see him there. "What a pleasant surprise."

"Lucy," he said. "Good to see you. What an odd coincidence." His voice betrayed the fact that he knew Lucy's coincidental arrival had been carefully planned. "Where's that husband of yours?"

"Home in bed. He has a hard time getting around nowadays." Lucy sat on the table's wooden benches across from George. "How have you been getting along? Don't see you around much anymore."

"Raising my granddaughter takes up all my time."

Lucy gave Candice a look. "Looks like you've done a great job."

"A man does what he can. You've got to protect those young ones. It's a vicious world out there."

"There's a lot of good out there, too, George," Lucy said.

"I suppose. The sun never shined much on the O'Brien household, though."

Candice squeezed George's shoulder, wanting him to change the subject.

When the steaks were cooked, Kirk tossed them on a plate, and Nicole brought them around for everyone. If not happy, George at least seemed content. Inviting Lucy was a nice touch. George no longer seemed like the odd man out. He left the steak alone and attended to his salad.

"You'll have to teach me your trick, Nicole," Lucy said. "I can't get my husband to fix anything but cold cereal."

"I'd save your compliments until you've actually tasted Kirk's cooking," Quinn said. "You're going to find that getting him to cook isn't exactly a good thing."

"Hey. I'm sweating over a hot grill for you guys. I want to see a little appreciation."

"Telling us you're *sweating* over our food doesn't exactly win our trust in your culinary skills," Nicole said.

"Eating your cooking doesn't exactly win our trust either." Quinn chewed on a mouthful of steak. "What is this, leather? My teeth can't even cut through this stuff."

"Here, try mine. See if they do any better." George slid his dentures out of his mouth and handed them across the table toward Quinn.

Candice let out a mortified gasp and grimaced at the sight of his teeth dangling from her grandfather's fingers. Quinn's face lit up. He looked stunned for a moment. Then laugher bellowed from his mouth. Tears filled his eyes, and he choked on the piece of steak he'd been chewing. He finally had to walk away from the table and spit the steak on the grass as he bent over wiping his eyes.

George casually slid his teeth back in his mouth and went back to eating his salad. But you could see that Quinn had won the man's heart. He didn't do anything but laugh, but George adored him. I think if George could have traded me with Quinn, he'd have done it without a second thought. They say imitation is the truest compliment. Surely, laughing at someone's odd sense of humor ranks right up there with it. George smirked, looking pleased with himself.

I envied Quinn. Most of us live our lives so caught up with ourselves that we can't truly enjoy other people's gifts. Quinn, on the other hand, had the ability to look at other people and see something great in them. And how can you help but like someone who sees something great in you?

We played touch football while George and Lucy sat on the bench talking.

Kirk told me later that, according to his grandmother, all George needed was someone from the community to listen to his gripes. He just wanted to be understood. Mainly, they talked about Candice and how she was the jewel of George's life. She was his second chance since he hadn't done so well with his Carolyn. Sure, he couldn't have been there with Carolyn every minute of every day. But he was her father. To him, he'd let her down by not being around to protect her when she needed him most.

CHAPTER 26

In the living room next to the piano stood an oak bureau dating back to the early 1920s. It had a fold-down desk, one drawer, and a cupboard on the bottom. The varnish had peeled off in several places and scuff marks adorned the front two legs and the side nearest the piano. When I opened the cupboard doors, a stack of papers spilled out. George groaned as he glared over my shoulder.

"I don't know what's in there, and I don't want to know." He hunched over his cane, staring at the mess. "Just throw everything in a box and get it out of here."

"What if there's something valuable in here?" Candice crouched and rummaged through the papers that had fallen out.

"When's the last time you used anything inside there?" George asked.

"I don't know. A long time, I guess."

"Then how valuable can it be?"

This didn't keep Candice from sorting through the old bills, crayon drawings, and scribbled notes as if they might be family heirlooms. They bore the musty smell of disuse, but overriding that was the scent of the strawberry shampoo Candice had used that morning as well as the Apple Blossom perfume on her neck. I had never smelled perfume on her before, nor had I seen the pink blouse she was wearing.

"Nice blouse," I said.

Candice gave me a thin smile, one that stated she was being mischievous and had just been found out. She looked up at her grandfather, who wrinkled his brow in confusion, not sure how to interpret her expression. The answer came in the form of a knock at the front door. He gave me an accusatory look. I shrugged as Candice got up to answer it. I'd been in Winter Haven for two months and I'd only seen two people come to the O'Briens' door: the boy delivering the groceries and the sheriff.

Candice pulled the door open, revealing Nicole McKnight, sporting a white blouse and tan Capri pants.

"You ready?" she asked and gave George and me a wave.

"Where are you going?" George frowned.

"Shopping." Candice gave him a little smile and stepped out the door, pulling it closed behind her.

George frowned at me

"I had nothing to do with it."

We walked to the window and watched Nicole and Candice climb into a red and white '55 Buick. She beamed as she settled into the passenger seat and rolled down the window. I shared George's ache at that moment, happy for Candice's ascent into adulthood, her declaration of independence, yet saddened by the thought that she no longer needed me to escort her into the frightening world.

I knelt again in front of the bureau, dragging out its debris and placing it in a box I'd retrieved from the attic. George sat on the sofa grumbling, talking more to himself than to me as he asked what Candice needed from town and what she was planning to use for money. "If she wanted something, she should have just asked me."

"Girls like to shop," I said. "They're not like us. They don't have to have something in mind that they want or need. They just like to wander through the stores looking at stuff and trying on clothes.

My sister could spend a whole day shopping and come home with nothing."

"Candice has always been above all of that."

I took the box out the back door and into the alley. Setting it on the ground next to the garbage cans, I saw that the city still hadn't hauled the larger items away. The boxes and bags had vanished, but the tables, boards, cinder blocks, and tires were still there, creeping farther into the alley and taking up the whole of the O'Brien fence. And there was still more to come, the largest item being the bathtub, which would certainly block part of the alleyway once I hauled it out of the yard.

I came back through the fence and went to work on the black garden. I was still using the little red wagon to assist me in transporting items from the yard into the alley. However, I had no idea how I was going to manage with the bathtub. George was in no condition to help, and I doubted Candice had the strength to be of much use. I left it alone for now, concentrating my efforts on the old phonograph. Tipping it onto the wagon, I wheeled along the sidewalk leading to the back gate. Phonographs from the 30s and 40s, like this one, were built to last, made of wood with speakers and cabinets build in. It must have weighed a hundred pounds. I pulled it up the gravel alley and dumped it onto the ground next to the Blanchards' fence.

By noon, Candice still hadn't returned from her trip to town. George was getting antsy. As we sat at the kitchen table, he looked at his watch a dozen times within the first five minutes. We ate Corn Flakes because it was the only thing either of us knew how to make. In college, I'd learned to make spaghetti, but the O'Briens didn't have any noodles or tomato sauce.

"I'm sure she's fine," I said.

He shoveled in another spoonful of Corn Flakes as the minutes ticked by. I filled my bowl with a second helping and was in the process of pouring on the milk when the front door opened and closed. George stared unemotionally across the table at me and then turned when the footsteps passed down the hall and stopped at the kitchen door.

Candice appeared with an expression of excitement and anticipation. George and I stared in stunned silence. She'd cut her hair so that it hung to the bottom of her ears. The bangs and sides were curled in the fashion we'd seen at Pete's Diner. She was wearing a dark blue poodle skirt, accented by a blue and white striped blouse, with the sleeves rolled up.

I set my spoon inside my bowl and said nothing as the milk soaked into my Corn Flakes.

"Well?" she said to encourage a response.

"Wow," was all I could manage to utter.

Candice's eyes were on her grandfather, awaiting his approval. From across the table, all I could see was the back of his head as he remained twisted in his chair, gazing at his granddaughter. I feared he was going to say something crass, something to wither this wonderful moment and bring Candice to tears.

"You're beautiful." The words caught in his throat, choking back tears.

Candice lit up as she grabbed the sides of her skirt, fanned it out, and twirled like a fashion model. She was radiant, basking for the first time in the beauty God had bestowed upon her. She curtsied before coming to her grandfather and kissing him on the forehead. George took her hand as she sat beside him at the table, both of them beaming.

"How did you pay for this?"

"Nicole paid."

"We'll pay her back."

"She said she doesn't want us to."

"We're paying her back anyway." He patted her hand and then touched her hair. "You look just like your mother." This wasn't true, but Candice's expression conveyed that George had just paid her the biggest compliment ever. She gave him a hug and another kiss on the forehead.

That evening, after George had gone to bed and the sun had drifted over the horizon, Candice and I sat on the front porch swing, staring out at the neighborhood that lay silent beneath the twinkling stars. Crickets provided the background music as Candice related the brighter side of her mother's history.

When Carolyn O'Brien was young, she and her parents would gather in the living room and listen to the radio, keeping informed on the progress of the war in Europe or cheering on the Red Sox as the announcer belted out the play by play action.

In her early teens, Carolyn became infatuated with music. She would put on her Tommy Dorsey album and dance around the living room, coaxing her father into dancing with her, begging him to teach her how to jitterbug. Once or twice a month, she and her mother, Dora, would climb in their Bentley and George would drive them downtown to the Apex Club, where they'd spend the evening swing dancing as they listened to big band jazz.

Carolyn's best friend was Myrna Jones, who spent so much time at the O'Briens' that George used to refer to her as his second daughter. She often spent the night, both girls dancing up and down the stairs like Fred Astaire and Ginger Rogers in The Gay Divorcee until Dora told them to go to bed.

"What happened to Myrna?" I asked.

"She married Jack Conway. You probably met her. They own the store where we buy our food. Her son is the one who delivers our groceries."

I did indeed remember Mrs. Conway. I remembered her standing behind the counter ringing up my groceries as she ridiculed the O'Briens, saying no one knew if Candice was George's granddaughter or daughter and that if she didn't know better she'd think they had a couple of warlocks and a witch living on Willow Lane. I said none of this to Candice. Instead, I lied and said Myrna had been friendly when she found out I worked for the O'Briens and that she'd asked how Candice was doing.

"I think her son has a crush on you."

"I know." Candice looked up at the stars. "What do you think about heaven and angels and all of that stuff?"

"I don't know. Some of it's probably true," I said. "I'm sure your mother's up there right now looking down on you."

"I hope not."

"Why not?"

"Would you want your mother watching everything you do?"

"No. I guess not."

Candice gave me a sly smile and looked again at the stars.

"How long ago was the accident?" I asked.

She squinted as though she wasn't sure what I was talking about.

"The car accident, the one that killed your mother."

"Oh, that. I don't know. I was just a baby. I don't even remember her."

"Your father wasn't actually with her at the time, was he?"

"Come here. I've got to show you something." She bounced off the swing, grabbed my hand, and pulled me after her. "Be quiet though. We don't want to wake Grandpa."

We crept through the front door, closing it quietly behind us, and went up the stairs, going slowly as Candice pointed out the squeaky steps so I'd be sure to step over them. Not only did we not want to disturb George's sleep, we also didn't want him coming upstairs and finding me in Candice's bedroom. I wouldn't be able to plead ignorance this time.

As she closed her bedroom door, I grabbed her and pressed my lips against hers, something I'd wanted to do since she spent the night in the studio. Now, with her new fashion, my desires grew even stronger.

"Lock the door," I said.

"No. If he comes up and finds the door locked, he'll get suspicious."

"If he comes up and finds us kissing, he'll have nothing left to suspect."

"Then no more kissing," she said and pulled away. Above her dresser was a shelf with framed photographs, a music box with a ballerina on top, some small figurines, and a tin canister slightly larger than a cigar box. She took the canister and lay facedown on the bed, where she peeled off the lid, revealing a stash of memorabilia. I took a seat on the other end of the bed as she pulled out some photos, rings, a key chain, and a watch that had a crack along the glass face.

"That's my mother," she said, handing me a photograph of Carolyn sitting at the kitchen table with a birthday cake in front of her, the candles still smoking. "She was beautiful, wasn't she?"

"Very." I looked at each photo as Candice handed them to me. It made me happy that Candice admired her mother so much, yet sad that she'd never had a chance to get to know her. "How old was she when she died?"

"Let's not talk about that." She put the photos back inside the canister. "These were her rings. This one's my favorite. I used to wear it all the time when I was a girl. I had to tie a string around the band to get it to stay on." She slipped the ring onto her finger and displayed it for me. It was silver with diamond-shaped glass embedded in it. Staring at the ring, a shadow of melancholy passed over her face. She erased it with a smile, pulled the ring from her finger and dropped it into the canister. "The watch doesn't work, but I keep it because it belonged to her." She stuffed everything back inside the canister and put the lid on.

She stared up at me with her blue eyes as I ran my fingers over her cheek. I bent forward to try to kiss her, but it was awkward since I was sitting while she was lying on her stomach. I ended up kissing her nose. She giggled as she got up and put the canister back on the shelf.

"Perhaps we should go to bed." She glanced at the dark window as she leaned against the dresser, facing me.

"I thought you'd never ask."

"I don't mean together." She raised her eyebrows.

I got up and took her in my arms, pressing her against the dresser, where my manuscript sat with its cover page slightly dog-eared. I stared into her eyes and kissed her gently on the lips.

"It'd be safer if you came out into the studio."

"It would be safer still if you went out into the studio and I stayed here."

"But it wouldn't be nearly as much fun."

"That's the safe part of it," she said and playfully pushed me away.

"Fine. Then you don't get to read any more of my manuscript." I grabbed it from the dresser and tucked it under my arm.

"I'm done reading it anyway."

"And?" I raised my eyebrows, awaiting her words of praise.

"It's good."

"That it? It's …" I fanned through the manuscript and stopped abruptly when I saw that she'd written in it. I felt sick, felt my stomach knot up as I stared at the pen markings, the crossed-out words and sentences, the notations scribbled in the margins, entire sections marked up with her alleged corrections.

"What have you done?" I turned through the manuscript and saw she had written on nearly every page.

"I made some suggestions. It's a good story so far."

"Now I've got to retype this whole thing." The words came out much sharper than I'd intended. I gritted my teeth and shook my head, unable to stay still.

"You were going to have to retype it anyway. It needs work, Mitchell."

"What do you know?" I said with restrained anger. "You never even went to school." The words hit her like a slap in the face. Pain dulled her eyes as her body stiffened. "Yeah, I know about that," I added. "So don't try telling me how to be a writer, okay? I've been to college."

Tears welled in her eyes, but she covered it by turning to her shelf and making a pretense of straightening out the figurines. She looked stunning in her new blouse and skirt, but I'd taken the joy out of her day. I felt ashamed, but my novel meant everything to me. It was my hope for the future, the one thing I took pride in. Criticizing it was the same as criticizing me. If I wanted a critique, I certainly could find someone better qualified than a grade-school dropout.

The door opened and George came in, wearing a blue robe and no dentures. He squinted at me as if he wasn't sure he could trust his eyes. "What are you doing in here?"

"Talking," I said.

"Talk in the living room. I'll have no fornicating under my roof."

"Sorry, Grandpa." The pain in Candice's voice gave George pause. His eyes shifted from me to her. He hummed and nodded, indicating that he realized he'd walked into the middle of an argument rather than a romantic interlude.

"You know better than this," he said to me. He started to close the door and then pushed it back open before walking away. I heard his footsteps pass down the hall but didn't hear them descend the stairs.

"I didn't mean to imply that you don't know anything," I said. "But do you realize how much work this is?"

"I'm sorry, Mitchell. I thought I was helping."

I let out a long breath and walked out the door with my manuscript under my arm.

CHAPTER 27

Winter Haven's favorite pastime was baseball. They had a field south of the park, complete with tall fences, grand bleachers, and a well-groomed diamond. According to Nicole, the city had eleven teams and held a game every Tuesday, Thursday and Saturday. George confessed he was a fan of the sport. He'd played often in his youth and still followed the Red Sox on the radio and in the newspaper. Yet he wasn't convinced that he'd enjoy watching a local game, not until Candice mentioned that Quinn was playing.

"You're really becoming quite the socialite," Lucy said to George as we entered the bleachers and took a seat next to her and Nicole, who had saved us a space among the crowd.

"I always read about these stupid games in the paper." George laid his cane next to him. "Thought I'd better come see one of them for myself. Who's winning?"

"We are," Lucy said, meaning the team that Kirk was on. "Nicole and I come to most of Kirk's games. They're the best in the league."

Candice sat between me and George, yet she leaned toward him, making it clear that she wanted nothing to do with me, just as she had done for the past two days. Around the house, she'd kept her distance. At the kitchen table, she served me breakfast, lunch, and dinner without a word. Nothing could have pleased George more. She had her arm around his shoulder as we watched a batter step up to the plate. The catcher crouched and punched his fist into his mitt, yelling: "Easy out. Easy out," as the pitcher took his position on the mound.

Even wearing his catcher's mask, it was plain to see that Quinn was the man crouched behind home plate. He had those broad shoulders and that playful attitude. The man holding the baseball bat was Kirk McKnight. He had his cap pulled over his eyes as he shoved the bat toward Quinn and said: "Stand clear, fat boy. I tend to swing wide. Took the last catcher's head plumb off." The two of them spoke loud, making a show of it. It sent a ripple of laughter through the spectators.

Quinn popped up out of his crouched position and turned to the umpire. "Hear that, Ump? The man's threatening me."

"You swing as wide as you want, Kirk," the umpire said.

"You playing favorites, Ump?" Quinn crouched back behind the plate. They were the Harlem Globetrotters of baseball, or rather softball, I discovered as the pitcher threw the ball underhand. It was a good fast pitch. Kirk swung and missed.

"Keep them coming like that, Jones," Quinn yelled to the pitcher. "We'll send this boy back to the bench where he belongs."

The next pitch came in and Kirk nailed it. It sailed into left field. Kirk made a dash to first base, where he stayed.

"Why are they playing on opposing teams?" I ask Nicole.

"It's city league. It depends which company you work for. Kirk works for Taft Paper, as does Todd Miller." She pointed to the man strutting up to the plate. This explained why they were the best in the league. Since Taft Paper was the largest employer in Winter Haven, they had the largest pool of prospective players to choose from.

Todd Miller, with his hair greased back, stepped up to the plate, cocked the bat over his right shoulder, and eyed the pitcher. He didn't handle himself any differently than Kirk, but I hated the way he stood and walked and tilted his head.

"Throw it slow, Jones!" Quinn yelled. "We've got a Girl Scout here!"

"That's right. You tell him, Quinn," George mumbled. His fists were clenched, and he was grinding his dentures. Nothing would have made him happier than to watch Todd Miller fall flat on his face. George leaned forward. His body tensed as the pitch came in and Todd swung. The sound of the wood connecting with the ball echoed into the bleachers, immediately followed by George's agonizing moan as the ball sailed over the shortstop, over left field, and over the fence.

"Girl Scout, huh?" Todd said as he tossed his bat in the dirt and jogged toward first.

"What you girls putting in those cookies nowadays?" Quinn yelled, but even this couldn't raise a smile from George.

"Like I said, they're the best in the league," Lucy said.

George moaned again. Seeing one team beat the other meant nothing to him. All he cared to witness was Todd Miller's personal failure.

Just when I thought George had reached his low for the day, three men climbed the steps into the bleachers and headed our way. One of them was Jordan Patrick. Not only was this bad news for George, it was bad news for me. George hadn't asked me about my conversation with Jordan, and I'd volunteered nothing. They hadn't seen each other in years, but there he was, coming right at us.

"Hey, George. Good to see you out," Jordan said as he and his two friends passed in front of us. George looked up with confusion. First, surprised to hear someone addressing him with kindness. Second, stunned to see that the kindness came from Jordan Patrick. The three men walked farther down the row and found some empty seats.

"I take it you gave that man a piece of your mind," George said to me.

"I intended to. I really did. But before I could get a word out, he started telling me how much he admired you and Candice, so I thought it'd be best if I kept my mouth shut."

Wrinkling his nose, George leaned forward and looked down the row. "Jordan Patrick never spoke a kind word in his life."

"I'm being totally straight with you, Mr. O'Brien," I lied as sincerely as I knew how. "He told me himself that he thinks this town has misjudged you."

Seeing George staring at him, Jordan offered a friendly smile and a wave.

George reluctantly waved back. "Well, I'll be damned."

I now felt safe in my lie. George would definitely speak up if I said Jordan had badmouthed him, but he wasn't going to confront Jordan now, not with the rumored of a compliment.

When the game ended, the flow of the crowd pushing toward the exits prevented George and Jordan from doing more than offering each other a farewell wave. Nicole and Lucy followed us down the steps of the bleachers and into the parking lot, where we met up with Kirk and Quinn, both sweaty and grass-stained. Kirk gloated over his eight to four victory, telling Quinn the plumbers were all washed up.

"The only reason you won," Quinn said, "is because old man Baxter paid off the umpire. He didn't want the whole town to know what a bunch of pansies he has working for him."

"You tell yourself whatever you need to make yourself feel good, Quinn." Kirk stopped at his car and unlocked the passenger door for Nicole. "We're heading over to the bar for a few drinks," he said, looking over at the O'Briens and me. "Would you care to join us?"

"You go ruin your livers," George said. "I'm going home. I've got a headache from all this sun."

"How about you, Grandma?" Kirk asked.

Lucy frowned and waved her hand at his foolishness as she got in the back seat of his car. It was nearly four o'clock with the sun streaming down from a cloudless sky. As we headed across the hot pavement, George pulled a handkerchief from his pocket and dabbed the sweat from the back of his neck.

Quinn passed us in his white Dodge Royal and gave two short toots of the horn, turned on to the road, and disappeared down the lane of trees, with Kirk's Buick behind him. George glared at several players and spectators heading toward us. They paid no attention to him as they got into cars and drove off, proving that most of George's fight was in his head and the average citizen of Winter Haven had no idea who he was and expended no energy contemplating the rumors about him.

As I unlocked the door of my Chevy, Todd Miller came up behind George and bumped him on his way past, nearly knocking him to the ground.

"Hey, killer," Todd said.

"What's your problem, Todd?" I stepped between the two men, expecting a repeat of the brawl I'd had with him in the theater parking lot. Only this time Vaughn wasn't around to help him out.

"Mr. O'Brien knows what my problem is. Don't you?"

"Of course I know," George barked. "You've got shit for brains, just like your uncle did."

"You think you're hot stuff now, strutting around like everything's fine. But we all know you did it."

"And you're next, Todd."

"What did you say, old man? What'd you say?" Todd's nostrils flared.

He started around me, trying to get at George. I pushed him back. Todd slapped his baseball glove against his open palm and turned to another ballplayer passing through the parking lot.

"You hear what old man O'Brien just said to me? He said I'm next! That's a confession, Mr. O'Brien. I think I'll take myself a drive down to the sheriff's office and tell him you confessed."

"You do that, Todd. While you're at it, tell him he can kiss my wrinkled ass."

Todd threw his glove on the pavement and came at George again. This time when I shoved him back, he took a swing at me. His knuckles brushed my chin. I took a jab, but he moved back.

Todd came at me with two quick jabs. I blocked the first one, but the second one caught me in the mouth. He stepped back and grinned as I licked the blood from my lip.

"You're out of your league, Massachusetts."

I spit a mouthful of blood onto the front of his white jersey. When he looked down at it, I stepped in and slammed my fist hard against his ear. He stumbled, shook his head, and then lifted his fists, ready to come at me again.

"What seems to be the problem here?" Jordan Patrick emerged from behind a truck and stood between us.

"No problem at all, Mr. Patrick." Todd stepped back and dropped his fists.

"You sure about that?"

"Yeah, I'm sure." Todd snatched his mitt from the ground and gave George and me one last look before walking away. There was more history between the O'Briens and the relatives of Howard Baxter than I'd realized. I knew about the rape, the trial, and how they had destroyed the lives of the O'Brien family. I even knew George had spent his weeks after the trial following the Baxters around with his camera. What had happened after that, I didn't know.

"He's just like his Uncle Grant," George said as Todd Miller walked to his car and opened the door. "Born with a silver spoon lodged up his ass."

"There's not a Baxter in this town smart enough to realize what a bunch of idiots they all are," Jordan said.

The look on George's face was the first real glimmer of hope I had for him. For years he had lived under the impression that it was him and Candice against the world, certain that Howard

Baxter's wealth had bought him the loyalty of everyone in town. Apparently, this wasn't so. His lips curved into a thin smile as he looked at Jordan Patrick with respect, an emotion I doubt he'd felt for anyone in Winter Haven since the trial twenty years ago.

CHAPTER 28

"I guess we now know who your rock thrower is," I said to Sheriff Cornell as we looked at the four flat tires on my Chevy. He stood on the curb with Deputy Fritz, shaking his head, while Candice stood next to me in front of my car. The puncture marks in my tires were as blatant as the broken front window on the O'Brien house. It had happened at 5:30 that morning, as another rock crashed through the new plate glass. When I told George I wouldn't call the sheriff again, I'd intended to keep my promise until I found that my tires had been slashed. It didn't take a genius to figure out who had done it. Todd Miller was the only person in Winter Haven who had a reason to hate me. I told George he could do whatever he wanted with his window, but I wanted Todd to pay for my tires.

I explained what had happened in the parking lot after the softball game. "The guy has it in for Mr. O'Brien, I'm telling you." I kicked one of my flat tires as the sheriff leaned on the roof of my car, filling out his report. "That there's your rock thrower. I can guarantee it."

"We'll look into it," the sheriff said. "But I'm not going to be able to get him to pay for this unless we can prove he did it."

"Not that proof carries much weight around this town," Candice said.

The sheriff smiled and shook his head without comment.

"Sure it does." Deputy Fritz came around the car and stepped off the curb next to Candice. "We ever find any signs of Grant Baxter, you'll see just how much weight proof carries in this town. Fact, I think we're pretty damn close to solving this thing right now."

The deputy's smug expression disappeared when Sheriff Cornell shot him a glance, wanting Henry Fritz to shut his mouth.

What the deputy had said bothered me, but the look on the sheriff's face drove it into the pit of my stomach. Whatever evidence they were looking for was not intended to help George O'Brien, but to condemn him.

"Come on. I'm sick of these people." Candice started toward the house and then looked back, waiting for me to follow her. She still hadn't forgiven me for the way I'd handled the situation with my manuscript, but my standing up to Todd had won me marginal respect. Not wanting to lose that margin, I followed her up the sidewalk.

"There's more to this story than you've told me, isn't there?" I said when I caught up to her.

"There's nothing else to know." She went through the gate and hurried up the steps, expecting me to do the same. Opening the front door, she stopped and looked back at me as I remained outside the gate. Her face was stern and disapproving. I hesitated, torn between what I wanted to do and what she expected of me. When I started back toward the sheriff and deputy, Candice frowned and went inside.

Sheriff Cornell had the door of his patrol car open and was about to get in when he looked up and saw me approaching. "Something else?" he asked.

"What happened to Grant Baxter?" I stepped into the street and talked to the sheriff while Deputy Fritz stood at the passenger door, staring at us over the roof of the car.

"I've been asking myself that same question for the past seventeen years," the sheriff said. "So far I haven't come up with an answer."

"But you think Mr. O'Brien had something to do with it."

"He does top our list of suspects, yes. He definitely had the motive after what happened to Carolyn."

"You mean the car accident?"

"I mean her suicide," he explained and could see that I didn't know what he was talking about. "About three years after the rape, Carolyn killed herself on Grant Baxter's front porch."

"How?"

"Shot herself in the head with her father's pistol. It was a real shame. She was such a lovely girl. She had her whole life ahead of her. Not long after that, Grant disappeared and was never seen again."

"And Mr. O'Brien mysteriously developed a limp about that same time," Deputy Fritz said. "Grant must not have gone easily."

I looked back at the O'Brien house, where Candice was watching from the broken window. The look on her face said she knew what we were talking about and that she disapproved.

"If you happen upon any skeletons in the closet, we'd love to hear about them," Fritz said.

"Henry." The sheriff shook his head, not sharing in his deputy's sense of humor. "We don't know if George O'Brien is responsible for Grant Baxter's disappearance or not, but it's our job to dig around and see that justice is served, even if it takes seventeen years to do so."

"And you think you've figured it out?"

Neither of them replied, but I didn't trust the thin smile on the deputy's lips.

For the second time, George and I dragged a pane of glass from his office out to the porch, cleaned the broken glass from the frame, and installed the new window. George said nothing about the sheriff's visit. In fact, he hardly said a word as we put the putty around the window. He glanced across the street at Margaret's empty rocking chair. Candice stayed in the living room, where she scowled at me, letting me know I'd lost my margin of respect.

After I'd swept the porch and put the tools away, I called the McKnights. Kirk was at work at Taft Paper, but I told Nicole what Todd had done to my car and asked if she'd have Kirk call me when he got home. Instead of calling, he and Quinn showed up late in the afternoon and inspected the damage to my tires. George came outside and sat on the porch swing and watched as we hauled the cinder blocks from the alley and set them under the axel of my car. Using my jack and lug wrench, we stripped off the tires and put them in the trunk of Kirk's Buick, each of us taking turns using Todd Miller's name in vain.

"Did you know that the police think Mr. O'Brien killed Grant Baxter?" I asked.

"You didn't know that?" Kirk said.

"You have no idea how tight-lipped those two are. I didn't even know Candice's mother committed suicide until the sheriff told me about it this morning. Candice said she'd been killed in a car wreck."

"Lot of people think old man O'Brien hacked Grant up into pieces and fed him to the little woodland creatures." Quinn waved at George, who was swaying back and forth on the swing. "Not that anyone would blame him. According to my father, Grant was one of those rich boys who was used to getting what he wanted. Apparently, Carolyn O'Brien was one of those things he wanted."

"You think he raped her?"

"My father thinks so. I asked him about it after the way Candice reacted to my campfire story. He remembered the trial. It was pretty big news at the time. There were lots of rumors, some blaming Mr. O'Brien, some blaming Grant. Perhaps we'll never know what really happened."

We climbed into the Buick, Kirk and Quinn in the front seat and me in the back. During the trip to Al's Auto Repair, Quinn filled us in on some of the gossip his father had passed on to him.

According to legend, on the day of the rape, Carolyn had been wearing a locket her father had given to her on her sixteenth birthday. It was sterling silver with a floral design on the outside and a photograph of Carolyn on the inside, along with an inscription George had had the jeweler engrave. Grant had torn it from her neck during his crime of passion and kept it as a memento of his conquest. The police searched his house and car, hoping to use the locket as evidence against him at the trial. They never found it.

A few years later, while George and Carolyn were in town shopping, Grant showed up and cornered Carolyn behind a rack of clothes while her father was in another section of the store looking at ties. When Mr. O'Brien saw Grant, he blew up in a rage, shoved Grant against the wall, and screamed at him, telling him to stay the hell away from his daughter. According to witnesses, Grant had walked away laughing. He went outside, walked down the sidewalk, and stood at a window where he could look in at George and Carolyn. With a grin, he reached inside his pants pocket, pulled out the locket, and let it dangle from his fingers. George went after him, but by the time he got outside, Grant was in his car driving away.

"Is that true?" I asked.

Quinn shrugged as we pulled into Al's Auto Repair and parked outside the open garage door. "From what my dad heard, George tried to get the police to put a restraining order on Grant, to keep him away from Carolyn. But Grant was a Baxter and George was a nobody. The police told him that Winter Haven was a small town and people are bound to run into each other every now and again. They didn't believe someone with Grant's good looks and money would waste his time chasing a single mother who didn't even like him."

"Have you ever seen pictures of Carolyn O'Brien?" I asked. "Kid or no kid, she was one beautiful woman."

While we waited for my tires to be repaired, we walked down the street to Nickel Pharmacy and stood at the soda fountain. People sat on the stools along the counter, devouring malts and hamburgers. We ordered our soda in bottles and drank them outside on the sidewalk while Quinn continued his father's tales of O'Brien lore, telling details that Candice would later confirm and elaborate on.

On the day of her suicide, Carolyn had brought baby Candice downstairs and made up a bed for her on the living room floor. An hour later, when Dora heard little Candice crying and went out and found her lying on the floor, she became hysterical. She knew immediately, the way mothers do, that something terrible had happened to her daughter. She ran upstairs to Carolyn's room and found a letter on the bed. In it, Carolyn apologized for the pain she'd put her family through. She said she hoped, with her gone, that the persecution would end. She was a very thoughtful girl. She'd even put on her Sunday best so the mortician wouldn't have to dress her, thinking this would cut down on the funeral costs. Unfortunately, blood stained the dress and George had to buy a new one to bury her in.

On the day of the funeral, Dora sent George to the mortuary alone.

"I don't want the last image of Carolyn to be of her lying in a coffin," Dora said.

Many people turned out for the service. They were surprised by the open casket since they knew the gunshot wound had been to the head, but the mortician had done a wonderful job preparing the body. Everybody said so. They listened to the minister lament the tragedy of one of Winter Haven's loveliest daughters. Later, they gathered around George and told him how sorry they were for his loss. Several even cried, but George was in no mood to hear their sympathy. These same people had looked down upon his daughter after the rape, had stopped inviting her to social gatherings and had spoken ill of the O'Brien family behind their backs. If anyone was to blame, it was the very people now filing past him paying their respects. George glared at them with glassy eyes as the emotions welled up inside of him as if spilling from his broken heart. Looking over at Carolyn's open coffin, he began to sob. A gentleman put his hand on George's shoulder to comfort him, but George slapped the hand away.

"It's all your fault," he said to those gathered around him. "You're all to blame. Each of you."

People stood back and looked at him with confusion.

"Carolyn was the victim of the crime, but you all treated her like the criminal. You abandoned her, just when she needed you most. Shame on you. Shame on all of you."

His bitterness had taken root before that day, but it was now in full bloom and had sprouted thorns. To him, the whole world was against him. Life had lost its color. He took notice of no one as he walked home from the funeral alone, with his head bent toward the sidewalk. Stopping at one of Winter Haven's three stoplights, he waited for the light to change and for the traffic to pass. A car pulled up beside him and the driver tapped at the horn to get George's attention. The sight of Grant Baxter sitting in his Plymouth made George's blood boil.

Grant rolled down his window. "Hey, Mr. O'Brien. I wanted to come to the funeral, but I was too busy cleaning blood off my front porch."

George gritted his teeth as the light changed. When he started across the street, the car pulled forward, keeping pace with him.

"You want this, Mr. O'Brien? Or should I keep it as a trophy?" Grant held his hand out the window with Carolyn's locket dangling from his fingers. He sped away before George had time to snatch it from him. Standing in the middle of the crosswalk, George stared around at the familiar sights: the stores, the parks, the tree-lined streets. It all looked out of focus now. Everything that had once brought him joy had become meaningless. Walking to the curb, he sat down, put his head in his hands, and sobbed.

CHAPTER 29

The moonlight streamed down over the trees and illuminated the trucks, tractors, and cement mixers, as well as the mounds of dirt and rubble. During the daylight, this was a hotbed of activity, with backhoes burrowing into the soil and trucks bustling back and forth, hauling away the dirt, while workers prepared the site for the foundation of a building that would fill a city block. But at night, all was tranquil and deserted.

"Howard Baxter didn't become successful by being nice to people," Kirk explained as we pulled up in front of the construction site. The headlights of his Buick shined out over the hole in the ground.

"I only met the guy one time," I said. "And right away I hated him. But still, I can't imagine him doing something like this."

"I doubt he set the fire. He's the type who would hire someone to do it for him."

I leaned forward in the back seat and stared out the windshield at the site that would one day be Baxter Center. For years, this piece of property had held the remains of Greenwood Paper, a mill that had burned to the ground in September of 1941, five weeks after Carolyn O'Brien shot herself.

Greenwood had been an eighth of the size of Taft, but Baxter and the leaders at the mill didn't want the competition, no matter how small. They used their political ties to try to get the city to shut them down, claiming Greenwood was in violation of city ordinances. When that failed, Taft spread rumors, claiming Greenwood produced low-grade paper. Slowly, the mill began to lose business. The Greenwood board of directors worked hard to restore their good name. Just when business had started to pick up again, the mill went up in flames. Howard Baxter and several other prominent figures at Taft were the prime suspects, but no evidence was ever found.

Now Baxter owned the land. It was on the outskirts of Winter Haven, in an area where the trees were being cut down and new houses were springing up. Most of the charred debris of Greenwood Paper had been removed. What remained lay in a pile of twisted metal and concrete at the far end of the site.

"You want to know what I think?" Quinn said.

"Here we go." Kirk looked at me and rolled his eyes. "Quinn's got a theory about everything. Ask him about the space aliens sometime."

"You know I've got a point about the space aliens." Quinn pointed a finger at Kirk before turning his attention to me. "I don't think Mr. O'Brien had anything to do with Grant Baxter's disappearance. I think Grant is the one who burned the place down, probably as a favor to his father. The Greenwood people found out and decided not to waste their time with the court system."

Kirk hummed out a half-hearted agreement. "It's true that they blamed Baxter. He wasn't the head of the company back then, but he was always the most ambitious. Maybe burning down this factory is why he has the job he has today." Kirk stared out at the tractors and rubble. "One of Greenwood's night watchmen died in the fire, but what could they do? You can't fight the Baxters."

"Somebody did," Quinn said. "And whoever it was did a damn good job disposing of the body."

We drove to Shady Bluff, where Kirk pointed out the white home where Grant Baxter once lived and where Carolyn O'Brien took her life. Grant was twenty-two at the time of his disappearance, a year younger than me, yet he'd already owned one of the nicest houses in one of the most expensive areas of Winter Haven. The sight of the home filled me with jealousy, accompanied by the sadistic satisfaction of knowing something awful had happened to Grant.

Five streets over, Kirk shut off the headlights and slowly cruised through the dark neighborhood. He pointed to another house, this one not as large or elaborate as the one Grant had owned. The red Thunderbird parked in the driveway revealed the identity of the owner. It was an older home, small and not as pleasant as I'd expected. Apparently, being Howard Baxter's grandson didn't pay as well as being his son. Yet according to Kirk, Todd made twice as much as any of the other foremen at the mill. He was always the last one blamed whenever production fell behind and the first one promoted when things went well.

Kirk made a U-turn at the end of the block and stopped at the curb, up the street from Todd's home. "You're never going to get him to pay for your tires. You know that, don't you?"

"What do you have in mind?" I asked, not trusting Kirk's tone of voice.

He pulled a pocketknife from his blue jeans, opened the blade, and handed it to me.

"Let's not get carried away now." Quinn took the knife and closed the blade. "I hate Todd Miller as much as the next guy, but this isn't the way to handle it."

"You just going to let him get away with slashing Mitch's tires?"

"Is this about Mitch's tires or about the promotion you didn't get?"

Kirk stared out the windshield at the Thunderbird.

"The Baxters can get away with that sort of thing," I said. "But I'm not so sure the police will treat me so kindly."

"Then don't get caught," Kirk said.

"Todd will know it was me."

"But he's not going to be able to convince anyone unless he owns up to slashing your tires. And I don't see that happening."

"The police already know I blame Todd for what happened," I said.

Kirk sighed and took the knife back from Quinn. From the side window, I saw a black cat crossing the lawn of the home next to where we were parked.

"But perhaps there's something else we can do."

"What do you have in mind?"

"Just wait here. I'll be right back." Leaving the door open, I stepped out into the night air and looked at the lighted windows of the homes lining both sides of the street. Not seeing anyone watching, I stepped onto the grass and approached the cat. Its eyes shined in the darkness as it stopped and looked back at me with its ears standing straight up. I crouched, patted my hand against my leg, and clicked my tongue. Cautiously, the cat turned toward me and stepped slowly through the grass.

"Come on, kitty. I got a job for you. How's that sound?" I let it sniff my hand and rub up against my leg before picking it up. "That's a good kitty." I petted it behind the ears and walked back to the car. "Where's the nearest market?" I asked as I climbed in the back seat, set the cat on my lap, and closed the door.

"What do you have in mind?" Kirk asked again.

"Don't worry, it's a good idea."

I didn't know if it was a good idea or not. In fact, during the drive from Todd's home to King's Market on Main Street, I had time to reconsider my plan and realize how stupid it was. Yet I didn't want Todd thinking he could get away with treating me the way he treated the O'Briens, so I made no mention of my misgivings as I went into the store while Kirk and Quinn waited in the car. I figured it was safer for me to go in alone since one person would be less memorable than three, just in case the police ended up coming around asking questions. Being a stranger in town also gave me the added benefit of not being recognized by most people, at least those not interested in the O'Briens' affairs.

When I came out and held up my brown paper bag as if displaying a prize, I got nothing but bewildered looks from the faces staring out through the Buick windshield.

"What did you buy?" Quinn asked when I slid into the back seat and shut the door.

I handed him the bag in exchange for the cat. His trust in me reached a new low when he pulled out a square blue tin of Ex-lax, the chocolate, chewy kind. He turned the container around and showed it to Kirk, who wrinkled his nose and looked in the bag to see what else I'd bought.

"Is this a joke?" He pulled out a can of cat food.

"I doubt Todd will find it funny," I said. "We're also going to need a can opener and a hanger."

I saw the light go on in Quinn's eyes as he realized what I had in mind.

"You wouldn't dare," he said and then started to laugh as only Quinn could. "I like the way your mind works."

"I hate to rain on your parade," Kirk said as he backed out of the parking space and headed down Main Street. "But they're still going to know it was you. You should have just cut his tires."

"No. This is a lot funnier," Quinn said.

"But how's this any different than my idea?"

"The man does have a point." Quinn turned in the seat and looked at me. "Either way they're going to know you were behind this."

"But can he prove it," I said, with little conviction.

"It's your call," Quinn said.

After stopping by Kirk's home for a can opener and hanger, we drove back to Todd's neighborhood and parked in the same spot as before. The cat scuttled back and forth across my lap, pressing its nose at the can of cat food as I cut the lid off. I let it take a few bites and then pushed it away as I opened the Ex-lax and smashed one into the food. I didn't know if animals liked the taste of chocolate or not, but the cat chewed it down with gusto.

Quinn started laughing again as the three of us exited the car. He had the cat in his arms while I carried the can of cat food and kept my eyes on the windows of the homes.

"I'd pay good money to see Todd Miller's face in the morning," Quinn said.

Kirk unraveled the wire hanger and formed one end into a hook. When we stopped beside the Thunderbird, he shoved the hanger down past the glass in the passenger door. "Don't touch the car," he said. "Knowing Howard Baxter, he'll have the FBI out here dusting for prints." He fished around inside the door, gave the hanger a tug, and up popped the lock.

"I think this can be construed as cruelty to animals," Quinn said.

"A defecating cat is a healthy cat," I said.

Using the tail of his shirt, Kirk opened the door and gestured to the seat like a gentleman inviting a lady into his car.

Quinn stepped forward with the cat and set it on the front seat. I dumped the cat food onto the floor mat.

"You be a good little kitty and leave lots of presents for Todd," Quinn said as Kirk used the tail of his shirt to relock the door and swing it closed.

CHAPTER 30

I lifted a porcelain gnome into the old wagon, wheeled it along the walkway, and dragged it through the back gate. At the end of the block, the sheriff's car turned out of the alley, onto the surface street, and disappeared around the corner. That was the second time I'd spotted the patrol car in the alley. It stirred a thought that had been nagging at me for the past month and had intensified after talking to the sheriff and deputy.

The garbage men came on Tuesdays. I would hear them around 5:00 a.m. as they parked in the alley behind the studio, throwing cans around and operating the hydraulics on their truck. Later, the trash began disappearing every day—not the big items, which still cluttered up the alley, but the small stuff: the boxes and the bags. I'd convinced myself that Winter Haven was better at garbage collection than Boston and that I had slept through the hum of the hydraulic truck on days other than Tuesday. Then one morning as I brought a box out the back gate, I saw the sheriff's car, just as I had today. I checked the garbage cans and found them both empty. That was on a Friday.

I pulled the wagon to a space behind the Blanchards' and abandoned it. It was of no use to me any longer. The only remaining item in the backyard was the bathtub, and it was too heavy and too bulky for the wagon.

I looked in Blanchards' garbage cans. They were full. I then checked O'Briens' and found what I'd expected: nothing. Staring into the empty containers, I saw the smug look on Deputy Fritz's face as he announced how close they were to solving the disappearance of Grant Baxter. The man had gone missing seventeen years ago. Now, his case was drawing interest again. I was beginning to understand why. Who knows what I'd thrown away? George didn't inspect each box I threw out, and I sure as hell didn't know what might or might not be incriminating.

I returned to the barren backyard and stood before the bathtub— one of those old-fashioned things that had legs with claw feet on the ends. It was filled with dirt and flowers and weeds that added an extra three hundred pounds to the already massive object.

Digging my feet into the dirt, I put both hands against the tub, thinking I could get it rocking enough to tip it over. It didn't budge. Walking around it, I observed how the claw feet had sunk down into the soil, holding it firmly in place. I grabbed the shovel and started uprooting one of the feet when the back door opened and George stepped out onto the porch.

"What are you doing?" he barked.

"Thought I'd see if I could move this thing out of here."

"Why?"

"It's a bathtub," I said.

"I think it gives the place character. You just leave it be." He went back inside.

As I returned the shovel to the shed, I stared back at the bathtub. It didn't give the place character. It looked as out of place as a golf ball in a bowl of pea soup. Staring up at the kitchen windows, I found George looking out at me. His expression troubled me. I was familiar with his different moods, which fluctuated between anger and bitterness. But this was an emotion I had never seen him express before. Fear.

I looked back at the bathtub and felt a horrible sensation creep the length of my spine. I suddenly believed George O'Brien had indeed killed Grant Baxter. I even believed I could predict where he'd put the body.

I took a rake from the shed and went to work on the patchy grass where the black garden had once stood. When I glanced at the windows again, George was still there, looking at me as though he could read my mind. He knew that I knew, and now he was waiting to see what I'd do with this knowledge. Would I scoop the dirt out of the tub and unveil Grant's remains? Would I run to the police? Would I confront him? What I did was set my rake against the fence, go out into the alley, and return with one of the empty garbage cans. Before walking away, George watched me put an armful of dried leaves and dead flowers inside the can.

I'd grown fond of George. He was bitter, but he had a good reason for that. Still, I found it hard to justify murder, regardless of the circumstances. Nothing got under my skin more than reading in the paper about how a jury had set a killer free because his lawyer had painted a picture of the criminal's terrible childhood as if that somehow made it all right. It seemed no one was accountable for his own actions anymore. But the people in the papers were strangers to me. George was someone I cared about. He was the grandfather of the girl I now loved. Knowing the details of the case, I couldn't help justifying George's actions in my own mind. But that's the problem with all crimes, isn't it? That the criminal somehow feels justified. Yet I still questioned the accuracy of my knowledge. I knew nothing firsthand. It was all hearsay molded to fit the view of the narrator. Surely, if I'd been hired to clean up Howard Baxter's house, then it would be George O'Brien who I saw as the monster.

I raked and mowed the backyard lawn, circling the bathtub, wondering if Grant Baxter was inside. When I finished, I went into the house and found George in the living room, kneeling on the sofa, looking out the side window.

"I hope he falls off and breaks his neck," George said as I entered the room.

I knelt on the sofa beside him. Next door, a tall ladder leaned against the tree in Blanchards' front yard. At the top of the ladder stood Carl Blanchard. He had a saw in his hand and was cutting away at one of the branches. Every time he pushed the saw forward, the ladder tottered and Carl looked as though he might grant George his wish by falling and breaking his neck.

"You realize he's going to kill himself, don't you?"

"I sure hope so," George said.

"I'd better go out there and give him a hand."

"The hell you are," George scowled. "You play saint on your own time. Right now you're punched in on my time clock."

"I'll put in my two hours when I get back."

"No. You'll put in your two hours right now."

I leaned toward the window, mainly so I'd be a little closer to George's eye level. "You don't honestly want a man's death on your hands, do you?"

George's eyes narrowed. He knew my comment had nothing to do with Carl Blanchard. "If he falls, it will be on his head, not on my hands."

I offered a wry smile and went out the front door. He yelled something about firing me, but I didn't care. He was all bark. At least, I hoped he was all bark. Perhaps Grant Baxter would have told me otherwise.

Over at the Blanchards', I found Harriet sitting on the front steps, watching her husband saw at the branch. Carl was more active than George, but he still didn't look at home in the tree.

"Could I lend a hand?"

"I think I've got it under control," Carl said, still looking precarious at the top of the ladder.

"Let him help, Carl," Harriet said.

"I don't need any help."

Harriet frowned. "The way he's huffing and puffing, I'm afraid he's going to have a heart attack."

"I'm fine," Carl said, not sounding happy with his wife for speaking ill of him to a stranger. "Go back before George finds out you've been consorting with the enemy."

"George is the one who sent me," I lied.

Carl stopped sawing and gave me a bewildered gaze.

"He even said he'd pay me," I added.

Carl's mouth fell open. He glared over at the O'Brien house as though it were a foreign entity. George had such a bad reputation in town that it was hard for anyone to believe he would do or say anything nice. I suppose if anyone ever told me he said something kind about me, I'd be equally shocked. I didn't feel bad about my lies. Someone had to turn the tide for George. Clearly, he would never take it upon himself to do a good deed.

Carl Blanchard came down from the tree and joined his wife on the steps. I suspected by the way he was rubbing his shoulder that he was happier to trade places with me than he let on. He had two large limbs and several small ones that he wanted cut. He'd only managed to saw about halfway through the first limb. This was mainly because his saw was about as sharp as a butter knife. I knew George had a saw of his own, and I was tempted to go get it. But two things kept me from it: first, I knew George wouldn't approve. Second, knowing the way George took care of his tools, I doubted his saw was any sharper than Carl's.

After I'd cut off both of the large branches and most of the small ones, Harriet came out of the house carrying three glasses of lemonade. She offered one to me, and I told her I wanted to finish with the tree first.

When I joined them on the steps, the three of us drank lemonade and talked about what a hot summer it had been. They said they'd lived in that house next to George for thirty years. They were friends for the first ten. They'd watched Carolyn grow from a small child into a lovely teenager. According to Harriet, Carolyn was one of those happy children who was always playing Hop Scotch on the sidewalk or chasing up and down the street with her best friend, Myrna Jones.

After Carolyn's rape, Myrna came over to check on her, to see if she could offer her support. George wouldn't even let her in the house. He kept her out on the porch where he could yell at her and humiliate her in front of the whole neighborhood. Carl said George was yelling so loud they could hear him over the sound of their radio. Carl and Harriet had gone out their front door to see what all of the ruckus was about. Even from next door, they could see that George had Myrna in tears. He kept telling her she should have been there with Carolyn, that she was her best friend and should have been there to watch out for her. Carl walked next door to see if he could help. He knew George was just upset and was merely taking his anger out on Myrna. But Myrna was just sixteen and took everything George said to heart.

When George saw Carl, he told him to get off of his property and go back home. Carl tried to reason with him and told him not to take out his anger on Myrna, which only made George angrier. He started telling Carl what a lousy neighbor he was and that he and Dora had always hated Carl and his wife and that the whole neighborhood would be better off if they'd just pack up and move.

Like Myrna, Carl took George's words to heart. Their friendship ended right there. As far as he was concerned, George O'Brien was the most despicable man alive. Anyone who would treat sweet little Myrna Jones that way was of less value than a bucket of dirt. George never did let Myrna in the house, even after she begged. He merely walked inside and slammed the door in her face, leaving her on the porch to cry.

"Don't get me wrong," Carl said as he finished his lemonade. "I wasn't happy to see the way things turned out with Carolyn. No man deserves to see those kinds of things happen to his daughter. But George ceased being human that day. And the way he's raising his granddaughter just isn't right." Carl set his empty glass on the step and pulled his wallet from the back of his trousers. "You tell George I appreciate him sending you over, but I'm paying you myself."

"No, no, no." I waved my hand at his money. "George told me you'd say that. He told me that if I allowed you to pay me that he would fire me. So I'm afraid I can't take your money. Besides, the only reason George is doing this is so you all can start a new relationship."

This time Carl and Harriet both stared at the O'Brien house. I could see they were moved by what I'd said.

"He says he hasn't been the best of neighbors since … you know … everything that happened. I think you should allow him to do this. It would mean a lot to him."

"He's sorry about what he said to me?" Carl asked.

"Yeah. I think he is. I mean, he never told me about yelling at you the way he did. That's not George's way. He's a very proud man. But he did say he felt it was time he made amends."

Harriet put her hand on Carl's shoulder and gave it a squeeze. Her eyes were glassy, and I felt good for having lied to her.

"Tell him, thank you," Carl said and put his wallet away.

CHAPTER 31

That Saturday morning I sat down at the desk near the window and opened my manuscript for the first time since taking it back from Candice. I wasn't looking forward to reading her comments and dreaded the thought of retyping the entire two hundred pages. Her recommendations progressed from a few minor typos to major overhauls that included character and plot changes. I didn't want to like what she had to say, but as I turned the pages, I found myself grinning at the cleverness of her ideas. Her brilliance opened my novel up to avenues I'd never considered. Knowing that Candice had dropped out of grade school and had lived most of her life in the seclusion of her home had led me to devalue her opinions and question her insights into the secrets of life. Reading her comments made me realize how gravely I'd misjudged her.

When I came through the back door of the house, I found Candice seated at the kitchen table reading *Of Mice and Men*, which I had lent to her the night before. She'd already read several of the books I'd brought with me and she planned to get through many more before the end of the summer, only three weeks away. I sat at the table across from her and waited for her to look up at me. She still wasn't happy about the questions I'd asked Sheriff Cornell, but she was beginning to realize I wasn't going to turn my back on her and George.

"You read a lot, don't you?" I said.

"That's all I ever do."

"I guess that's a pretty good education in and of itself."

The glint in her eyes said she understood what I meant.

"Do you want to run downtown with me? I need to get some more typing paper."

The glint darkened as she closed the book and laid it on the table. "I'm sorry you have to retype everything, Mitchell."

"Don't be. I read your comments. I suppose I'm just a bit sensitive about my writing."

"I wasn't criticizing you."

"I know that. What I'm trying to say is that sometimes I take things wrong because my writing means a lot to me. But you were right: my novel needs work. And your comments were brilliant. One of my professors at the university read the first three chapters and his advice wasn't nearly as insightful as yours."

Candice beamed. "Let me run upstairs and put on some shoes."

We drove downtown to Scott's, a small store that sold books and cards, as well as office supplies. The stiffness I'd seen in Candice the day I took her to the theater had disappeared. Winter Haven had become her element. Her world had expanded from the blue Victorian house on Willow Lane to the shops along Main Street and the surrounding neighborhoods. I saw confidence in the way she moved, in the way she smiled at other customers and laughed at my attempts at humor. Yet all it took was a judgmental glance from a stranger for the confidence to fade and the stiff awkwardness to take its place.

The judgmental glance came from the man behind the counter. He was attending to a woman standing in front of us, ringing up her construction paper, glue, and pencils. His eyes gazed past her, focusing on Candice, who was laughing as I told her about the time the back of my pants split open while I was in church. Suddenly, she fell silent and stared at the floor. I turned my head and found the cashier glaring at me through his Buddy Holly glasses.

My first thought was to return my ream of paper to the shelf and take my business to a store where the employees didn't eye their customers with contempt, but that wouldn't help Candice regain her confidence or teach her not to hide her face in shame whenever anybody looked at her with disapproval.

"You know, Candice, I just can't get over how brilliant your comments were."

She looked up from the floor with surprise, not just at my odd transition from one subject to another, but at the volume of my voice, which was louder than usual.

"Even after three years of college, I don't have the insight that you have. I don't know many people who do. It's a natural gift. I envy you."

A thin smile graced her lips as her eyes left mine and glanced up at the cashier. He pushed his glasses to the bridge of his nose and turned his attention to the customer in front of us, who looked over her shoulder to see who had won such praise.

"I'm having trouble with a couple of other scenes. When you have some time, I'd love to have you look them over and see what you suggest."

Candice kicked my foot to tell me to stop with the compliments. But she was grateful. I could see it in her attitude as we stepped up to the counter and I paid for my paper. The cashier hadn't warmed up any, but it didn't matter. Candice paid no attention to him. Instead, she turned to me and said: "Perhaps we should put my name on the book as the coauthor."

"Don't press it," I said, tucking the ream of paper under my arm as we walked to the door.

"I should at least get a cut." She raised her eyebrows as I opened the door for her and we stepped outside. "Don't worry. I don't expect fifty percent. Forty-five ought to do."

"How about a kick in the pants?" I nudged her with my elbow. "And if you're really nice, I'll even throw in an autographed copy of the book."

"You're much too kind," she said, elbowing me back. "So what are we going to do to celebrate when your book gets published?"

We. The word hung in the air like a note composed by Mozart, a note so perfect that it brought the whole world into harmony. I thought about the word and its implications as we drove back to Willow Lane. I jumped to every possible conclusion a young man in love could jump to. I imagined Candice in Boston, meeting my parents and sister. I imagined us walking hand in hand across the campus, sharing classes, and looking for an apartment together. Suddenly, life made sense. Everything happened for a reason: I'd broken up with Marie, I'd fled Boston, I'd moved to Winter Haven, all for the purpose of meeting Candice O'Brien. The clouds had parted and had left me with nothing but sunshine, which remained with me right up until I turned onto Willow Lane and saw that the clouds hadn't gone far. They hovered over the O'Brien house.

The sheriff's brown and white cruiser was parked at the curb, near O'Briens' front gate. I pulled up behind it and could see George sitting on the porch swing with Sheriff Cornell standing in front of him. Deputy Fritz wasn't with him.

Candice didn't even wait for me to put the car in park before jumping out and hurrying through the gate and up the steps.

"What's going on, Grandpa?"

"Got myself a babysitter," George said.

"Howard Baxter's threatening to make trouble." The sheriff turned his attention to me as I entered the yard.

"What's he threatening to do?" Candice asked.

George gave me an accusing stare as I climbed the steps. "Some idiot threw out Carolyn's locket, and Baxter sees that as proof that I killed his dimwitted son."

"You threw out my mother's locket?" Candice asked, looking at me.

"I don't know. What did it look like?"

The sheriff pulled a locket from his shirt pocket and held it up for me to see. This confirmed my suspicion that the sheriff had been collecting the O'Briens' trash. I took a close look at the sterling silver locket with its floral design. It didn't look familiar, but I didn't doubt that I'd thrown it out. I'd tossed out so much stuff I couldn't keep track of it.

"Can I have that?" Candice asked.

"I'm afraid that's evidence," the sheriff said.

"I thought Grant Baxter stole that from Carolyn," I said.

"Precisely." Sheriff Cornell dropped the locket back into his shirt pocket. "So if Mr. O'Brien here had it in his possession, it could only mean that he somehow got it back from Grant. Isn't that right, Mr. O'Brien?"

"He sent it to me in the mail," George said dryly as he eased the swing back and forth.

"I'm sure he did." The sheriff looked at Candice as though his heart was breaking for her. She'd already lost her mother and grandmother. George was the only person she had left. The way things were going, Candice would soon lose him as well. The sheriff removed his hat and scratched his head as if trying to figure out how to solve a problem that couldn't be solved.

"I'm sorry for what happened to your daughter, Mr. O'Brien— believe me, I am. If I felt there was something I could do to set things right, I'd do it. But my hands are tied."

"Hand me the locket and pretend you never saw it."

"We don't work like that."

"Sure you do. Your father performed all sorts of magic tricks with the evidence I provided him. The man was a true Houdini. He waved his wand and everything disappeared." George glared at Sheriff Cornell but got no reply. "I've been around long enough to know how things work. Men like Howard Baxter pull the strings and everybody dances—including our good old justice system. The rich are innocent and the poor get fed to the dogs."

The sheriff rubbed his eyes. He looked tired. Talking to George had probably given him a headache. "You give me a call if there's any trouble, won't you? And I'd suggest you have Mitch spend the night in the house."

"I think I can handle the sleeping arrangement of my own house, thank you." George moved forward on the swing. "Though what would make me sleep a little better is if you'd leave your gun here for the night. Those Baxters never did respond too well to small talk, but you put a couple bullet holes in them and they perk right up."

"That sounded mighty close to a confession, Mr. O'Brien."

"Rough crowd." George grabbed his cane and stood up. "Tell a bad joke around here and they hang you for it."

The sheriff sighed and shook his head as he started down the steps. Then as an afterthought, he turned back to me and said: "You wouldn't know anything about a cat in Todd Miller's car, would you?"

Both George and Candice gave me a look of surprise. I'd told neither of them about the cat cleansing experiment—not that I didn't think they would appreciate it, but I feared it might come back and bite me later on, as it was doing now, and I didn't want them involved.

"I'm not sure what you're talking about, Sheriff."

The sheriff bobbed his head as though I'd given the answer he'd expected. I figured he was good at spotting liars, especially those who lied poorly, like me. He tipped his hat and walked to his car while the rest of us went in the house.

Candice stared out the window, watching the sheriff drive away. "What's going to happen, Grandpa?"

"Baxter's threatening to drop by later on with some of his friends. But I wouldn't worry about it. He's all talk." George went to the sofa and grabbed a newspaper.

"How did you get the locket?" Candice sat on the coffee table. When he didn't respond, she put her hand on the top edge of the paper and folded it toward her.

"There's nothing to worry about, Candice. Everything is okay."

"Did you do something to Grant Baxter?"

George stared at the floor as he folded his paper on his lap. With a deep sigh, he shook his head and looked up at Candice. When he reached out his hand, she took it in both of hers, bent forward, and kissed him on the knuckles.

"Grant Baxter disappeared. He was a bad man and then he disappeared. That's all anybody knows." His eyes met with mine and displayed a trace of fear, accompanied by what I felt was a plea for me to keep my secret, the one I thought I knew.

"What did you mean about giving the sheriff's father evidence?" I asked.

"His father was the first Sheriff Cornell. That family's always been tight with the Baxters. Howard has them in his hip pocket. Always has. Howard Baxter funded Jim Cornell's campaign for sheriff and his father's before him. Baxter figures that gives him the right to tell them what to do. They're nothing but lapdogs. Baxter throws a stick, and they fetch it for him. Right now, I'm the stick."

"What evidence did you give his father?"

"What difference does it make? It's all water under the bridge now." George patted Candice on the knee. "Why don't you get in the kitchen and fix us up some lunch? All this nonsense has stirred up my appetite."

Forcing a smile, Candice stood, kissed George on the forehead, and went to the kitchen, while I remained in the living room, wondering if I should mention the bathtub.

"What can they do?" I said. "I mean there's no way of saying how you got that locket from Grant, right?"

George nodded, but his face gave nothing away.

CHAPTER 32

I had a photo album my mother had insisted I bring with me. She claimed it was to remind me of the loving family I had back home. But I knew better. It was another one of her ploys designed to remind me what a bad son I was. She'd pleaded with me to stay in Boston for the summer. When I refused, she poured on the guilt, accusing me of abandoning my family. "It's only for three months," I'd said in my defense, and she pretended to agree with me while nodding sadly and telling me how she'd hoped to keep the family together a little longer. She gave me the photo album, telling me it might give me comfort whenever I felt homesick. In truth, the album wasn't intended to cure homesickness but to cause it.

I sat on the bed with the album open on my lap, looking at pictures of me when I was a child. My hair was always messy, and I was constantly pulling faces at the camera. One photo showed Ann and me scowling. Another showed my father holding a tie I'd bought him for Christmas. Rather than feeling homesick as I turned through the pages, I felt gratitude for the childhood I'd had and the normal family I'd shared it with. I'd taken it all for granted until I met the O'Briens.

A knock came at the studio door. It was Candice, carrying the weight of the world on her shoulders. I stared past her, out the open door, to the kitchen windows.

"Don't worry. He's asleep," she said. She came in, sat on the bed, set the photo album on her lap, and started turning through the pages. But her mind was elsewhere. Worry showed in the creases around her eyes and in the stiffness of her movements.

"He's going to be okay," I said.

Her eyes were emotionless and distant when she looked up at me, as though she hadn't understood what I meant. Then she said: "He has the locket, but that doesn't mean anything, does it? It doesn't prove that he did anything."

"It doesn't prove a thing."

She nodded and turned a few more pages, casually glancing at the pictures and biting at her lower lip. "Is this your mom?"

I sat beside her and looked at the photograph of my mother posing in her beige dress and matching jacket. It was an old picture, taken when I was a baby. My mother looked so young, so full of smiles and playfulness. With melancholy, Candice ran her fingers over the photograph, touching my mother's face.

"I don't remember my mother," she said. "I was only two when she died."

"I'm sure she loved you very much."

"But that didn't stop her."

"What she did had nothing to do with you," I said.

Candice looked at me as though my stupidity disappointed her.

"Okay, so it had something to do with you, but not because she didn't love you."

Again, she turned through the photo album, watching my family grow older, observing the changing fashions, seeing friends enter our lives. She studied our expressions, our silliness, and our laughing faces. She looked sad. This was the life she had read about in books, the one she dreamed about but would never have.

"I often think about how things would have been without me," she said. "And no matter how I look at it, I always know it would have been better. My mother would still be alive. Grandma would have stayed. And everything would be okay for Grandpa."

"Your grandmother left?"

"She moved to Albany. I think Grandpa always hoped she'd come back. She died about a month before you came. I think cleaning out the house is Grandpa's way of letting go."

"Why did she leave?"

"Because of me."

𝄢𝄡

George and Dora divorced six years after Carolyn killed herself, when Candice was eight. The suicide had devastated Dora. She'd become moody and judgmental, just like her husband. However, unlike George, Dora couldn't tolerate the rumors. Wherever she went, she could feel the eyes of the town on her, crawling beneath her skin like a disease. People whispered behind her back, wondering how she could stay with a man who had raped their own daughter, and how she could raise a child that had come out of such a sinful union. In the beginning, she defended her husband. But the years wore on her. She began to regard Candice as the source of her problems.

By the time Candice was in the second grade, her grandmother started distancing herself from her. By the third grade, Dora refused to take Candice to town or church or school. When the kids at school picked on Candice, calling her a devil's baby, Dora said: "Kids will be kids."

But George knew the problems ran deeper than that. The words had come from the mouths of the children, but the adults had planted the ideas. The parents claimed the O'Briens were a family destined for hell and refused to allow their children to be friends with Candice. Yes, children could be cruel, but the real difference between them and the adults was that the children spoke the words to your face while the adults whispered them behind your back.

Whenever Candice would come home from school crying, George's heart would break. She was such a pretty little girl, but suddenly she stopped smiling and hardly ever spoke. She'd go into her bedroom and stare at the walls. She often cried herself to sleep. George began showing up after school to pick up Candice. He'd yell at the other children, telling them how horrible they were and telling them to keep their filthy mouths shut. The principal came to the O'Briens' door one evening and asked George to stop his behavior, claiming he was frightening the children.

"If you'd do your job, I wouldn't have to do if for you!" he shouted.

"You can't treat children like that, Mr. O'Brien."

"What about the way they treat my granddaughter? That doesn't seem to bother you any. She comes home from your school crying nearly every day. She barely eats and doesn't sleep at night. I don't see you doing anything about that!"

"I can't control what the children say to one another."

"If you can't control little children, then what makes you think you have the right to come here and tell me what to do? I won't stand for it. And I won't stand for any more of the nonsense you let go on at your school either. If you and your teachers can't do your jobs, I guess I'll have to do it for you."

Candice never stepped foot in another classroom. George knew nothing about educating a child, but he was certain he could do a better job than the Winter Haven school district. When George showed up at the school the next morning, the teacher and students were horrified to see him. He was polite and merely asked the teacher if he could get Candice's school books, claiming she was ill and he didn't want her to fall behind on her work.

Dora was sweeping the kitchen floor when George came in and set the books on the table. He'd said nothing about his intentions. When he'd left the house that morning, Dora had assumed he went downtown to his photography studio.

"Where's Candice?" he asked.

"I thought you took her to school."

"No."

"Then she's still up in her room." Dora looked at the school books with concern. "Don't you have appointments today?"

"I canceled them. I've got more important things to worry about. I need to straighten things out for Candice. I'm not sending her back to that school. Those stupid teachers don't know what the hell they're doing. They can't even control a room full of eight-year-olds for crying out loud. It wouldn't surprise me if every kid in that school came out illiterate."

Dora's face turned red. Her hand was shaking when she grabbed the dustpan, swept the dirt into it, and emptied it into the garbage. From the time of Carolyn's rape, Dora's life had begun to unravel as her friendships fizzled and her nerves frayed. She used to enjoy going down to Redding's Department Store and trying on the latest fashions. People would say hello to her and pass along the latest gossip. Now *she* was the latest gossip, and she saw judgment and pity in the eyes of her friends. The money for new clothes, food, and common household necessities became scarce as George began to lose business to a man named Mark Maley, who had opened his own photography studio and was capitalizing on George's bad name.

"The only fleeting moment of happiness I get anymore is when she's off at school," Dora said as the discussion between her and George escalated into a shouting match. "You're not going to take that away from me."

"I can't subject her to the kind of treatment she's getting from those kids. I just won't do it." George limped as he paced the kitchen floor. His leg was getting worse. It wouldn't be long before he would have to rely on the support of a cane.

"And what about me?" Dora yelled. "What about the way people look at me and talk behind my back? What about that, George? You think I don't hear what people say? How my husband impregnated our own daughter? How do you think that makes me feel?"

"Just ignore them and their filthy lies."

"Are they lies?"

George stopped pacing. The anger went out of his face, replaced by hurt and betrayal. It had always been him and Dora against the world. Now, even she had turned on him. "How can you ask me that?" He felt the tears gathering, but he fought them back. "After twenty-six years of marriage, how can you even ask that question?"

"Get rid of her, George. If she's not your child, then get her out of this house. She doesn't belong here."

"She's Carolyn's child."

"And she was conceived in sin."

"Not by any fault of her own."

Dora was trembling now, out of pain and grief and exhaustion. She knew her request was ridiculous, but she couldn't go on like this. She wanted her old life back, when she wasn't the joke of the neighborhood and wasn't scorned by the religious zealots, who claimed they spoke for God when they declared their condemnation on the O'Brien household. George was equally exhausted. He wanted to hate his wife for what she was saying, but he couldn't. He understood her pain and knew he had failed her with his inability to turn the tide that had swept in upon their family.

"Put her up for adoption," Dora said. "Give her to the Baxters. I really don't care. Just get her out of my house."

"I'll do no such thing," George said. Now, the tears were flowing freely.

"Either she goes or I go."

"Be reasonable, Dora."

"Either she goes or I go."

"It's going to pass. Just wait and see. It's going to—"

"Either she goes or I go." Dora stood near the refrigerator with her hands on her hips and her eyes locked on George, awaiting his reply. She didn't care about his tears or the deep sorrow in his face. All she wanted was for this nightmare to end.

"Then you go," George said and felt the spirit drain out of his body. He swallowed the lump in his throat as he turned away from his wife and sat down at the table, where he opened one of Candice's schoolbooks. He would need to ask her how far along the class was so he'd know where to begin. Or perhaps he'd just start from page one. A review might do her some good.

What George and Dora didn't know was that their screaming had brought Candice down from her bedroom. She'd started down the hall toward the kitchen when she realized she was the topic of discussion. Returning to the living room, she sat on the stairs, learning for the first time how her own grandmother felt about her. Dora had never been affectionate, but this was crushing.

She knew her grandfather loved her. He was often depressed or grumpy, but whenever she'd come into the room, he would brighten up and take her onto his lap, sometimes holding her a little too tight as though he was afraid to let her go. She was his jewel, the only thing that gave his life meaning. But as Candice sat on the stairs listening to her grandmother talk about her as though she was the family dog that was no longer wanted, she knew her grandfather would have no choice but to get rid of her. When Dora mentioned giving her to the Baxters, Candice's heart sank. Her grandfather had always said awful things about the Baxters, and the last thing Candice wanted was to be handed over to them.

Three days later, Dora's sister and her husband arrived to take Dora back to Albany with them. Candice stayed upstairs in a room that looked out onto Willow Lane. She watched from the window as they loaded the suitcases into the trunk and drove away. Her grandmother hadn't even said goodbye. No one talked about divorce. In fact, Dora said she just needed some time away so she could breathe. George told Candice not to worry, telling her that Grandma would be coming back home just as soon as she had time to clear her mind and realize what was truly important to her in life. Even after the topic of divorce was broached and executed, George still talked about how nice it would be when Dora returned. "She'll be back. Just you wait and see. Your grandma's not the kind of person to give up on her family." For eleven years he held out hope.

He and Candice didn't attend the funeral.

CHAPTER 33

As Candice laid her head on my shoulder and cried, I understood George's desire to protect her and take away her pain. I wanted to go back into her childhood and erase the bad memories. I wanted to show Winter Haven how wrong they'd been, how childish and cruel. And I wanted to yell at Dora O'Brien for turning her back on her family and for being such a coward. I understood Dora's reaction, but that only made it worse, because it made me hate myself. It made me feel spineless and stupid for every time I'd done anything remotely similar.

I brushed the tears from Candice's face and kissed her on the forehead. "You can't blame yourself for that," I told her. "That argument wasn't about you, not really. It was between your grandfather and grandmother, and the stupid old hag was using you as a scapegoat."

"Don't call her that."

"That's what she was, a gutless coward who wasn't willing to stand up for her own family." The passion in my voice startled Candice, but I didn't care. I was angry, not just at Dora or at myself, but at Candice for taking responsibility for her grandmother's weakness, for allowing her grandmother to use her as an excuse to run away from her problems. "It's about time you started putting the blame where it belongs."

"But I—"

"You what?" I gazed at the sad beauty of Candice's face. "What did you do? You were eight years old for crying out loud. If you're going to take credit for destroying your family then we should be building monuments to you because you were one powerful little kid."

"But look at what happened to my family."

"You think you're the only family with problems?" I grabbed my photo album and opened it up to a random page, to a photograph of me and my childhood friend Randy, both of us with goofy looks on our faces. "You look at those pictures and think, 'Wow, look at these happy people living perfect lives.' Well, they're not. We're all screwed up in one way or another, but that's fine. That's life. You go out there and you live. That's what you do. Sometimes things work out great. Sometimes they don't, but that's okay. You learn from it and you move on."

"You don't know what I've gone through."

"I know enough. And yes, I have to admit that you've had a lot of crap thrust on you that you didn't deserve. But that doesn't make you any less a person than those who were born into families who don't have so many problems. You're still a wonderful girl, Candice. You're still beautiful and charming and someone I happen to love."

"Really?"

"Really." I wiped a tear from her cheek. Another one flowed down to take its place. The tears now sprang out of happiness and gratitude as the sorrow dissolved from her face. "I've loved you for a long time now. I thought you knew that." I bent forward and kissed her softly on the lips, feeling her wet cheek press against mine.

Her hands were on my shoulders, pulling me toward her, so I laid her on her back and held her beneath me. Her blue eyes glistened as she looked up at me with a faint smile. I basked in her beauty and could smell the scent of her perfume as I put my cheek against hers and breathed into her ear. She shuddered and murmured something I couldn't understand. Her hands caressed my back. The soft heat of her body warmed my chest and abdomen. Our bodies moved in rhythm, flexing and relaxing. Again, my mouth was on hers, and her fingers gripped through my shirt and into my flesh.

I thought of the door, wishing I'd locked it and fearing George would come through it at any moment. But that thought didn't stop me from working my hands behind Candice's back and pressing my body against hers.

"Why don't you come to Boston with me?" I whispered. "It'd be a new life for you. You'd just be another stranger on the street there, which isn't necessarily a bad thing."

I could see by her face that I should have kept silent. Instead, I'd brought her back into the reality of what had taken place that day.

"I couldn't. Grandpa needs me—more now than ever."

"He'll be fine." I kissed her again, but rather than kissing me back, she pushed at my shoulders, wanting me to let her up.

"I should go in." She sat up and smoothed out the folds of her skirt.

"Your grandfather's a grown man. He can take care of himself."

She gave an ambiguous nod as she got up and went to the window, where she parted the curtains and looked out at the house. "Walk me to the door, will you?"

The air was still warm when we stepped outside beneath the stars. The light was on in the kitchen and it flowed out across the barren backyard, revealing the patchwork of grass and soil where the black garden had once stood. The white bathtub, overflowing with weeds and flowers, remained the sole reminder of the bygone wasteland.

"Think about what I said about Boston," I said as we climbed the back steps. When she didn't respond, I said: "How long is this going to go on, Candice? There's got to be a limit to your obligation."

"Don't make me choose between the two of you."

"'Cause I'd lose, wouldn't I?"

"He chose me over my grandmother." She gave me another kiss and went inside. Even after she turned out the kitchen light and disappeared down the hall, I remained on the back porch, staring up at the night sky. Candice hadn't answered my question about her obligation to her grandfather, but I knew the answer. Her love ran deep, and her obligation would last until George O'Brien was in his grave. As stubborn as that man was, I figured he'd probably live another thirty years.

I was halfway to the studio when I saw a head peering over the gate that led into the alley. It startled me. In the dark, I couldn't make out the face, but I saw the hand wave and heard the voice of Sheriff Cornell bidding me a good evening. He opened the gate for me, and I stepped out into the alley. His cruiser was parked behind the studio.

"Looking for some more garbage to rummage through?"

"Just thought I'd better keep an eye on things. Don't want anybody out here trying to take the law into their own hands." Still dressed in full uniform, he looked as if he needed to get home and get some sleep. "You've really got this place looking nice."

"Yeah. It's a fine home." I looked up at Candice's window. Her light was now on, and the curtains were closed.

"You know I've been keeping an eye on that bathtub, wondering what George planned to do with that old thing." He gave me a knowing glance, and I felt my stomach knot up.

"George is thinking of going for a bathroom motif," I said. "He's hoping over time to get a sink or two and a couple toilets, perhaps even a urinal."

Sheriff Cornell smiled. "Did George give special instructions not to move that tub?"

"No, not really. Why?"

"Oh, just a theory I have." He leaned forward on the wooden fence and stared in at the bathtub, sitting alone in the shadowy yard. "Seventeen years ago, the day Grant Baxter went missing, I came up here and had a look at the place. I suspected George right away. That bathtub was propped up against this back fence, and there was a patch of fresh sod where the tub now stands—as if someone had dug a hole right there in the lawn, then covered it back over with the grass. The next day, when I came back, George had moved the tub over the fresh sod and had filled the tub with dirt and had planted flowers in it. He'd also planted flowers all around its base. What really struck me, though, was that he'd stuck a few weeds in there as well, and since it was fall, he'd taken leaves and scattered them over everything to make it look as though it'd been sitting there a while." The sheriff gave me a long look as if waiting for a response, but I said nothing. "It was amazing how, as the police stepped up their investigation, the amount of odds and ends accumulated around that tub. Next thing you know that bathtub didn't look the least bit out of place. Just another item among a heap of trash."

"Were you a police officer back then?"

"No. Just a distraught young man whose best friend had suddenly come up missing. And like everyone else in this town, I suspected George O'Brien."

"Grant Baxter was your best friend?"

"Yup." Sheriff Cornell rubbed his fingers over his bottom lip and gazed up at Candice's window as the light went out. I thought he would do anything to convict George O'Brien of murder, but that obviously wasn't so.

"Why didn't you tell anyone about the tub?"

"Ah." The sheriff waved a dismissive hand in front of him. "You know how friends are. You get together and you talk about things. Sometimes your friends do stupid things. Sometimes these things come back and bite them."

"Grant told you he raped Carolyn O'Brien, didn't he?"

Cornell shrugged. "My father was the sheriff at the time. This case was a thorn in his side until the day he died. Now it's a thorn in mine."

"You should have spoken up during the trial," I said, certain he could have stopped this whole thing from escalating out of control.

"Grant Baxter was my closest friend."

"His father lied under oath. He wasn't with his son the day of the rape, was he? That's perjury."

The sheriff stared up the alley.

"You're the sheriff. You've got an obligation."

"I also have an obligation to see what's buried there beneath that bathtub. But I'm not going to. How about you? You want to go grab a shovel and start digging around and see how much worse you can make George O'Brien's life?"

I looked at the bathtub, thinking now that Grant Baxter wasn't in it but under it. "I happen to like George O'Brien."

"And I happen to like Howard Baxter," he said. "He's the father of one of the best friends I've ever had."

"You realize, of course, that you're letting your best friend's killer walk free."

"George O'Brien isn't free. He's been in prison for seventeen years, and that's fine with me. Sad thing is, though, he's locked his granddaughter in there with him. I'm no matchmaker, and I sure don't want to tell you how to run your life, but you and Candice look good together. I think the best thing you could do for that girl is take her away from here."

I gave the sheriff a raise of the eyebrows, seeing now that I'd misjudged him. In his mind justice had been served, even if it wasn't the government administering the punishment.

"Why'd you put that cat in Todd Miller's car?" he asked.

"I still don't know what you're talking about."

He smiled. He knew I was guilty, but he wasn't about to get a confession out of me. Though I suspect he wouldn't have done anything even if I had admitted it. He told me about the investigation, about how Howard Baxter had pressured them to start digging around through the O'Briens' trash after he learned I was cleaning out the house.

"I told him no, said that we didn't have the manpower for something like that, but Mr. Baxter can be pretty persuasive. So we started digging around. We found that locket several weeks ago. I didn't tell Baxter about it because it's not hard evidence and I didn't want him to make a federal case out of it like he's doing now. But after this thing with the cat, he got all riled up and Deputy Fritz let it slip about us having the locket. Now I'm stuck trying to deal with the consequences."

"What do you think is going to happen?"

"I don't know. But Howard Baxter isn't the kind of man to let something like this slide."

CHAPTER 34

The sun was fading behind the mountains, out beyond the rooftops and trees. The sunset painted the sky deep red with streaks of orange and yellow cutting through it. There was no breeze, just the stagnant heat of August. Summer was coming to a close. In two weeks I would be sitting in a university classroom scribbling down notes while a professor filled my head with knowledge I would forget shortly after taking the final exams.

"You move up here, I could probably help you get a job at Taft Paper," Kirk said, toying with me. The only positive thing I'd ever heard Kirk say about his job was that it paid the bills. Even if he'd loved it, I could never go to work for Howard Baxter, not if I expected George and Candice to keep speaking to me.

"Personally, I'll be glad to see you go," Quinn said. "As soon as you're out of here, I'm going to be moving in on your girl and taking her out on dates."

I gave him a scowl and sat back in the wooden chair without commenting. We were sitting on Kirk's patio in his backyard. It was a boys-night-out, just the three of us sitting around drinking and telling stories about our youth, always making ourselves sound cooler than we really were. Nicole had gone to a movie with one of her friends, and Candice stayed home with George, probably sitting in the kitchen studying a game of chess.

I stared at the sunset, feeling good about life and thinking that the situation between the O'Briens and the Baxters would probably blow over, as it had years ago, until Kirk said something that sent a chill up my spine.

"Rumor has it that Sheriff Cornell knows where Grant Baxter's body is." He took a sip of his beer and set the bottle on the patio railing next to him. His tone and casual manner made it clear that he didn't put much stock in the rumor.

"Where did you hear that?" I asked.

"Out at the mill. Anything to do with the Baxter family spreads like wildfire through that place." He swiped at a mosquito buzzing around his ear. The backyard was filled with them.

"Where does he think it is?" I knew the answer to that question better than anybody, but I wanted to see how seriously to take this rumor. Kirk shrugged and told me about a meeting Baxter had held at his house the other night, trying to drum up support in his campaign against George O'Brien. Kirk McKnight had learned the details of the meeting from a man named Bill Wechsler, who worked with Kirk at the mill. According to Wechsler, Baxter had invited about twenty of his closest friends to his home. Bill Wechsler was among the attendees, along with Deputy Henry Fritz. The sheriff hadn't been invited. According to rumors, Mr. Baxter was grooming a new candidate for sheriff, one that didn't ignore crucial evidence when it turned up in George O'Brien's trash.

To me, Deputy Fritz had always seemed too eager to please to make much of a leader, but that was probably what Howard liked about him.

Todd Miller and Vaughn Deval were also in attendance. Todd's mother, Rita Baxter Miller, sat on the sofa next to Barbara Baxter, Howard's wife. Barbara was well acquainted with money and enjoyed flaunting it. She'd won her share of beauty contests in the early 30s, which had won her the admiration of the young Howard Baxter, who had already made a name for himself in Winter Haven. Barbara no longer had the figure she'd had in her youth, but she always dressed in style and was well known for her large collection of shoes and fur coats.

"This is the very locket that George claimed my son Grant had," Howard said as he paced through the living room, surrounded by friends and family. "Yet somehow George had it to throw away. So how'd he happen to have it unless he killed my boy to get it?" This got the response he hoped for: a lot of nodding and some groans of agreement. "Yet Sheriff Cornell is planning to do nothing about it. Instead, he's protecting George O'Brien as if he's the victim here."

"Jim Cornell told me himself that he considers this case closed." Deputy Fritz, dressed in his uniform, sat on the piano bench enjoying his role as Howard Baxter's new right-hand man.

"Perhaps he's right," said Barbara Baxter, who seemed less supportive than one would expect of a mother whose son had gone missing.

"That's enough, Barbara." Howard shot her a sharp look. They had clearly had this discussion before and he didn't want to rehash it in the presence of friends and relatives.

"I'm not the only one who thinks this way, Howard." Barbara had a glass of wine in her hand and several more glasses in her stomach, enough to loosen her tongue and free her inhibitions. "You're validating Mr. O'Brien's story," she continued, much to her husband's chagrin.

The Baxters' living room was spacious, filled with elegant furniture and a white carpet they had shampooed twice a year, whether it needed it or not. They'd brought in several chairs from the dining room so everyone would have a place to sit. Barbara's eyes left her husband's for a brief moment, long enough to see that the guests were anxiously awaiting her explanation.

"This is neither the time nor place," Howard said.

"This is exactly the time and place," she shot back. "You're convinced the discovery of the locket makes George O'Brien a killer."

"It does."

"How could it unless our son raped Carolyn and stole the locket from her like Mr. O'Brien claimed?"

Bill Wechsler and the other supporters no longer looked so supportive. Instead, they stared at Howard as if it'd never occurred to them that Grant had actually raped Carolyn O'Brien and hadn't considered how Howard's obsession with the locket reflected on his son's guilt.

"He killed our son," Howard said to his wife, and then turned his attention to his guests. "The man killed my boy!"

"I love you, Howard." Barbara sounded as though she honestly meant it. "You're one of the smartest men I've ever known, but for the first time in my life, I'm ashamed of you."

"For what? For wanting to put our son's killer in jail?"

"Your reaction to the locket is a confession of Grant's guilt. And that means you lied on the witness stand that day."

"I didn't lie about that," he said.

"It's been seventeen years, Howard. Perhaps it's time we let it go."

"This is our son we're talking about."

"She's right about the locket, Mr. Baxter," Deputy Fritz said. This time he wasn't so comfortable voicing his opinion. "It'd never stand up in court. Grant was found innocent of the crime, so as far as the court is concerned, he never had that locket."

"You sound just like Jim Cornell," Howard said.

"If we had the body, that'd be a different story."

"But we don't have the body!" Howard trembled with anger. "And we have no idea where to find it."

"But I think I know somebody who does," the deputy said. This time he looked happy with what he had to say.

As I sat on Kirk McKnight's patio, I thought about the conversation I'd had with Sheriff Cornell and wondered if he'd had a similar discussion with his deputy, telling him everything except the exact location. I thought of it again later that evening as I sat in the dark studio, staring out the window at the bathtub. A rational man wouldn't put the body of his victim in his own backyard, would he? Of course, a rational man wouldn't actually kill someone either. Thus, who knows what was going through Mr. O'Brien's mind at the time, if he had indeed been the one responsible for Grant's disappearance. In my heart, I believed George had done this, and I feared it was now catching up with him. Soon his tragedy would play itself out and his world would come crashing down. However, the true victim would be Candice.

CHAPTER 35

When the sanitation workers arrived the following Tuesday morning, they brought a large truck to haul away the remnants of the black garden cluttering up the alley. I was still in bed, but I heard the men yelling as they hoisted the items off the ground. The cinder blocks, the bicycle, and the phonograph all fell into the truck with a crash, followed by the shattering sound of the porcelain gnome meeting its demise. They cursed George for the extra work. One of the men yelled: "It won't be long now." I couldn't say for sure what he meant by that, but the interpretation I gave it made me sick to my stomach.

I called Kirk that afternoon to see if any new rumors had made their way through the Taft Paper grapevine. From what Kirk had heard, Howard Baxter refused to believe the locket wasn't enough to convict George O'Brien of murder. Thus, he had taken his case to the highest authority in Winter Haven: Judge Ellington.

ഇൗരു

Baxter argued his case while Ellington sat behind his desk in the judge's chambers. Sheriff Cornell had also come along to the meeting. He leaned against the wall, going through the motions, hoping to appease Baxter, but Baxter wouldn't be appeased, not until justice had been served. To Baxter, that meant George O'Brien spending the rest of his life behind bars.

"We could arrest him," Ellington said, "but we couldn't make it stick, not without a body. For all we know, Grant ran off to Canada."

"You know damn well Grant's not in Canada!"

"Yeah, but can you convince a jury of it? That's the question. The locket would raise a lot of suspicions, but it's not going to convict anyone of murder."

"From what I understand, the sheriff here knows where the body is."

"How would I know that?"

"You told Deputy Fritz that you had a pretty good idea where Mr. O'Brien buried my son," Baxter said.

"I said no such thing."

"He's lying to us. I can see it in his eyes." Baxter gritted his teeth and looked at the judge for support. "Us Baxters are the foundation of this community, and when I ask for something to be done I don't appreciate being pushed aside as if I were your average Joe Citizen."

"If you think you know where the body is," Ellington said to Cornell, "it's your obligation to lead us to it."

"I once told Henry that if I dug the body up that it wouldn't change a thing, that Grant would still be dead. You know Henry. He's always jumping to conclusions. He took it wrong and thought I was saying I knew where Grant was buried, but that's not what I was saying." Cornell spoke to Baxter, who eyed him with contempt. "When are you going to let this go, Mr. Baxter?"

"Let it go?" Baxter screamed. He got in the sheriff's face, but the sheriff didn't budge or show any emotion. "You're asking me to forget that my boy is dead and that George O'Brien is responsible?

The only reason I helped you become sheriff is because my son was your best friend. Do you want me to forget that, too?"

The sheriff said nothing.

"You're just as worthless as your old man. If he'd been better at his job, this would have been over years ago."

"And if you hadn't lied about being with your son the day he raped Carolyn O'Brien, perhaps he'd still be alive today. Probably be out of prison by now, too."

Baxter brought his open palm hard across the sheriff's cheek and grinned at the look of shock it left behind. Suddenly, the sheriff no longer cared about appeasing Howard Baxter. His fist came up, ready to defend his honor. Instead, he merely put his hand on Baxter's chest and pushed him away.

"I realize you're under a lot of stress right now, Mr. Baxter, but don't you ever lay a hand on me again."

Baxter gritted his teeth and jabbed a finger toward the sheriff's face. "One thing is painfully clear, Jim, and that's that you no longer deserve to wear that badge. Next election you can bet my support will be behind someone else." He marched to the door and slammed it behind him as he left the room. The sound hung in the air like a dirge sung in honor of Cornell's final days as sheriff of Winter Haven.

"I think he meant that," Judge Ellington said.

"I'm sure he did." Cornell rubbed his hand over his cheek, still baring the sting of Baxter's anger. "I was hired to uphold the law, not to be Howard Baxter's patsy."

"The law isn't all about who's right and who's wrong. It's about doing what's best for the community. Howard Baxter is the foundation of this—"

"If I hear one more person refer to the Baxters as the foundation of this community, I'm going to shoot somebody."

Ellington glowered. "Howard Baxter provides a lot of jobs in this town. What has George O'Brien ever done?"

"I've done plenty for Howard Baxter. So did my father. Things we shouldn't have done. But with Howard, it's never enough. He's the kind of man who does you one favor and expects ten in return."

"And if you're smart, you'll keep on delivering those favors," Ellington said.

Sheriff Cornell left the courthouse that day feeling the full weight of politics pressing down on him. He had a wife and children to think about. He had to put clothes on their backs and put food on the table. He had house payments to make and bills to pay. He wasn't going to be able to do this if he lost his job. Though it went against his better nature, he knew he had no choice but to carry out the job he'd been elected to do.

CHAPTER 36

That Friday evening, Jordan Patrick held a birthday party for his wife at his home. He'd called on Thursday and invited George, Candice, and me, and apologized for the short notice. As a self-proclaimed procrastinator, he had decided on the party at the last minute. Though George had changed his opinion about Jordan, he was still reluctant to accept the invitation. He stood near the refrigerator chatting on the phone while I sat at the table with Candice, watching her annihilate me in another game of chess.

"Who else is going to be there?" George asked several times, followed by a list of reasons for hating whichever person Jordan had mentioned. He'd then listen, grunt a few times, and agree that the person might not be so bad after all. "Yeah, okay, I suppose it might be fun," he said. "Candice bought herself a really nice skirt, but I don't know about Mitchell." He looked at me and put his hand over the receiver. "You didn't bring a suit with you by chance, did you?"

I shook my head.

"He didn't bring anything," George said into the phone. "But maybe I have something that will fit him."

By the next day, George had lost his enthusiasm for mingling with a group of people he hadn't seen in years and hadn't missed. The two O'Briens were in George's bedroom and hadn't heard me come in through the kitchen. I stepped into the hall and stopped short of the open bedroom door, where I could hear George saying how I'd interrupted their lifestyle, claiming everything had been much simpler before I came along.

"The party was Mr. Patrick's idea," Candice reminded him.

"I'm sure Mitchell had a hand in it. Always meddling like an old woman. I'll be happy when he goes back to Boston."

I waited for Candice's rebuttal, but she said nothing. But I knew she would be sad to see me go—almost as sad as I would be to leave. We planned to make the best of my last weekend in Winter Haven, with the party this evening and a fishing trip tomorrow. Quinn, Kirk, and Nicole planned to stop by in the morning, and the three of us would follow them to the lake. George claimed to hate fishing as much as I did. He said fishing was about as exciting as watching a silent movie with a blindfold. He only agreed to go because Jordan Patrick was coming and had promised to bring his rowboat. Apparently, George was fond of the water. He'd served in the Navy before getting married. He said he passionately hated the service, but really missed being out there surrounded by nothing but ocean.

When I heard the knock at the front door, I hurried into the kitchen and waited around the corner where I listened to Candice open the door, say hello to Jordan, and invite him in.

"Grandpa's almost ready," she said. "How good are you at tying ties?"

"I think I've got it," George said as he left the bedroom with his cane tapping on the linoleum. "I haven't worn one of these things in years. I forgot how to put them on."

"You look sharp, George," Jordan said. "Good thing you have that cane. You'll be needing it to keep the women away."

George groaned. "Where's Mitchell?"

"I'll go see if he's ready," Candice said.

With that, I rounded the corner and headed to the living room. Candice was walking toward me, dressed in the skirt and blouse Nicole had bought for her. She looked stunning. Both men were decked out in suits and ties. I, however, was sporting a pair of jeans and a T-shirt.

"Why aren't you ready?"

George turned as I entered the living room. He frowned at my attire and checked his watch. "What happened to the suit I gave you?"

"I don't feel so good." I rubbed a hand over my stomach. "I think I'll stay home and work on my novel."

"I don't care how you feel," George said. "Go get dressed. You're coming with us."

"I don't think that would be wise. Not with the way I'm feeling."

George grumbled. "Then let's just cancel the whole damn thing. You're the only reason we're going in the first place."

"You don't want to go to my wife's birthday party?" Jordan sounded hurt.

"Yeah, I'm mean, of course. It's just that Mitchell really had his heart set on it."

"I'll be fine, Mr. O'Brien. Go out. Enjoy yourselves. You wouldn't want to let Mrs. Patrick down."

"She is looking forward to seeing you," Jordan said. "In fact, I mentioned to a few others that you were coming and they were pleased to hear it. They would all be disappointed if you didn't show."

When Benedict Arnold betrayed the Continental Army by plotting to surrender his fort to the British forces, I doubt he received more contempt than I was getting from the two O'Briens at that moment. I walked outside with them and told Jordan to wish his wife happy birthday for me as they went out the gate.

"Lock the door," George said. "And turn out the lights." He gave me one final scowl before getting in the front seat of Jordan

Patrick's car while Candice got in the back. As I watched them drive away, I felt the pain tighten inside my stomach. It was a clear night. The stars shone like a million eyes, all looking down at me, watching me step through the front door, lock it, and turn off the lights in the living room. A moment later, they watched the kitchen lights go out, followed shortly by me stepping out the back door. I looked up at those stars, wondering what they were thinking, wondering if I had made the right decision.

That night I slept the sleep of the dead. My whole body ached, but I was at peace. I dreamed of a field of red flowers with a black dot in the center. I believe they were poppies. In the middle of the field stood a white bathtub with a circle of crows perched along the rim. They drank from the tub, overflowing with cranberry juice. It streamed down the sides of the tub and disappeared among the flowers. As I approached, the crows turned into doves and flew off into the blue sky. I waved my hand through the tub of cranberry juice, cupped some in my palm, and brought it to my lips. It tasted like copper, but I swallowed it anyway. Soon the juice faded from red to pink and then lost its color altogether. It was nothing but clear water now, bubbling up from the drain and spilling out over my feet. This was the last image I saw before the knocking woke me from my sleep.

I opened my eyes and saw the sun streaming through the curtains. Another knock came at the door. I popped out of bed and pulled on a clean pair of jeans. I had no shirt on and my hair was a mess when I pulled the door open and glared at George, already dressed and wearing his Boston Red Sox baseball cap.

"Don't tell me you're still sick," he said, "because I have no intention of entertaining your friends on my own."

I stared at my wrist, trying to figure out what time it was, but I wasn't wearing a watch.

"It's almost eight."

"Give me ten minutes," I said and started to close the door, but George stopped it with his hand.

"What did you do to the tub?" He looked back at the bathtub, which now looked distinguished, with dozens of bright flowers sprouting up from the soil.

"I weeded it," I said. "I figured if you were going to keep it, it might as well look respectable."

George moaned and walked away.

By ten o'clock, we were gathered at the shore of the lake, squinting as the water reflected the sun into our eyes. Kirk baited his hook, tossed it out into the water, and then handed his pole to me. That way, if the fish didn't like my scent, which seemed to be the consensus, then we would beat them by not letting me near the hook or line.

"How was the party?" I asked Candice as Kirk baited her hook for her.

"Okay, I guess. I think Grandpa liked it. Everybody there was old."

"I wouldn't have been much fun at the party," I said.

"And how would that have been different than any other time?" she asked.

Kirk laughed as he handed her the fishing pole. "She got you there, Mitchell."

We settled along the shore and watched Kirk reel in three fish in the first hour while the rest of us caught nothing. He'd open up his blue cooler, drop the fish in, rebait his hook, and cast his line back into the water, as we sat wondering what he was doing differently than any of us. He swore it was a talent, and perhaps it was, but it was one of those talents that couldn't be detected by the naked eye.

By one o'clock, Candice and Nicole each caught a fish and Kirk caught two more while Quinn and I remained fishless. Once again I'd be going home empty-handed. I'd like to say I tried, but what exactly is trying when it comes to fishing?

"It's a conspiracy," Candice said, right after a fish had jumped about ten yards out. "He was sent out to check out the situation," she said to me. "Did you see him? He looked right at you. He's down there right now telling everyone to stay away from your hook."

"Fish don't like getting eaten by ugly people," Quinn said.

"Then why did you bother coming?" I asked.

"Fish love me. They think I'm the sexiest thing alive. So do the women. Isn't that right, Candice?"

"She only has eyes for me," I said.

"Soon, you'll be back in Boston, my friend. And it'd be a pity to have Candice sit home all alone on a Friday night."

I shook my head at Quinn, warning him to stay away from Candice, while she grinned at the attention. Kirk sprang to his feet, yanked the rod back, and reeled in the line, as he pulled in yet another fish.

"Have I told you recently how much I hate you," Quinn said, which made Kirk grin wider.

"Now this is the life." Kirk grabbed his net to scoop the fish out of the water. "I think I'll quit my job and spend my time here at the lake and let Nicole support me for a while."

"Oh no you won't," Nicole objected. "I only married you for your money. Without that, what good are you?"

"We'll still eat. I'll be out here catching our dinner every day."

"It's going to take a lot more than fish to keep me happy."

"She wants a new car," Kirk said, looking at me. "Don't ever get married, Mitch. You neither, Quinn. All women are the same. They only want what's in your pants: your wallet."

I smiled and stared out at the lake, at the rowboat floating far away from shore. I could see the top of George's baseball cap as he bent forward and stared into the water. Jordan was also bent over the side of the boat as if trying to scout out the fish.

About fifteen minutes later, they came sloshing through the water, rowing toward us. They were in low spirits. My first guess was that they hadn't had any more luck with the fish than I had. The two of them looked different, older somehow. I couldn't put my finger on it at first, and then I realized that neither of them had any teeth. They were nothing but gums and wrinkled faces.

Kirk and Quinn waded in the water and pulled the boat in so George and Jordan could step out onto the rocks.

"Grandpa, where's your teeth?" Candice asked.

George gave Jordan a hard look.

"How was I to know?" Jordan said, apologetically.

George had no response. He pulled his cane from the boat and started up the hill toward the vehicles. This was George's way of letting us know he'd had enough for the day and wanted to go home. We looked at Jordan for an explanation. He sat on a large rock and rubbed the bald spot on his head.

"How was I supposed to know?" He put his hands out in a questioning gesture. "George seems to think I'm the biggest idiot to walk the Earth, but how was I supposed to know those were his teeth?" He looked at George, making his way slowly up the hill. "I was tossing my line out and my dentures fell right out of my mouth and into the water," Jordan explained. "That was a fine set of teeth, too. They aren't even paid for yet. Wasn't a thing we could do, so we went back to fishing. About ten minutes later, there's George with a set of dentures dangling from his hook. It was a damn miracle. That's what I thought. The man caught my teeth. So I take the teeth and stick them in my mouth, and what do you know? They're not mine. Completely wrong fit. Well, I don't know whose teeth George caught, but I sure as hell ain't keeping them in my mouth. So I spit them right back out into the water. George doesn't say a thing. He just sits there looking over the side with this horrified look on his face. That's when it dawned on me that those were George's own teeth. Damn old fool's joke backfired on him, and now he's mad at me."

Quinn looked at Kirk and let out this nasal sound of suppressed laughter. Then he lost it. And that contagious laughter got us all going. Maybe George and Jordan didn't find it amusing, but the five of us couldn't quit laughing.

Most of us weren't ready to pack it in quite yet, but with George in a foul temper and waiting for us by the vehicles, we decided not to protest. We carried Jordan's rowboat up the hill and put it in the back of his pickup truck. All the cars were locked. George was sitting on the front bumper of my blue Chevy. He frowned and looked at his watch as if we'd taken far too long making our way up the hill.

"So Mr. O'Brien, you catch anything out there?" Nicole asked. I honestly think she was referring to fish, not teeth, but Quinn broke up laughing all over again, and he just wouldn't stop. He was completely red in the face by the time we got the boat tied down.

It upset George that we found his misfortune so hilarious. He didn't want to talk to us, so Nicole offered to let him and Candice ride in the car with her while Kirk and Quinn rode with me. They hounded me the whole trip back to Winter Haven, calling me the "Queen of the Wild Frontier," whatever that was supposed to mean. I thought it was corny, but they seemed to think it was pretty funny. They'd declared the entire day a success. Of course, at the time, neither of them could have foretold what was coming.

CHAPTER 37

The noise that drifted through the neighborhood this particular afternoon came from an unusual place: the backyard of 613 Willow Lane, a place that had been mute for the past seventeen years. The home had begun to take on an air of respectability, at least from the front view. The sides and the back still needed painting, and the grass in the backyard was patchy, but to the casual driver cruising down Willow Lane, it was just another lovely home in the quiet neighborhood. In the backyard, kitchen chairs sat on the erratic patches of grass that rose up among misshaped plots of brown earth. A folding table held a pitcher of lemonade, baked potatoes, and three different kinds of Jell-O. A barbecue grill Quinn and I had hauled up from the basement sent up waves of smoke and the smell of fried fish. Kirk stood at the grill with a long fork in one hand and a container of spices in the other. He enjoyed cooking, as long as it was done outside, and he was far superior to the rest of us when it came to filleting a fish, so we let him command the grill.

"All these fish and no teeth to eat them with," George said to Jordan, seated on a chair next to him. "I've been thinking of putting one in the blender. You want one?"

"Tempting, but I think I'll pass."

Both men had their plates filled with Jell-O and mashed potatoes. Without their teeth, they looked like a couple of Muppets from *Sam and Friends*. The two men sat on their chairs, chewing the fat and sucking down Jell-O, while the rest of us ate our fish. Harriet Blanchard looked out the window of her home, surprised to see activity in the O'Briens' backyard. She smiled. George made a guttural noise but tipped his hat at her.

"What did you say to the Blanchards?" George asked me. "They're being all sweet and gooey."

"I told them you wanted to make amends." I sat cross-legged on the grass, holding my plate on my lap since we didn't have enough chairs for everyone.

"No, you didn't."

"I also told them it was your idea I help with the tree."

"You meddling little shit."

Candice came out of the house carrying a porcelain cup that had a flower design on it. Giving me a wink, she descended the steps and handed the cup to her grandfather.

"What's this?" he asked, looking in the cup and finding it empty.

"It's Margaret's. I think you should take it back over to her before she thinks we stole it."

"You take it over." He shoved the cup back at her, but she refused to take it. "Then give it to Mitch. He's the one who borrowed it in the first place."

"You're the one who wants to talk to her," I said.

"Who are we talking about?" Jordan asked. "Margaret Hansen?"

"These two have it in their heads that I got the hots for the old woman."

"She's younger than you, Grandpa," Candice said.

"Yeah, but men hold their age better. I'm looking for someone in their late thirties or early forties."

"I doubt Margaret's a day over forty-five," I said.

"She's pushing sixty and you know it."

"Go on over and talk to her, George," Jordan urged. "She's a nice lady. She comes in the store all the time looking at the plants."

George fidgeted in his chair and stared down at his assortment of Jell-O. "I wouldn't know what to say to her. Besides, I don't even have my teeth in."

"Want me to invite her over?" I asked. "She doesn't even need to know it's your idea."

"It's not my idea. And no I don't want you to invite her over here. I didn't hire you to play matchmaker. Ever since you showed up, you've been sticking your nose where it doesn't belong. I can't wait until Wednesday when you go home and we finally have some peace and quiet around here."

"We've all been saying that same thing, Mr. O'Brien," Quinn said.

George gave him a toothless grin. But the smile died as easily as it came, chased away by the sight of Sheriff Cornell and Judge Ellington coming around the side of the house. The sheriff was in uniform while the judge wore slacks and penny loafers.

"How's it going, Mr. O'Brien?" The sheriff's tone and expression said he wasn't comfortable with the position he found himself in.

"I lost my teeth," George said. "Other than that I have no complaints."

The sheriff glanced around at the festivities and nodded at Quinn and the McKnights. Kirk was still at the barbecue, where more fish sizzled on the grill.

"Looks as though you've got a party going on here."

"I'd have called and invited you," George said, "but I'm not sure we have enough fish to go around."

The sheriff feigned a smile, but it looked more pained than amused. His eyes drifted to the bathtub, still filled with dirt and brimming with flowers. Cornell's eyes caught mine, and I saw a look of apology in his face, sorry for what we both knew he had to do. Ellington nodded at him, encouraging him to state his business, but the sheriff gave him a mild shake of the head.

"I'm afraid we're here on official business, George," Ellington said.

George's face filled with worry.

Vehicles pulled up in the alley and soon several men came through the gate carrying shovels. Among them were Todd and Vaughn, carrying themselves with self-importance. Todd, with his shovel propped over his shoulder, gave Quinn a nod as he passed through the yard.

"You got a warrant for this?" Jordan asked.

Ellington handed it over.

"This is based on what?"

"George threatened Todd at the baseball game. He said he was going to bury him in his backyard beneath the bathtub right next to his Uncle Grant."

"Horseshit," George barked.

"I was there," I said. "Mr. O'Brien never said that."

"He whispered it in my ear," Todd said.

Everyone knew it was a lie, yet here they stood.

Deputy Fritz came through the gate carrying a shovel of his own. He avoided eye contact with the sheriff, who watched him with contempt. Behind Fritz came Howard Baxter, dressed in shirtsleeves and dress pants. By the look on his face, you'd have thought they were digging up a lost treasure, rather than the remains of his murdered son. He remained near the back fence next to his wife, Barbara, who kept staring at the grass as though she didn't want to see what they were about to pull out of the ground. I could see the beauty in her face, hidden behind the worry and the sadness.

It took six men to get the bathtub rocking and finally tip it on its side. I expected George to protest, to claim they were destroying his flowers or the serenity of his backyard. Instead, he quietly climbed the steps and settled down in his rocking chair, watching the men take up their shovels and start the slow process of exhuming what was left of Grant Baxter. Candice went up the steps and stood behind him with her hands on his shoulders.

Kirk pulled the remaining fish off the grill before sitting on the edge of the porch with Nicole and Quinn. They looked at me for an explanation, but I said nothing as Jordan and I went up the steps and joined Candice at the back of George's rocking chair.

A vein pulsed at George's temple. He gripped his cane as though he was afraid it would get away from him. "That Baxter's trying to ruin my good name," he said.

"You have a good name?" I asked and won a frown from Candice.

Deputy Fritz went to work with the rest of the men, digging into the soil where the bathtub once stood. There were eight men with shovels. At first, they were all in there together, bumping into each other, eager to be the one to discover Grant Baxter's remains. Finally, Deputy Fritz paired the men up and had them work in shifts, giving them all a turn at the shovels and a chance to catch their breath. A few of the men had brought picks, but they discovered the ground was softer than they'd anticipated, so they put the picks aside and stuck with the shovels.

The sheriff and the judge stood on the walkway, watching the men sink their shovels into the earth. A dozen faces stared over the back fence, people from the neighborhood who had come to see what the activity was about. A few had even wandered through the gate. In all, I counted thirty-two people, both inside and outside the fence. Behind Ellington and the sheriff, Carl and Harriet Blanchard stood in their backyard, gazing over the fence with concern.

Seeing the stress in the sheriff's face, Baxter wandered over and put a hand on his shoulder, like a father comforting a son. "Sorry it had to come to this, Jim, but damn it, I couldn't just stand by while you sat around on your ass."

"Get off my property, Howard," George said. "And take your friends with you."

"We'll leave all right. Just as soon as we pull my son's body out of the ground there."

"Go to hell!"

"I would, but I understand the O'Briens have already spoken for all the seats down there." Howard's comment sent a ripple of laughter through the crowd. He looked around at his friends, pleased with himself.

"There's always room for a Baxter in hell!" George yelled. "That's where your son is."

"You son of a bitch!" Baxter charged toward the porch.

George came up out of his chair and started down the steps with his cane in hand. Verbally, George could take on the best of them, but he didn't stand a chance against Howard Baxter in a physical confrontation. Rushing down the steps, I wedged myself between the two men, putting a hand on Baxter's chest to hold him back.

"Out of my way!" he barked.

"Let him by," George said. "No pampered little Baxter ever scared me."

"Go wait by the back gate, Howard." The sheriff took him by the arm.

Howard pulled away. "I'm not leaving until I see some justice done."

"And what's your idea of justice?" I asked. "Beating up an old man?"

"I'm not old." George popped me in the back with his cane.

"Wait by the back gate, Howard," the sheriff repeated. "I mean it."

"You're nothing but a coward, Jim. You always have been."

"You sound just like your son, Howard, a big crybaby," George said, and that got Howard started all over again, but the sheriff stood in front of him to stop him from climbing the steps.

"You still tucking your granddaughter in at night, Mr. O'Brien?" Todd grinned at the crowd. He was taking his turn resting while Fritz and a burly man handled the shovels.

This time Candice started down the steps, but I grabbed her by the arm and held her back.

"That was uncalled for, Todd," Sheriff Cornell said.

"I think everyone here has a right to know," Todd went on.

"You still sleeping with your dog, Todd?" Quinn asked, as he sat on the edge of the porch.

"Shut your mouth, Quinn!" Todd pointed his finger.

"I think everyone here has a right to know," Quinn persisted.

People chuckled. Todd looked around with anger, glaring at the laughing faces. He started toward Quinn with his fists ready.

"You want to go for it, let's go." Quinn popped up off the porch and started across the lawn. I was looking forward to seeing Quinn Judson pulverize Todd Miller, but the sheriff got in between them before either one could throw a punch.

"Knock it off! Both of you!" The sheriff's face grew red and serious. "Either conduct yourselves like civilized human beings or get the hell out of here. That goes for everybody here!" he yelled, looking around at the crowd. "One more outburst like this and I'll send all of you home."

"Got something," Deputy Fritz announced, and everybody lost interest in the squabble.

"What did they find, Grandpa?" Candice asked.

George took her hand and squeezed. They were both standing behind the rocking chair now. I climbed the steps again and stood beside them, feeling their pain. George's face was heavy with worry as he leaned forward on his cane, watching the deputy tap the nose of his shovel on a piece of wood buried in the dirt.

Sheriff Cornell looked up at us and shook his head. To him, George had already paid for his crime. His punishment was losing his wife and daughter and living as an outcast in his own community. Yet he knew the law didn't see it that way. The only punishment the government would recognize was the one it personally brought down upon George O'Brien's head.

The crowd pushed forward, wanting to see what the deputy had unburied. The only sound in the backyard was that of shovels scraping the dirt away from a wooden crate. George let go of Candice's hand and started around his rocking chair. As he passed me, he put a hand on my shoulder, leaned toward my ear, and whispered: "Take care of my girl." He then settled in his chair with a look of resignation on his face.

A couple of men dug around the crate and helped lift it out of the hole. It was a wine crate, not big enough to house a body. After brushing the dirt off with his hand, Deputy Fritz used a crowbar to pry open the lid. As the nails squeaked loose and Fritz lifted the top off, Cornell and Ellington walked over to take a look inside. Howard Baxter was already over there, scowling, while Barbara Baxter remained by the back fence.

The sheriff reached inside the wooden crate and pulled out a black garbage bag, which brought on looks of confusion from those standing around the yard. Even George leaned forward in his chair as though he couldn't figure out what was going on. The confusion intensified when the sheriff removed a Tupperware container from the bag. The crowd tightened in around him, heads peering over shoulders, trying to see inside the container as the sheriff peeled off the lid. From the porch, we could hear the gasps and mumbles and saw the sheriff shake his head at Howard Baxter, who looked genuinely horrified. Judge Ellington looked at George as if looking at an alien. Everyone around him bore that same expression.

"Sorry, Howard," the sheriff said. "Looks like we dug up a whole new set of problems here."

"You conniving little son of a bitch!" Howard yelled at George.

"What's in there?" Candice squeezed her grandfather's shoulders.

George shrugged as he watched the sheriff walk toward him. He tried not to let it show, but I could see the amusement on the sheriff's face as he stopped beside the porch and stared up at George.

"Did you take these, Mr. O'Brien?" The sheriff handed him a stack of photographs. Now it was George's turn to be confused as he leaned back in his rocking chair and thumbed through the photos. They had been taken at night and weren't the best quality, but the younger Howard Baxter was recognizable as he squeezed through a hole in a wire fence. In the background stood the blurry image of a large white building. The next few photos showed Howard dragging two canisters of gasoline through the fence with him. Then came the pictures of the fire—starting off small, but quickly spreading across the ground floor of the building. When Howard squeezed back through the fence to his awaiting car, the building behind him was ablaze and his expression was one of pure delight. The final shot showed Howard Baxter standing at his open car door, looking back at the burning Greenwood Paper Mill lighting up the night sky.

Looking up from the photographs with a look of bewilderment and gratitude, George eyed the sheriff, who remained stone-faced as though he could read George's thoughts but refused to give anything away.

"That was years ago," George said as he handed the photos back to the sheriff.

"Why did you bury them in your yard?" Judge Ellington asked as he approached the porch. By the tone of his voice, I was certain he expected George to deny burying the photographs, that he expected George to claim he'd handed those photos to Jim Cornell's father seventeen years ago and hadn't seen them since.

For a moment, I also felt this was what George would say. Instead, he said: "I figured someone has to look out for those Baxters. God knows they're not smart enough to take care of themselves." George looked over the judge's shoulder at Howard. The animosity lay thick between them, and for the first time in his life, George had the upper hand. Getting up from his chair, he turned toward me with the same look he'd given the sheriff, one of suspicion and gratitude.

"Those are some nice photos, Mr. O'Brien," I said. "They're worth framing."

He patted me on the arm. "Let's go in the house, Candice. It's been a very long day."

Later that afternoon, after everyone else had gone back to their homes, I was alone in the space I'd once dubbed the black garden. The sun faded and twilight settled over Winter Haven.

Gazing past the side lawn and the willow tree, I could see Ellington and Sheriff Cornell standing by the patrol car. The judge seemed frustrated and suspicious. He'd probably seen those photographs himself, seventeen years ago. How did they end up in the O'Brien backyard unless someone planted them, or unless George had made a duplicate set? He was Howard Baxter's friend, his protector, but what could he do now? A night watchman had died in the Greenwood fire, which meant Howard Baxter was facing charges of manslaughter.

The yard looked barren, lonely. Even the bathtub was gone. Kirk and Quinn had helped me carry it out the back gate. It now sat in the alley, where it would remain until the sanitation workers once again arrived with their truck.

After finding the photographs of Howard Baxter's misdeed, his friends had lost their enthusiasm for work and left without refilling the hole. I didn't mind. I needed the physical labor to help me burn off the restless energy I'd built up over the past few days. As I returned to the hole and began shoveling in the dirt, the back door opened. George O'Brien stepped out onto the porch. He looked peaceful as he leaned on his cane and gazed down at me.

"Did you have something to do with this?" he asked.

"I have no idea what you're talking about, Mr. O'Brien."

He pressed his lips together and nodded. I could see he wanted to say more. Instead, he turned and went back inside the house.

CHAPTER 38

The night before I drove back to Boston, a light rain fell over Winter Haven, ushering in the cooler nights as autumn approached. Candice sat on my bed watching me pack my bags. The curtains remained open. Through the drizzle, I could see George milling around in the kitchen, occasionally glancing out at us.

"Are you going to miss me when I go?" I asked.

"Probably not." Candice had her shoes off and was sitting cross-legged on the bed.

"I probably won't miss you either, but I'll miss your grandfather." I put my typewriter in a box. "I don't know what I'll do without someone following me around telling me what to do."

She giggled like a little girl and fell back against the pillows. Not that my joke was that funny, but she was giddy and confused and was trying hard not to let me know how sad she was to see me go. I understood her emotions. I felt the same. Turning around, she lay on her stomach with her elbows on the bed and hands cradled under her chin, watching me wrap a rubber band around my manuscript.

"Perhaps when I get back to the peace and quiet of Boston, I'll actually find time to finish this damn thing," I said as I stuffed the manuscript in the box beside the typewriter.

"You probably know lots of pretty girls there at the university, don't you?"

"Yeah, I do, and they're all crazy about me. But who can blame them?"

She smiled with sadness in her eyes. "I wish you didn't have to leave."

"I wish you didn't have to stay." I grabbed an empty box from a pile near the door and set it on the floor in front of the bookshelf. Scooping a handful of books into my arms, I bent down and began placing them in the box. Candice was still lying on the bed, watching me with her sad blue eyes. I loved her so much that I hurt, but I couldn't stay, not with just one year left of college.

"If you'd like, I could leave these here?" I said, indicating the books. "I can pick them up later."

"You're thinking of coming back?"

"Try keeping me away."

She smiled and her eyes became glassy. As she sat up, I went to the bed and sat down beside her. I could hear the rain falling harder now, tapping against the roof of the studio.

"I don't want you out finding another boyfriend in the meantime, okay?" I put my arm around her. "And if Quinn calls, tell him you're already taken."

"Okay." She squeezed her arms around me and kissed my cheek.

"Your grandfather's watching." The rain on the window blurred my view, but I could see George standing in the kitchen looking out at us.

"We still have our clothes on," Candice said and kissed me on the lips. I laughed and held her in my arms. Her mother's silver locket hung from her neck, still holding the small portrait of the young Carolyn O'Brien and the inscription George had asked the jeweler to engrave: *To my beloved daughter, Carolyn.* The sheriff had shown up at the door the day after they dug up the backyard. He said the department no longer had any use for the locket and offered it to Candice. She was ecstatic. The sight of her joy put tears in George's eyes. He thanked the sheriff for his kindness, but I don't think the locket was the only thing he had in mind. The discovery of the photographs told George that Sheriff Cornell had spent some time digging around in the backyard, prior to the night before.

According to the story Cornell told me, seventeen years ago, after photographing Howard Baxter setting fire to the Greenwood Paper Mill, George had promptly handed the photos to Sheriff Cornell Sr. His spying had paid off, and now Howard Baxter would pay for the lies he'd told at his son's trial. Weeks passed as George awaited the news of Baxter's arrest. But nothing happened. Then one morning George showed up at his photography studio downtown and found that someone had broken in through the back door and had stolen all of his negatives and many of his prints. Everything pertaining to Baxter's arsonist days had disappeared. He went to the sheriff's office to report the crime and to ask what was happening in the case against Howard Baxter. The sheriff gave him a confused look and told him he knew nothing about a case against Howard Baxter. Instead, the sheriff took that opportunity to present George with a restraining order, telling him to stay away from the Baxters.

The following week, Grant Baxter disappeared.

CHAPTER 39

"Are you leaving?" Harriet asked as Candice and I stuffed boxes into the backseat of my car.

"Candice said she's had enough of me," I said.

"He's been nothing but trouble since the day he showed up," Candice said, and both of the Blanchards laughed. They were seated on their porch. During the bulk of the summer, their porch had remained empty. But within the past few weeks, two kitchen chairs had made an appearance. They were up against the wall, in the shade, and Harriet and Carl occupied them for a few hours each day. They always made a point of saying hello to me, and I'd see them glance toward the O'Briens' porch as if expecting George to materialize and offer a sign of friendship. So far, that hadn't happened, but I had hope.

George was outside now, sitting on the porch swing. He paid no attention to the Blanchards. Instead, he watched me take his granddaughter's hand and escort her through the gate. He was still toothless and would be until his new dentures arrived in twelve days. Yet there was happiness in his face as he eased the swing back and forth. When Candice and I climbed the stairs, he took a check from his shirt pocket and held it out to me.

"You never got around to cleaning out the basement, but other than that, you worked out fine."

"I'm glad to hear that." I didn't bother looking at the check, just folded it and stuffed it in my own shirt pocket. "If you're ever in Boston—"

"I won't be," he cut me off.

"Well, if you are, you're welcome at my home anytime. Both of you."

George's cane lay across his lap and Margaret Hansen's cup sat behind him on the windowsill. "Do you have plans for Thanksgiving?"

"My family usually has a big dinner. We sit around the table and stuff ourselves until we can't move. If you'd like to come down, I think my parents would have room for two more."

"I was thinking more along the lines of you coming up here."

"That'd work, too," I said, and Candice squeezed my hand.

"We'll count on you then." George moved his cane and patted the spot next to him, wanting Candice to join him on the swing. "One more year of school and then what?"

"I'm going to be a writer."

"That's commendable." George patted Candice's leg as she took her seat beside him. "Heaven knows there aren't enough starving artists in the world."

"I've also been thinking about teaching," I said. "At least until I get my big break. I've been taking education classes in case I need something to fall back on."

"They've got schools up here, you know. They could use a decent teacher." George took Candice's hand. "Jordan Patrick is a member of the chamber of commerce. He may have some pull with the school board. I could talk to him and see if he can pull a few strings for you."

"I'd really appreciate that, Mr. O'Brien."

He grabbed his cane and stood up from the chair. "You drive safely. We'll look forward to seeing you on Thanksgiving." He grabbed the cup from the windowsill and started down the steps.

"Where are you going, Grandpa?"

"There's an old prune across the street I owe a visit to." He winked at her and smiled.

I kissed Candice goodbye before getting in my car and driving down Willow Lane. In my rearview mirror, I could see her standing at the curb, waving at me. Rolling down the window, I put my hand out and waved as I honked my horn. A hint of autumn tinted the trees that lined the narrow street. It wouldn't be long now and the neighborhood would be filled with yellow, orange, and red. Brittle leaves would sweep across the street, and then the snow would begin to fall. And while nature went into hibernation, the O'Briens would blossom.

I turned left on Maple Avenue and drove to the outskirts of Winter Haven, where the town was expanding as construction workers laid the foundation for the new shopping center. An orange cement mixer faced the road. The drum was spinning and gray cement flowed from a shoot extending from the back.

I parked next to a white car and watched as one man guided the flow of cement while others used shovels to spread it evenly across the earth. The large sign to my right read: *Future site of Baxter Center.* To my left, the passenger window of the white car squeaked as Sheriff Cornell rolled it down. He was wearing a blue T-shirt and chewing on a stick of beef jerky. Beside him, behind the steering wheel, sat Jordan Patrick.

"You coming back next year?" Cornell asked.

"Probably. George said he'd talk to Mr. Patrick about helping to get me a teaching job."

"I'll act surprised when he brings it up," Jordan said.

"How long are you going to wait around?" I asked.

"Until they get the foundation laid." He didn't hate the Baxters, and he didn't like cementing his best friend's remains in the foundation of Baxter Center, but it seemed a fitting resting place.

The night I sent George and Candice off to Mrs. Patrick's birthday party, the sheriff and I scooped the dirt out of the bathtub before we could tip it over and shove it out of the way. I prayed we wouldn't find Grant Baxter's body buried beneath the bathtub. But we did. It was wrapped in a sheet of plastic that had deteriorated over the years, as had the body. Cornell had brought a tarp, which we laid out on the ground to hold the remains. Most of the skeleton was still inside the ragged plastic, but we dug around for an extra half hour to assure that we hadn't left any bones behind. When we hauled the tarp into the alley, Cornell removed the wine crate from the trunk of his family car and we set the body inside. After shutting the trunk, he grabbed the crate and led the way back through the gate.

The sheriff said he had first seen the photographs six years ago while cleaning out his father's home after he'd died of heart failure. They were in a shoebox on a shelf in the bedroom closet. Jim Cornell had sat on his father's bed and studied the photos, sensing the pain and betrayal George O'Brien must have felt years ago. Howard Baxter had just helped Cornell win his second term as sheriff. He didn't want to repay him by sending him to prison. So he said nothing. He merely put the photos back inside the shoebox and held onto them for a rainy day, just as his father had.

By the time we refilled the hole and replaced the bathtub, it was nearly 11:00. Jordan had promised not to let the O'Briens leave the party until then. Since they'd gone in his car, we felt safe that they wouldn't be able to sneak out early. It took us another two hours to bury the body at the construction site. The ground was packed tightly and Cornell wanted a deep grave.

"So Grant can rest in peace," he said.

As I watched the cement fill the wooden frame that stretched out across the dirt, I noticed how calm the world had become. Machinery and workers were running at full speed, but it seemed more uniform today than it had before. Everything had its place and purpose as if the cosmos had left nothing to chance. Beyond the hustle of the construction, the trees swayed gently with the wind as birds fluttered from the branches. I felt a sense of peace that had abandoned me the past week.

The sheriff and Mr. Patrick also looked at peace. They had been strangers to me a few short months ago, but now they'd each won a spot in my heart. Saying goodbye, I put the car in reverse and backed out onto the road and prepared for the long drive back to Boston.

Please Review This Book

Reviews help authors more than you might think. If you enjoyed The Black Garden, please consider leaving a review at Goodreads. It would be greatly appreciated!

Say Hello

You can connect with Joe online at www.joebrightbooks.com. Also, he posts book updates and amusing anecdotes on www.facebook.com/joebrightauthor. For a writer, he's rather fickle with his social media activity. He's vowed to do better. We'll see how that goes.

ABOUT THE AUTHOR

While attending university on a fine arts scholarship, Joe Bright spent a lot of time playing the guitar, writing songs, and performing with a band. He won the KFC songwriting contest while in college, and no, he wasn't writing jingles about chicken. He also won a battle of the bands.

To support his artistic pursuits, he took time off from college and worked in the oil fields of Wyoming, where he met some interesting characters he could draw upon in his writing. He also spent a few years with a dance group, touring Canada and Europe.

After receiving his English degree, he went to work as a technical writer for Thiokol, the manufacturer of space shuttle rocket boosters. Yes, they're the ones responsible for the 1986 Challenger disaster, long before Joe worked for them.

Joe later taught English in Honolulu, Hawaii, and Berkeley, California. During this time, he began focusing seriously on his writing. He currently resides in Studio City, California.

Made in the USA
Las Vegas, NV
28 February 2021

18769120R00138